THIS JUST IN . . .

"I'm afraid there's some unfortunate news," Rick said, interrupting. "As tireless as our city workers have been, on alert for the safety of all"—he turned to address Erin—"I'm sorry to say that we have our first casualty, Erin."

Erin's face took on a somber look, and I noticed a discreet gulp and a soft clearing of her throat. "What do we know for sure, Rick?"

Probably nothing, ever, I thought, but a negative outlook was the last thing we needed today.

"Emergency workers arrived on the scene in downtown North Ashcot just moments ago, and have confirmed that the storm has claimed one life in that town," Rick said.

Erin took over, facing the camera. "This might be a good time for a break while we seek out the details. We'll be back shortly with more news on this devastating storm."

In a minute, the storm had gone from "dud" to "devastating." And my attention went from a dull interest to full alert.

One life lost will do th

Prime Crime titles by Jean Flowers

DEATH TAKES PRIORITY

CANCELLED BY MURDER

JEAN
FLOWERS

CANCELLED BY MURDER

BERKLEY PRIME CRIME
New York

BERKLEY PRIME CRIME
Published by Berkley
An imprint of Penguin Random House LLC
375 Hudson Street, New York, New York 10014

Copyright © 2016 by Camille Minichino
Penguin Random House supports copyright. Copyright fuels creativity, encourages
diverse voices, promotes free speech, and creates a vibrant culture. Thank you for buying
an authorized edition of this book and for complying with copyright laws by not
reproducing, scanning, or distributing any part of it in any form without permission.
You are supporting writers and allowing Penguin Random House to continue to
publish books for every reader.

BERKLEY is a registered trademark and BERKLEY PRIME CRIME and the B colophon
are trademarks of Penguin Random House LLC.

ISBN: 9780425279113

First Edition: September 2016

Printed in the United States of America
1   3   5   7   9   10   8   6   4   2

Book design by Kelly Lipovich
Interior map by Richard P. Rufer

For my husband and greatest support, Richard Rufer

ACKNOWLEDGMENTS

Thanks as always to my critique partners: Nannette Rundle Carroll, Margaret Hamilton, Jonnie Jacobs, Rita Lakin, Margaret Lucke, and Sue Stephenson. They are ideally knowledgeable, thorough, and supportive.

Special thanks to Linda Plyler, retired postmaster with a thirty-year career in the postal service. I received the full benefit of her professional experience as a training and development specialist in a large city and as a postmaster in a one-woman office in a small town. Linda is also an award-winning quilter, whose *Zip Code Quilt* received national recognition and media coverage.

Thanks also to the extraordinary Inspector Chris Lux for continued advice on police procedure, and to the many other writers and friends who offered critique, information, brainstorming, and inspiration: in particular, Gail and David Abbate, Sara Bly, Mary Donovan, Ann Parker, and Karen and Mark Streich.

My deepest gratitude goes to my husband, Dick Rufer. I can't imagine working without his support. He's my dedicated

ACKNOWLEDGMENTS

webmaster (minichino.com), layout specialist, and on-call IT department.

Thanks to Bethany Blair for her expert attention, and to all the copy editors, artists, and staff at Berkley Prime Crime for their work on my behalf.

Finally, my gratitude to my go-to friend and editor, Michelle Vega, who puts it all together. Michelle is a bright light in my life, personally supportive as well as superb at seeing the whole picture without missing the tiniest detail. Thanks, Michelle!

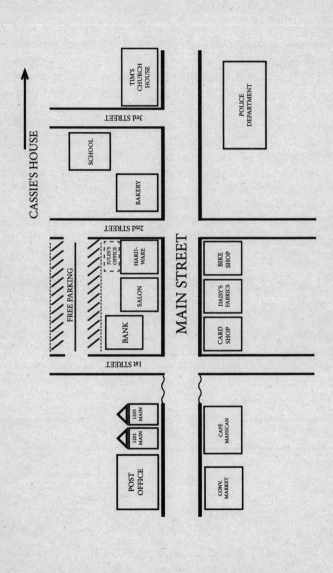

1

August—the peak of the Atlantic hurricane season. The Monday-morning sky above the post office in my hometown of North Ashcot was heavy, and becoming darker by the minute. Or maybe my perception was influenced by the news, dominated by warnings of a severe storm heading our way. This was nothing new. Here in the Berkshires of western Massachusetts, serious flooding and wind damage were a major threat all year long.

I had a decision to make. The flagpole in front of my building stood waiting. One of my favorite duties was the morning ritual of raising the flag, but I didn't want to hoist Old Glory at eight a.m., only to have to pull her down before noon.

I pinned my badge—CASSIE MILLER, and under it, POST-MASTER—to my regulation blue-striped shirt, and stepped out through the side door of the post office, an old redbrick

Colonial, the folded flag under my right arm. No gusts, and not a drop of rain. Yet.

Current predictions varied from a low-category hurricane heading straight toward us, to a storm that might turn south, or north, and produce only heavy rain, or none. In other words, it was New England, so anything could happen weatherwise. It wasn't unusual, at any time of the year, to have a sudden downpour with no warning. Dry sidewalks one minute, and a curtain of water the next. ETAs today ran the gamut from late morning to early evening. The common wisdom: Batten down the hatches, just in case.

More often than not, my experience as a lifetime resident of New England was that the more news there was about the pending arrival of bad weather, the more likely it was that we'd never see it. Especially so now that we were treated to a twenty-four-hour news cycle. As my predecessor and mentor, former postmaster Ben Gentry, would put it, "The news of the storm lasts longer than the storm itself these days."

I attached our flag to the rope and, hand over hand, ran it up the pole.

An hour into a busy retail morning, most of the muffins I'd brought in were gone. I'd begun the custom of feeding my customers once a week a year ago when I was feeling my way as a prodigal daughter. I'd left North Ashcot after high school and stayed away until my only living relative needed my help in her last days. Baked goods from our local bakery, A Hole in the Wall, originally a donut shop, were my way of pandering for acceptance by those who'd never strayed from home. Whether the pastries helped or not was anyone's guess, but it was clear that there was no way to end the tasty custom now.

After a year back in my hometown, I finally had my footing as sole operator of the North Ashcot Post Office. I also had a new BFF in Sunni Smargon, the chief of police, and a new boyfriend in antiques dealer Quinn Martindale. I even had a hobby—I had been talked into taking a quilting class and joining a group on Tuesday evenings. Things were looking good.

The weather held out longer than the muffins, and the morning passed quickly. My usual pet lovers Carolyn and George Raley came to the counter around eleven thirty, each holding an infant African genet wrapped in a swaddling cloth. The old couple were volunteer wet nurses of a sort, raising small exotic animals to the point where they would be comfortable in venues like petting zoos or school programs. Assigning the label "service animals" to accommodate post office rules for pets worked for me.

"We have twins today," Carolyn said as she stroked the spotted gray fur of a large-eyed catlike animal barely filling the palm of her hand. Its ears were too big for its tiny head, but I knew from experience that all parts of its anatomy would soon be in proportion.

"Morning, Cassie. Say hello to Abby and Tabby," George said, his unruly gray hair in need of attention. I might have been more sensitive to George's locks since I'd just had my own long, untamed mop cut and styled appropriately for a professional woman halfway through her thirties.

I weighed each animal and Carolyn entered the numbers into her logbook while George told me once again how grateful they were that I was willing to let them take advantage of the most accurate scale in town.

I'd just passed the animals back to their keepers when a loud noise resounded through the lobby, shaking us all into a state of alert. A gust of wind had blown a tub of mail from the hands of a customer entering the front door. The white plastic container hit the glass door, dozens of pieces of mail spilling over the entrance. Anyone within three feet of the door was treated to a shower as heavy rain came on the tail of the wind.

"Maybe there's something to those storm warnings after all," George said.

"Let's move," Carolyn said, and, in fact, I'd never seen her move so fast as she and George rushed out with Abby and Tabby tucked under their arms.

What had started as a smattering of rain a few minutes ago now appeared as a sheet of water slamming down on the trees and cars in the parking lot. Customers inside moved closer to one another as if seeking protection from the sudden (except for the newscasters' warnings, but who believed them?) cloudburst.

Weather words flew among the people gathered.

"I hope I can find my hurricane kit," from an older woman as she abandoned her place in line and headed for the door.

"I'm right behind you," from a woman in a business suit and stilettos, whom I recognized as one of the financial officers at the bank in town. "I think this downpour is payback from my boss. He didn't like that I was taking an early lunch."

"Yeah, you never know who might be in charge of climate around here." Sarcasm, from a young guy in a Red Sox cap. Even here, one hundred and fifty miles from Boston, where I'd spent the first decade or so of my career, there was no shortage of red-and-blue Sox apparel.

Our high school science teacher tried to take advantage of the situation to give us an impromptu (and unsolicited) lecture on wind speed and high- and low-pressure areas.

"Which are red and which are yellow?" a young woman asked him, scrolling through satellite pictures on her smartphone.

"And don't forget the storm now raging on Saturn," the teacher continued, ignoring the weather map question. "It's big enough to swallow four earths," he reminded us.

At that, several people snapped to attention and looked up at the sky. Three more people turned and left the building, toting their unprocessed packages with them. I pulled my regulation blue cardigan closer around me and took care of mail from Harvey Stone, the second-oldest man in the Berkshires, or so he claimed.

Harvey had been laughing through it all. "This is nothin'," he said. "I've seen worse storms before breakfast many a time." Harvey stood his ground now, and very quickly became the only person in the lobby once the teller, the science teacher, and all the other North Ashcot natives left the scene.

Harvey was on his usual errand, with a package to his youngest "boy" in Michigan, who was probably only in his seventies. I knew I'd be treated to a few storm stories while I weighed and labeled the box.

I'd already heard the one about the huge maple that fell on his station wagon during a microburst in the nineties, and about the time in the eighties when downed utility lines left the town without power for ten days. Harvey's most dramatic tale, told many times, included the Great Hurricane in September of 1938, when his family's home had been destroyed.

"That was before they named hurricanes," he reminded us every time. "But I was a hellion of a small boy, and my daddy used to say they should have named the storm Hurricane Harvey." He laughed, and ended his visit with another word of wisdom from his daddy. "No matter what you do, the storm is going to win."

As if in response, a woman seemed to be blown into the lobby when she opened the door from the outside, also serving up another torrent of rain.

It was time to take the flag down.

I looked out the front door and saw that Ben, my pseudo-retired predecessor, was way ahead of me, already taking down the flag. For once we were of the same mind.

Ben was kind and generous on the one hand, and a first-class curmudgeon on the other. He'd opposed every ounce of modernization I'd brought to the office, from updated equipment to broader customer service, such as accommodating the Raleys' young four-legged charges. But when it came to pitching in when I needed a hand, Ben was on the job, often unsolicited, as now, even though he'd long since stopped receiving a paycheck.

With the rattling of windows in the background and a brief respite from customers, I answered quick texts from Quinn, who was off on a treasure hunt through New England, scouting for antique treasures for his shop, and from my friend Linda Daniels in Boston. I knew both of them would be watching the weather map.

The weather could be vastly different from north to south, east to west across our state even though Massachusetts ranked forty-fifth out of fifty in size, only a little more than eight thousand square miles. ("You can fit twenty of them inside California," Quinn bragged, comparing our native states.)

Today Linda reported only scattered showers in the state's capital, while Quinn's return message to me from the far suburbs was

cruising around Taunton today. wild winds starting up here. good bargains. miss u.

I smiled and immediately acknowledged.

miss u 2.

A few brave stragglers ventured in before I could hang the CLOSED sign, which would usually be for the lunch hour, but today was until further notice. I took care of an express mailing headed for the Florida Keys and a media mail package on the way to New York, and then Ben and I struggled together with the shutters.

"Reminds me of the summer of '04," he said, his rain-soaked hair and bedraggled face leaving me to wonder which century he was referring to. "I was on vacation in Nantucket when Jeannie hit."

"Do you think this storm will get a name?"

Ben looked at the sky with a practiced eye. "I doubt it."

We admitted one last customer, Olivia "Liv" Patterson, an expert quilter and a member of the circle I'd joined. I felt my face flush, since, for a variety of reasons, I hadn't done my sewing homework for the week.

When I first returned to town and met Liv, I'd foolishly admitted to her that I needed a hobby. She'd been delighted, smoothing the way for me to join her group, reminding me that my new best friend, the chief of police, was also in the group.

"I don't have a sewing machine," I'd said.

"You can borrow one of mine."

"*One* of yours? How many do you have?"

She'd smiled. "Don't ask."

With Liv now stepping up to the counter with a stack of mail from her card shop, I preempted her potential query about my progress by asking about the enormous quilt she'd been working on for her daughter who was headed for a college in the Northwest. She'd been collecting fabric with a Western theme. Usually, Liv would have no shorter than a five-minute answer to any question related to her quilts. Not today.

"It's fine," she said.

"I'll bet you have a hundred hours invested in it."

"Right," she said.

I made one more attempt. "Did you ever find that fabric you were looking for, with a stagecoach?"

She shrugged, a deep frown creasing her brow. "Yeah, well, let's not talk about fabric, okay?" She waved her hand at my counter, pointed to her pieces of mail, which I'd been working on as we talked. "I'd like to be done with this, please."

"Okay," I said. I wondered what had upset Liv enough to produce this mood, but it was none of my business. She was probably nervous about the storm, and besides, I had shutters to put up and howling wind to battle.

While Liv walked away, Ben, who'd crept up behind me, whispered, "Even the grouchiest customer is always right."

It was always nice when Ben and I agreed on something.

We set to the next task, complying with the request of one of our town selectmen that we check the emergency supplies in the community room adjoining the post office. The all-purpose room ran the whole width of the building, with a connecting door to the retail floor. The closets were always in a ready state for emergencies, with necessities like blankets, flashlights, bottled water, packaged goods, and first-aid kits.

Quinn said the stash reminded him of growing up in San Francisco, where they learned at an early age to be prepared for when the Big One might hit. Not a hurricane or a blizzard, but an earthquake.

"At least there's warning with our storms," I boasted.

"But earthquakes last only a matter of seconds, not days," he countered.

Thus had begun a short back-and-forth on hurricane damage versus earthquake damage and finally we agreed that whatever the detailed statistics, when it came to natural disasters, it was lose-lose for humans.

Now, with the supplies checked, and the shuttering of the front doors complete, Ben and I packed up our things and went our separate ways to take care of our own homes. All we had to do first was wade through the enormous pond that was the parking lot to our cars.

2

After what seemed like a swim through a regulation swimming pool, I shook myself out of my soaking wet rain jacket, threw it in the backseat of my car, and wrung out my newly styled hair. I thought how much worse the repair work would be if my curls were still past my shoulders as they had been a couple of weeks ago. I started my car and watched my windshield wipers struggle to keep up with the deluge. The wipers were losing.

The heavy rain made for poor visibility on my way home, even in the middle of the day. Wings of water flew up on both sides of my car as I drove through puddles that were more like tiny lakes creeping up to the level of the curbs. The gutters were no more successful than my windshield wipers against the downpour. I swerved more than once to avoid small branches and other debris—no fewer than four umbrellas, for example—that had lost the battle with the gusting wind.

I kept my car radio tuned to a station with weather every ten minutes on normal days, but was dedicated to storm announcements full-time today. The banter between radio news personalities matched that between television anchors, as two newscasters debated which did the most damage—wind or rain? Hadn't I studied that issue when I was exposed to the ancient Greek philosophers in college? Apparently, the issue hadn't been settled.

"It's six of one, half dozen of the other," a female newsperson said, with all seriousness.

"A good point, Bonnie," her male counterpart answered, equally serious, as if he'd been considering the answer for a while, perhaps consulting his old Western culture textbooks, and Bonnie had just offered the words of wisdom he'd been waiting for.

"We're lucky in Massachusetts, Jeff," the radiowoman noted. "We're in the enviable position of receiving all three hurricane threats."

"That's right, Bonnie. Depending on the track of the storm, we're subject to coastal inundation, inland river flooding, and widespread wind damage even far inland."

I figured it took a lot of training to give bad news while maintaining an upbeat cadence to his voice.

Now Bonnie and Jeff were resorting to weather history, reminding us that it had been a good year, without a backbreaking winter storm—lots of snow through January and February but nothing that brought major outages.

"We should have known there'd be August to pay," Bonnie said, before Jeff issued warnings for all in the commonwealth to take precautions.

I switched to another station, where a nameless female lifted our spirits with human interest stories, like the one about a young boy who braved the wind and a flooded back-yard to rescue his neighbor's wayward puppy. A South Ashcot woman had made an enormous pot of soup and delivered portions to residents of a block that had lost power, and our own Main Street Hardware man, Pete Clarkson, had offered to deliver emergency repair supplies to anyone in the city limits of North Ashcot.

My drive was slow, probably also thanks to the many other workers who'd decided to leave their posts and wait out the storm at home. Most of the shops—the convenience market, bank, nail salon, and bakery—had already closed, or perhaps the owners had taken the forecast seriously and never opened this morning. There were no signs of life, either, in any of the offices above the shops. The lights were on only in Daisy's Fabrics, on the south side of Main Street, in reality a shop stocked half with bolts of material and half with gift items, and where I'd spent some time lately. I saw the petite Daisy, draped in a yellow anorak, exit the shop, presumably to pull in the container of decorative banners displayed under her canopy. I waved, but apparently she didn't see me.

I recalled my first trip into the back room of Daisy Harmon's shop. I'd almost walked into an ironing board, set up near the doorway, a semicircle of chairs behind it. I hadn't ironed since my days as a Girl Scout, thanks to permanent-press fabrics and a modest budget for dry cleaning. The modern wrinkles-are-stylish trend didn't hurt, either.

Daisy had grabbed my arm as I was turning to leave. "It's okay, Cassie. Newbies get issued already pressed fabric." I wondered if she had more than one ironing board, the way most quilters had more than one sewing machine.

Daisy, about a foot shorter and a few years older than me, with twice my energy, was a born teacher, delighting over small achievements, like when I finally produced a true quarter-inch seam of straight line stitches. Two classes into the course, I'd stopped wishing I'd tried the knitting class instead; I was hooked. I loved working with different textures and so many colors and patterns. For the last several months I'd been laboring steadily on a red, white, and blue block quilt. (Not only was I a postal employee, but I was also a pushover for all patriotic designs.)

"Who's the quilt for?" members of the circle had asked me.

"It depends on how it turns out," I said.

"We hear you" was the comforting response.

I thought of stopping now to see if Daisy needed help shutting down but figured her husband would be on hand, since Cliff worked as a security guard in the elementary school across the street. I continued on. At least it was summer and he wouldn't have classrooms full of students to worry about today.

On the same side of Main Street as Daisy's was the darkened Café Mahican I also knew well; the card shop run by Liv Patterson, another quilter (so grumpy today); and Mike's Bike Shop on the corner of Main and Second. Stopped at a light, I noticed a row of bicycles that were still on the sidewalk in front of Mike's Shop. Strange, I thought at first, but then figured today's new materials probably rendered bikes indestructible in the face of wind and rain. The shop looked dark, but with my rain-streaked windows I couldn't be sure.

My final acknowledgment was to the police station on the next corner, where my friend Chief Sunni Smargon would not be free to leave her post. I gave a mental wave to her and most likely all four of her officers on duty today, and after a few more blocks of stunt driving through debris and overflowing gutters, I pulled into my rock-strewn driveway.

Aunt Tess had willed her home to me, and teased that she might not have, if I weren't the only living relative she had left. And one who looked like her, tall, dark-haired, and thin, to boot. I'd spent my late teenage years in her loving care after my parents died, and was happy to come back and make her last weeks as comfortable as possible. It was still hard to think of her without tearing up.

I'd recently had the exterior of the house repainted in the same pale yellow Aunt Tess loved, and with Quinn's help, I'd updated the interior with some of his own handcrafted pieces.

When I opened my car door in the driveway, it was pulled from my hands by a gust of wind. I exited hunched over, the hood of my jacket over my head, and used two hands to shut the door. I climbed the front steps with my head down, unlocked my door, and practically fell into my living room.

My landline was ringing, a good sign—North Ashcot wasn't disconnected yet. I dumped my purse and briefcase on the carpet, threw off my dripping jacket, and checked the caller ID display. Linda Daniels from her 617 area code in the heart of Boston, checking in again.

"I didn't think I'd get through," she said. "Your storm is all over the news, not a half hour after I thought you said you were clear. Are you okay?"

I gave her a quick rundown, kicking off my soaking wet shoes while I talked. "So far, no big problems," I assured her. "What's it like there?"

"All we have is some fairly heavy rain. They're saying the eye is going to turn south." She laughed. "Or north."

I walked the phone over to my front windows, where torrents pelted against the glass. "I wish you could hear this."

"You said you didn't want anyone to make a fuss over your first anniversary in North Ashcot, but I guess Mother Nature is overruling you. She must know how much you love the sounds of storms."

"I do, but I'm hoping it will be calm by next weekend for the parade," I said, immediately regretting my reference to our upcoming celebration. "For your trip, that is," I added.

Too late. Big-city Linda chuckled as she always did at the idea of a small-town event. I remembered a time when I couldn't imagine it, either—settling back into a town with a population of three thousand. Some days I missed the urban environment I'd lived in with Linda, my coworker at Boston's main postal facility. Every evening we had a choice of entertainment—passive, like watching a play at one of the many theaters; or active, like dancing the night away at a club. As for restaurants, name an ethnic group and its cuisine was showcased somewhere among the tall buildings.

I knew Linda's sarcastic tone came partly from wishing I'd return to Boston, where our daily contact was a highlight of our busy lives.

"Oh, right, the big parade is next weekend, isn't it?"

Linda asked, as I feared she would. "Of course. It's in honor of the famous Henry . . . who was he again?"

"Henry Knox, as you know very well. As if Boston doesn't have its share of Revolutionary War monuments and heroes."

"You want to compare Paul Revere with Henry Knox? The statue at the Old North Church to the little plaque in the park on Main Street?"

"Never mind." It was useless to try to convince Linda that just because Paul Revere's midnight ride was more famous than Henry Knox's journey across the state to deliver needed artillery to the battlefields, that didn't make him more important in the war for independence. "Did you know that Henry Knox was the first secretary of war?" I asked, unable to quit defending my small town and its heroes.

"I did not know that."

"You mean, 'Who cares?' right?"

"It's nice that you have Quinn, your California native, now," Linda said, backing off, but only a bit. "He probably knows nothing about the Revolutionary War and will listen raptly."

It was true that Quinn had let me go on and on about the legendary General Knox, my current favorite commemorative stamp honoree. He inserted a "Wow" at appropriate times in my simple version of the tale: twenty-five-year-old Knox on an ox sled, dragging fifty cannons from Fort Ticonderoga in New York, across ice and snow, to deliver them to General George Washington, waiting in Boston to win the war. It was enough to set a patriotic heart thumping.

"Hey, do I hear a John Philip Sousa march?" Quinn had asked a few times. In turn, I let him teach me about the many missionaries who'd shaped California history. I was still struggling to pass his test, naming the twenty-one missions.

I hadn't anticipated all these treks through history on my phone call. It took a minute to get my mind back to Linda in the present.

"I think the parade is the last thing on the minds of the government here right now," I said to Linda. "It's all about storm damage control. But I'm still planning to put up the display of Knox stamps as soon as they arrive."

"I thought they were out of print."

"They are. But I have my sources."

I refrained from mentioning that I'd also hoped to have my patriotic quilt finished in time for the display in the community room on the day of the parade. I'd greatly under-estimated the time it would take to finish even a relatively small quilt. Linda had been less than enthusiastic when I told her of my new hobby. Finally, she'd reminded me that there were quilting bees in Boston, too, whenever I was ready to return.

"As if you would know" was my retort, just before we called a halt to the my-town-is-better-than-yours banter.

We wrapped up with a mutual hope that the weather would allow her to visit next weekend.

After I clicked off, I made a tour of my house, checking windows and doors, making sure my flashlights were all in working condition, my candles and matches in strategic locations—all while toweling my hair. A look in my cabinets had me wishing I'd made a stop for groceries. With Quinn, my favorite cook, on his business trip, there was little in the way of leftovers. Peanut butter and homemade (not by me) lemon marmalade would have to do for lunch. Dinner was many hours and many inches of rain away. Maybe it would be clear enough by then to venture out again.

I carried my PB sandwich and a mug of coffee to the living room and turned on the television. Nothing but talk shows until the top of the hour. For distraction, I left the set tuned to the roundtable talk of five celebrity women, as they were billed. Never mind that their only celebrity as far as I knew was this talk show. I fell asleep halfway through my sandwich and a discussion of how DNA testing was going a long way toward settling problems of paternity in Hollywood. *Glad that's off my mind.*

The sound of an ambulance blaring past my front lawn jolted me awake. Sirens followed close behind—a North Ashcot Police Department patrol car, I knew by now.

I looked out the living room windows, through sheets of rain, in time to catch sight of a fire engine and a second police cruiser joining the convoy traveling west—in the direction of the post office. And an entire downtown of shops, I reminded myself, wondering if I should check on my building.

I tried again for television news, lucky this time. Our local anchor team, Rick and Erin, took turns reading from notes to update viewers on the state of the storm. Erin was in the middle of a boilerplate paragraph urging the citizens of North Ashcot and vicinity to err on the side of safety and stay indoors.

"And please, folks, refrain from heavy power usage, even though this storm may turn out to be a dud, and not one for the books. Also, we want you to know—"

"I'm afraid there's some unfortunate news," Rick said, interrupting. He held up a sheet of paper that had been handed to him. Erin looked genuinely surprised and eager to hear the tidbit. Rick continued. "As tireless as our city workers have been, on alert for the safety of all"—he turned to address Erin—"I'm sorry to say that we have our first casualty, Erin."

Erin's face took on a somber look and I noticed a discreet gulp and a soft clearing of her throat. "What do we know for sure, Rick?"

Probably nothing, ever, I thought, but a negative outlook was the last thing we needed today.

"Emergency workers arrived on the scene in downtown North Ashcot just moments ago, and have confirmed that the storm has claimed one life in that town," Rick said.

Erin took over, facing the camera. "This might be a good time for a break while we seek out the details. We'll be back shortly with more news on this devastating storm."

In a minute, the storm had gone from "dud" to "devastating." And my attention went from a dull interest to full alert.

One life lost will do that.

I kept myself busy with paperwork I'd brought home from my PO desk and sat facing the muted television set, ready to tune in again when Rick and Erin or their counterparts returned with news. My mind kept drifting to the question: Who was the casualty of the storm?

I couldn't put a number to how many of the three thousand townsfolk I knew. Certainly the dozens of my high school classmates who had never moved away. Now I handled their mail and knew a lot more about their lives than I did twenty years ago. I knew who had relatives out of town (in important jobs, unemployed, in prison), where and how often they took vacations, which catalogue companies they bought from, which magazines they read, what kinds of puzzles they were hooked on. Such was the life of a postal worker in any city, but especially so in a small town.

When Terry Thornton, another quilter, walked up to my counter last week with a stack of "Save the Date" postcards, I became one of the first to know that she and Justin had set a wedding date. I made a private bet with myself that Terry would begin subscribing to a brides' magazine, and, sure enough, I'd been right, though I would never have revealed her pseudoprivate business. I also knew the length and birth weight of former resident Mabel Foster's new granddaughter. The more than two dozen postcard announcements, addressed to select people on her mailing list, passed through my hands and into the homes or PO boxes of her chosen recipients.

Day after day, I learned things about North Ashcot citizens that perhaps only their closest friends were aware of— late payments, a high- or low-end shopping spree, a returned item, a prescription drug.

Now one of those citizens was dead as a result of the wind and rain outside my door. Did I know the person, more than as his or her mail handler? Was he or she an old friend? A new friend? A customer? Selfishly, I hoped not. I wanted it to be a stranger, a drifter perhaps, realizing full well that any "stranger" to me would still have family and friends who would grieve. But I'd been back only a year and had already experienced the loss of my aunt and a friend from high school. That should have been enough for a while.

Rick and Erin never showed up again. Eventually, two beefy men took over the screen and treated us to a sports roundup—not even a storm could stop the tide of sports information. Impatient for more local details, I called Ben.

"Wouldn't your friend know who was killed?" he asked. "Isn't she the chief of police?" Ben wisecracked.

"I thought she might be a little busy right now," I said.

"And I'm not?"

"No, you're not."

"Dang right," he said, chuckling. "I heard it was branches."

"Excuse me?"

"Branches of a big old maple got lopped off by the wind and hit someone. Don't know who."

From my television, which had finally caught up, I heard similar words. Branches. A tree in the backyard. A visual showed the flashing lights of the ambulance, fire truck, and patrol cars on Main Street from a couple of hours ago. It was impossible to tell exactly which address was the scene of the accident, but it was surely on the route I'd driven only an hour ago, between the post office and my home. The police department building was in that same stretch of properties. How sad that someone had died within the shadow of those who might have been able to protect him. But as old Harvey's daddy had said, one way or another, the storm was going to win.

I called a few people and left messages or not, deciding on the spot. I'd run out of options for getting information on who the storm victim was and thought I should do something productive. I wasn't usually home in the daytime, and though I'd often claimed the opposite, I had no intention of giving my house a thorough cleaning, sorting through old photos, or organizing my files. Maybe in retirement.

I tried Quinn to see if a Skype session was possible but then remembered today was a big travel day for him, up to Bangor, Maine. I knew the storm was still rattling around the East Coast in various stages of severity, and hoped he was not in its path.

I'd finished my office work, gone through all my magazines, worked on my quilt until the point where I needed Daisy's advice on color matching, and almost given in to a vacuuming session when my doorbell rang. Though the wind had died down significantly, the rain was still pretty heavy and I suspected some of our streets were flooded. Who could be ignoring the warnings to stay off the roads? Whoever it was rang again, more insistent.

I peeked through the blinds in the living room, then opened the door to the chief of police. She brushed by me carrying a large covered plastic container. "Chicken soup. I knew you wouldn't have anything good."

Sunni was the quintessential small-town woman. She did it all—cooked (not just your everyday chicken soup), quilted, baked from scratch, and held down one of the most responsible jobs in the county. Maybe that was why I'd left town after high school. I knew I couldn't measure up to images like hers. Living in the Fenway District of Boston, where all supplies and services and all the major food groups were a phone call away, had made me even more lazy.

A typical conversation between Linda and me would bear that out.

Scene: a living room, hers or mine, on a weekday evening after work.

"I wish I had something good to go with coffee." (Her or me.)

"We could whip up a coffee cake. They're not hard to make." (Me or her.)

"Do you have any flour?"

"I'm not sure."

"Or we could go to Dunkin' Donuts and have one of their banana chocolate chip muffins."

"And take back a few extra for the rest of the week."

In the next scene, we'd be at the nearest coffee shop, having called a couple of buddies to join us.

"Next time, we should bake ourselves," one of us would say, pulling a muffin apart. "How hard can it be?" And the others would laugh.

Now I watched the slight-framed Sunni, her auburn hair dripping from the rain, standing over my stove. I loved that she knew its idiosyncrasies better than I did. She poured servings of hearty soup into two bowls, carried them to my kitchen table, took a seat, and indicated that I should do the same.

I motioned toward my clock. Five fifteen. "Is this a late lunch or an early dinner?" I asked.

"I don't know about you, but for me, it's the rest of my breakfast."

Her first words since she took over my stove. She looked as though she'd been out in the storm, from its beginning to its near end, which was promised to be within the hour.

She retreated to silence for a few spoonfuls of hot soup. "I have something to tell you," she said.

I looked at her bedraggled body, her face that had been somber since her arrival. I should have known. I wasn't just a convenient place to prepare her meal, though that happened before and would have been enough for me to welcome her. She could have stopped a few blocks from here and used the microwave in her own break room at the police station.

I felt my stomach clutch, every muscle tense. "It's about the casualty."

She nodded.

I ran through the possibilities, grateful to be able to eliminate a few key people—Ben, Sunni herself, and my traveling boyfriend—as potential victims.

"Daisy," she said in a near whisper, her head bent over her bowl.

I let my spoon bounce into my bowl, splattering the table with globs of soup. "Daisy Harmon?" I asked, as if there were another Daisy in our circle. "I just saw her. I waved to her on my way home."

That ought to do it. That should clear things up. Daisy couldn't be dead.

3

I t wasn't the first time I'd tried to bring someone back to life simply by willing it to be so. The first time was at the news of my parents' death in a car crash. This time it was a friend who, like my parents, I'd assumed would be around for a long time. How wrong could I be? How often?

"Daisy Harmon died in the storm," Sunni said, from another world. "I just talked to Cliff. He's been at some kind of training program for private security forces in Springfield."

Daisy's husband. "He's supposed to be across the street." He was supposed to be on hand to help her, was what I meant.

Sunni gave me a strange look, perhaps the first eye contact she'd made. I saw her gaze wander toward my living room and out the door. I realized she was trying to focus on my reference to "across the street."

"I mean when I saw her on my way home, once I closed up. I figured Cliff must be at the school across from her shop."

She shook her head. "He's been out of town since Wednesday. He drove back after I called him, and got here a couple of hours ago. Her parents are in Florida, and except for some cousins in the Midwest, she has no other relatives."

"Cliff must be devastated."

"No one's prepared for something like this."

I couldn't get my last image of Daisy out of my mind. I wished she'd waved back at me. Foolish thought. She'd been in front of her shop, alive, not long after noon when I drove by. Then she was dead. How could that be?

"When did it happen?" I asked.

"Around one thirty. Tony found her."

"Bike shop Tony?"

"Yeah, the young guy, going to school at night. He went out back to drag the trash barrels into the little covered area and he saw a branch of the tree on Daisy's property was down. He thought he heard activity, so he yelled over, and"—Sunni picked at a twig of grapes from a bowl on my table—"when she didn't answer, he hoisted himself on the fence and saw her under the branch, and ran down the alley to the street and then up the other alley into her backyard. When he got there she was dead. Tony thinks if he could have climbed the fence, he might have saved her. But there's no telling when the branch had fallen."

Cliff, Tony, and I—how many other people were now second-guessing their decisions, thinking they could have prevented Daisy's death somehow? I thought how this must be a regular occurrence for Sunni, trying to go back and figure out how she, the chief cop, could have done better in a disaster, even prevented a death.

The wind and rain had stopped. They had done their damage. I wished there were someone to be angry with. I gestured to the living room where the chairs were more comfortable. "Can you stay awhile?" I asked Sunni.

"I shouldn't. I need to give Ross a break."

Not that I would remind her, but Officer Ross Little was about twenty years younger than Sunni, and well able to handle an extra shift or two.

"Just a few minutes," I said. "You've had a rough day already."

If I were being honest, I'd have admitted to her that I didn't want to be alone just yet. Thus my relief when she let out a heavy sigh, followed my directions, and sat on one of my rockers.

"It wasn't that bad a storm," I said, sitting across from her. "We've had so many that were worse, not just the past year, but also my first years here as a kid. Nor'easters. Hurricanes. Blizzards." I ticked them off on my fingers, almost mentioning earthquakes in my distress. "There wasn't even widespread power loss with this storm. And Daisy was killed by it?"

"Maybe," Sunni said. Maybe? Was this my fantasy speaking? Was Daisy in the ICU, with a chance of recovering? Had I misunderstood from the beginning? "I'm waiting for a call from Barry."

The medical examiner. North Ashcot was one of the few small towns with its own ME, a local doctor who performed double duty in cases of suspicious death. What was suspicious about Daisy's death, other than it was a senseless loss from a storm that probably wouldn't even require government assistance?

"You mentioned you saw Daisy during the storm?" Sunni asked me.

I nodded and described my ride home. "The visibility was so poor, I'm not sure now. The person I saw was the right size, with that yellow anorak Daisy always wore in the rain, but I suppose anyone could have thrown it on for a minute to grab the banners."

"One of her employees," Sunni suggested.

I thought for a minute. As far as I knew, Daisy's helpers were all part-time students. "Mia is way too tall. Barb is much heavier. Katie is visiting a friend in Philadelphia for two weeks. But no, she's back already." I threw up my hands. "I guess I just assumed it was Daisy."

"But you're sure whoever it was, they were handling the merchandise, taking it inside?"

"Yes," I said, glad to be firm on one thing at least. "I'm sorry I can't be certain of much more. Is this important?"

"Could be."

"Now I wish I'd pulled over and offered to help her."

"Maybe it's just as well you didn't."

"What do you mean by that?"

Sunni's phone rang. I wanted to quash the call. I doubted I'd be able to survive a long wait for clarification on her questions to me.

I heard her side of the conversation only.

"Yeah, Barry."

A long, never-ending pause.

"That's final?"

A shorter pause. A few "Okays." Another pause. And finally, "Then I guess we have a lot of work to do."

Sunni clicked off her cell and looked past me. "Daisy was murdered."

Not the clarification I'd hoped for.

Sunni was out the door before I could ask how or who or any of the growing list of questions about Barry's message. When she popped her head back in a moment later, I thought she was going to take it all back. Instead, she said, "Not a word, okay?" and left again without waiting for an answer.

All I could do was climb into bed, fully clothed, and hope for sleep.

I woke on Tuesday morning with none of the restful feeling that should start a day. Not wanting to wake Quinn, I texted him sad news. call when u r up and got ready for work. Not that he knew Daisy as well as I did, but I needed to share my grief with someone other than the chief of police.

Thanks to an efficient town government and committed business owners, there were hardly any signs of storm debris along my commute path only one day later. Even faster than a twenty-four-hour flu bug, the storm had come and gone. I sent a silent thank-you to the men and women in orange vests who'd worked through the night to clear the way for business as usual.

All the more striking, then, was the yellow-and-black CAUTION tape strung in front of Daisy's Fabrics. The cheerful yellow-and-white CLOSED sign quilted by Daisy herself still hung on the door and made a mockery of the last twenty-four hours.

I thought of security guard Cliff Harmon, Daisy's husband, and how awful it must have been for him to be notified of her death. I wanted to call and offer my sympathy but decided to wait until the final ME report was in. I wasn't sure whether Cliff had been made aware of the suspicious nature of Daisy's death; glad I didn't have Sunni's job making decisions like that.

I wondered what Cliff had been doing at the time he learned of his wife's death. Listening to a boring lecture on advances in surveillance techniques? Engaged in a high-impact practice drill? Enjoying a relaxing break in his hotel room?

I knew too well how life could change in a moment, with one phone call. Like the one I received while I was at my best friend Crystal's surprise sixteenth birthday party. My surprise trumped hers when a call came from Aunt Tess, tearfully informing me that there had been a car accident, a very bad accident. I remembered everything from that one still frame of my life—the taste of coconut from Crystal's favorite German chocolate cake; the striped sweater vest my mother had helped me knit and wrap for my friend; a crowd of teenagers' bodies moving to the music of the Macarena; how the sunflower clip I wore in my long, thick hair fell to the floor as I pushed the phone against my head in anguish. It seemed a lifetime ago. Or one minute ago.

As with Cliff Harmon, I'd had no warning, no chance for one more "Good-bye" or a final, tender "I love you."

I thought, Poor Cliff, and poor everyone who suffered great loss.

* * *

The mood at the post office on Tuesday morning was a strange mixture, hushed sadness over what was still thought to be Daisy's accidental death, and overreaction to the relatively minor wreckage the storm had left in its wake.

Sunni had sworn me to secrecy about the ruling that our friend had been murdered. She needed an official written report from ME Barry before the verdict could be made public.

"I'm glad you were there," she said in a message left on my voice mail this morning. "And I also wish you weren't."

I got her meaning and wanted to assure her she could trust me not to enter the gossip fray. She knew me well enough to trust that. If there was one thing a postal worker understood, it was the importance of confidentiality.

Everyone in the post office lobby today had a storm story to tell. I had a strong suspicion that some citizens had whipped up letters and packages for the sole purpose of coming into town and meeting their friends. You never knew what might help or hurt a particular business day. The North Ashcot Post Office had a lot going for it—it was larger than the coffee shop and cooler than the park behind the school, now baking again in the August sun, as if there hadn't been a big departure from the weather norm only yesterday. Another factor in the townspeople's choice of venue was that Mahican's fancy espresso equipment had suffered from a power surge during the storm, one of the few breakdowns in utilities in town, making the menu less desirable. I thought of installing a watercooler in my lobby, but it was hardly necessary to encourage gathering and chatting.

Stories worked their way down the line along the length of the lobby, overlapping and competing with one another for drama.

"Tore up every flower, but darned if the weeds aren't tall as ever."

"Ashie's doghouse collapsed like it was made of feathers."

"Our big waste container toppled over and smashed a basement window." This speaker clapped his hands to make a sound that suggested shattering glass.

A little boy enjoyed the laughter following his report: His little sister's crib was in the same room as his bed, and the crib "shaked and shaked."

"She slept right through it," the boy said. "Prolly thought our mom was rocking her."

It seemed Daisy's friends and customers hadn't yet come to grips with her death. Well into the morning retail hours, there was still no shortage of tsk-tsks and tales of frightened pets and flooded gutters, but talk of Daisy remained limited to mumbled expressions of dismay over the loss of "such a vibrant young woman," "a gifted teacher," and "a generous businesswoman." I thought the toned-down nature was out of respect for Cliff, who might have walked through the door at any minute.

The intensity of remembrances took a turn when Gigi, the young woman who ran the florist shop down the street, came in with a large vase of daisies and sunflowers, accompanied by a memorial card.

"Okay if I put these on the counter in memory of Daisy?" she asked me. "Maybe people can sign the card for Cliff?"

I pushed aside what Ben, a stickler for rules, would think

of the departure from policy. "This is not a public meeting place," he'd say.

"What a nice thought," I said, and for convenience, added a post office logo pen to the display.

Tuesday night should have been quilt night in the back room of Daisy's Fabrics, where a group of six to ten women gathered weekly in our version of a quilting bee. A true "bee," according to Daisy, involved women sitting around a homemade wooden frame with a single large quilt stretched across it. All the women would work on the same project. In our group, there was often sharing of blocks and patterns, but for the most part, we brought our own materials and enjoyed twenty-first-century treats from a sturdy crafts table, not a rickety frame supported by a rough sawhorse.

After a flurry of e-mails, texts, and phone messages during the day, the consensus among the group had been that we should get together tonight as usual, as a way of remembering Daisy. Eileen Jackson, a retired middle school teacher and longtime quilter, offered her home for the meeting. It turned out that her husband, Buddy, played cards on Tuesdays, so the timing was perfect and the house was ours. Not surprisingly, Eileen had already delivered a food basket to Cliff's home.

Eileen's home was more modern than I would have expected from a North Ashcot native of her generation. I saw none of the dark paneling and heavy furniture so common in the older houses in town. We brought our snack contributions into a kitchen that was bright and open, with white appliances and light maple floors and cabinets. Tonight's offerings included a cheesecake, assorted crackers and cheeses, and brownies from me, via the freezer section of the market.

My incorrect expectations were driven by what my aunt Tess's home had looked like until I finally made it my own over the past few months. Although my aunt was modern in her thinking, the décor in her home remained in the style of her own mother's era, with thick carpets, heavy drapes, and elaborate furniture. Even Quinn had been astonished by the weight of a dark oak dresser that was almost immovable until he detached the mirror, ornate posts, and extra drawers that rested on the top surface. A rolled-arm love seat with delicately carved wooden trim also presented a physical challenge to Quinn and the crew he worked with at Ashcot's Attic.

Six of us assembled at Eileen's home at the west end of town tonight. Sunni had expressed her regrets at missing the meeting. We all understood how busy she must be, and I figured she was also not ready to face a firing squad in the form of a group of quilting women eager for the latest information.

Eileen, tall and stately, with a teacher's commanding voice, assumed Daisy's role and called us to order. We carried our sewing totes and works in progress into the living room and took seats in the same configuration that we chose in Daisy's back room. Frances Rogers, a middle-aged woman who worked as a teller at the Main Street Bank, sat to my left; beauty salon owner Molly Boyd, to my right. Molly, a short, heavy woman, was on crutches this evening.

"My brand-new porch chair, a big Adirondack, got tipped

over during the storm and landed on my ankle," she explained. "Don't ask why I didn't go inside as soon as the wind picked up. Now I have a broken ankle, just because I wanted to sweep up outside in honor of the new furniture. How dumb can I be? And now it's a mess out there anyway, of course."

We all expressed our sympathies and hoped Molly would be walking normally soon.

Someone suggested a moment of silence for Daisy. I joined in, though I'd already had many moments of silence and meditative thought inspired by Daisy's passing. For a minute or two, all we heard were the Westminster chimes from the Jacksons' grandfather clock, the only gesture to the past among the modern furnishings. We resumed normal chatter slowly, with murmurs that our mourning wouldn't really be over until we knew what had happened behind Daisy's shop.

Terry Thornton, our youngest member, got us started on the future. Excited about her upcoming bachelorette party, Terry asked for advice on whether she should wear her long blond hair up or down. She demonstrated both styles for us. My first thought was of the inappropriateness of a cheerful bride-to-be conversation, but I quickly realized that we needed something to help focus on the future and whatever good news might be on the way. The vote was nearly unanimous that Terry should take advantage of her natural curls and let her hair cascade past her shoulders.

I never would have guessed that the next bit of good news would be the start of what old Ben would have called a "catfight."

Andrea Harris was a veteran quilter whose niece was

expecting her first child. This evening, Andrea was ready to put the finishing touches on a baby quilt in different shades of yellow and pale green.

"They don't want to know the baby's gender before the birth," she moaned, referring to her niece and nephew-in-law. "So I have to use these so-called gender-neutral colors."

We all uttered a version of "It's still beautiful."

"But look what I had to pass up," she said, her short, pudgy fingers extracting a swatch of very pink cloth from her tote. "Look at these adorable pink creatures."

Liv Patterson looked closely at the piece of fabric and screwed up her nose. I felt another version of yesterday's unpleasant mood coming on. "A mermaid and a hippo on the same piece of fabric? Maybe they do know the gender, Andrea, and that's why they won't tell you," Liv suggested, drawing a nervous chuckle from most of us. Emboldened by the response, Liv went on. "Aren't you supposed to be the color expert for paint supplies in your brother Pete's hardware store?" She looked around. "Who here wants a pink bedroom?"

The laughter stopped and so did Liv, finally. Andrea looked up from her sewing and seemed understandably put out by the comment. "You're in a good mood, Olivia. Could it be because the storm has made your life easier?"

"What's that supposed to mean?" Liv asked. She removed her fifties-style sewing glasses, which matched her wardrobe, I noted, and cast an angry glance at Andrea.

"I mean your worries about Daisy's shop encroaching on your customer base are gone now that she's out of the picture," Andrea said.

All the noise in room ceased; it seemed quieter than it

had been during our moment of silence. Liv's face turned red. She put her fabric across her lap and opened her mouth to speak.

"What a terrible thing to say," Molly Boyd cut in, followed quickly by overlapping comments from everyone except me. I was too stunned to join the chorus and was glad when Eileen stepped in.

"Let's try Molly's new cheesecake recipe," Eileen said, holding up her hand as if that would be enough to block further unpleasantness. A trick she'd learned from years of elementary school classes, I was sure.

Molly, in spite of her bad ankle, put down her sewing and hobbled over to carve a delicious-looking raspberry-bedecked creation. In deference to Molly's lameness, and to mask my nervousness, I took over the job. The clatter of china dessert plates and silverware became the only sounds in the room, but not for long.

Andrea hadn't finished, starting up again to address Liv, but in a normal conversational tone. "Well, we all know you've been losing money since Daisy added a line of cards to her inventory."

"Excuse me?" Liv asked, her whole stocky body stiffening.

"I get it," said Terry, the youngest in the group, ready with an explanation. Was she naive, thinking one was needed, or was she trying to keep the pot of trouble boiling? "Andrea is referring to how you think Daisy should have stuck to fabrics and not tried to be a card shop, too, since you already run one. Everyone heard you two arguing."

Apparently, she liked the boiling-pot option.

"Not everyone heard anything," Eileen said, scrambling her negatives. She cleared her throat and pulled out her schoolteacher voice again. "Maybe we should change the subject. Did I show you my latest?" Our hostess bravely held up a block we hadn't seen before, a star quilt in shades of green. "Do you think this will be okay for a guy's dorm room? My grandson hinted that quilts were not just for girls, so I'm taking him up on that."

"I think it's perfect," I offered. As the newest person in the group, and inherently averse to conflict, I'd have said anything to get us back to quilting.

"It's manly," Molly offered.

Liv, however, had more to say on the controversial topic. She turned to face Andrea straight-on. "Are you saying I'm glad Daisy is dead?"

Fran, who'd been quiet until now, gasped. "What a terrible thing to say."

Bride-to-be Terry looked eager to say something else, but bit her lip instead. Good choice, I thought.

Liv kept her eyes on Andrea. "If anyone is glad, it's probably you. That's one less obstacle in the way of Reggie's proposal for a farmers' market."

More gasps and words of explanation for those not in the know. Like me. By listening carefully to the snippets of conversation around me, I was able to piece together the story. Reggie Harris, Andrea's husband, a big developer in the county, was spearheading a proposal for a farmers' market in town, every weekend between Memorial Day and Labor Day. The plan called for blocking off the cross streets at both ends of the business district on Main Street on Saturdays and Sundays. Though nothing would happen until next spring, tempers were already running high. I learned that Daisy had led the opposition, maintaining that a farmers' market would severely impact all the businesses between the post office and the police station and beyond.

Almost a full year back in North Ashcot, working in the center of town, and I still had a lot to learn about city politics. It wasn't enough to listen to my customers; I needed to work on the stack of local newspapers by my rocker, especially the op-ed pages.

Liv and Andrea packed up and stormed out of Eileen's house within five minutes of each other. No one wondered out loud whether they'd come to an impasse or were taking their fight somewhere else.

Eileen made an effort to pull the rest of us together by reminding us that we needed an extra meeting on Monday evening next week to prepare for the quilt display as part of Henry Knox Day. We'd meet in the community room adjoining the post office around seven to take measurements and otherwise prepare the room.

I'd had grand plans to be part of the show, unaware at the time of how much work was involved in making just one quilt.

"Next year," I told Eileen in an effort to lift her spirits. "For now, I'll just be part of the backstage crew."

Tonight we beginners (Terry and I) were supposed to learn how to choose and prepare sashing—the strips of fabric that separated the main blocks of a quilt. We approached the lesson, to which everyone usually contributed advice and tips, only halfheartedly. The altercation had gotten us off to a bad start that we couldn't seem to recover from. Not even Molly's special cheesecake or the other snacks could get us out of our funk. Eileen offered a fresh pitcher of iced tea, but no one had the heart to stay much longer.

Poor Eileen looked as if she'd done something wrong.

I thought of calling to her attention that the unpleasant evening wasn't her fault, and that at least no blood had been spilled on her soft white sofa.

4

By Wednesday afternoon, the world knew that Daisy Harmon had been murdered. Or so it seemed in my post office in the middle of the day, with everyone gasping and gulping as the awful news spread. I wasn't surprised that a murder provoked more distress among our citizens than an accidental death. I hadn't heard the final word directly from Sunni—just because we were BFFs didn't mean she had to keep me in the loop, crime-wise, I told myself—and I hadn't watched television at lunch as I sometimes did.

But, as the old bumper sticker says, *there may not be much to see in a small town, but what you hear makes up for it.*

If all that I heard was correct, Daisy was already dead when her killer rolled a large, heavy tree branch over her body, a branch that had conveniently fallen to the ground in the backyard of Daisy's Fabrics. Police thought (said the townsfolk) that there'd been an argument.

"Ya think?" asked Moses Crawford, our oldest citizen, hitching up his baggy jeans. "That must have been some danged argument. Don't know what this world is comin' to."

I regretted that I couldn't take notes, then realized that the chatter I'd heard all day was hearsay at best and I'd lose nothing of value if I forgot some of it.

Between locking the front doors at closing and packing up to leave the building, I played my cell phone messages. I clicked through the usual check-ins from Linda Daniels in Boston ("Any big news in the little town?") and Quinn Martindale, now on the North Shore near Gloucester ("Miss you. Back as soon as I can.") Sunni's voice promised she'd drop in soon (to "explain a couple of things"). The most surprising was a call from Cliff Harmon, Daisy's now-widowed husband. I knew Cliff as well as I knew any of my regular customers, but I wouldn't have expected to be at the top of his list in a crisis.

"If you can spare a few minutes, I'd like to talk to you, Cassie," Cliff said. "Any time that's convenient." His voice was cracked and hoarse as he gave me his cell number.

Curious, as well as eager to help in any way I could, I decided not to wait until I got home. I sat at my desk, surrounded by posters of commemorative stamps of the Civil War, this month's special. I looked past the lobby through the double front doors to the outside, still light, and calm as a late-summer afternoon should be. The storm was long gone, but I knew its aftermath was just beginning for some. I took a deep breath and called Cliff's number.

"Thanks for getting back to me, Cassie. I know you're busy," he said.

"If there's anything I can do for you, don't hesitate to ask. I'm so sorry for your loss."

"Thanks," he said, his voice understandably weak. "I was doing okay at first, you know. Then when I heard . . ." He left unsaid the fact that a murder verdict had compounded his grief over his wife's death.

"This has to be really hard for you. I don't know what to say or how I can help."

"I do have a favor I want to ask. Can you come by this evening? Or I can go to your place. Or some place neutral if you want."

I thought a minute. "Let's meet at Mahican's. That way neither of us has to waste time getting drinks or anything."

Selfish, I admitted to myself. It was less likely that I'd have to deal with an emotional outburst from a grown man—a beefy one, at that—if we were in a public place. My psych classes and further training with the USPS went only so far in enabling me to handle extreme distress, which I imagined was Cliff's current state.

"Whenever you say."

I looked around and saw nothing urgent on my desk. "A half hour?" I asked.

"I'll see you there. Thanks, Cassie."

I finished packing up paperwork that I could take care of at home later and prepared myself to meet Cliff. I doubted I could be of help, but I hoped I could at least be a good sounding board if that was what he needed.

* * *

Cliff was at a corner table in Mahican's, talking to Jules Edwards, his and Daisy's accountant, a middle-aged man I'd met a couple of times in passing. They were head-to-head and seemed quite serious, and I figured that condolences were involved. I wasn't sure if Jules intended to be part of my meeting with Cliff, so I ordered an iced drink at the counter and headed for an empty table where I could wait. Cliff saw me and waved me over.

Jules, maybe an inch taller than my five-nine, greeted me with "How are you doing, Cassie?" and before I could answer he turned and addressed me over his shoulder as he was leaving. "See you around," he said. Not part of the meeting apparently.

Cliff stood, all six feet four of him. His muscles strained the fabric of his army green polo shirt. I put my plastic cup on his table and we shared a brief hug. I'd often thought that Cliff was the poster boy for a bouncer in a tough neighborhood, except that after a few minutes in his company, everyone knew that he was a gentle man and not about to abuse his gift of physical strength. It was well known that the small-framed Daisy was the more aggressive member of the family, the more involved in community issues, the more likely to speak her mind.

"He just walks around and carries a big stick," Daisy often said of her husband.

I pointed to where Jules had been seated and where I'd placed my mug. "I didn't mean to interrupt," I said.

"We were done for now. Daisy's the one who handled all the finances, for the house as well as the shop." He rubbed his forehead, stressed. "I have so much to learn. I don't know where to begin. I guess I figured she'd always be around."

I was at a loss to respond verbally and hoped taking his hand and guiding him to sit down again would do the trick.

When we were both seated at one of Mahican's more scratched-up wooden tables, Cliff handed me a memorial card. On one side was an image of an angel in white, arms (wings?) raised to heaven; on the other a poetic tribute to Daisy Harmon and the important dates in her life. Her birth, marriage to Cliff, and death. A small photo of her was included; in it she looked much younger than her forty-four years. By contrast, Cliff, ten years older than Daisy, I'd heard, looked old enough today to be her father.

"This card is lovely," I said. "I'm surprised you have it so soon."

"The funeral parlor prints the cards themselves, would you believe? Pretty much while you wait."

"I guess I would believe it." I thought of Aunt Tess's memorial last summer and how many services the mortuary offered, right on site. Turnkey shopping was the rule, complete with sheet music to review, and several designs of memorial cards to choose from, like the one I had in my hand.

"They're making the arrangements to have her flown to Miami where her parents are, as soon as"—he closed his eyes and swallowed—"the police will give her back to us."

I let Cliff take the lead in the conversation. He seemed to want to chat for a while. I heard how determined Daisy was to make the shop work, how passionate she was about everything she became involved in. Her husband extolled Daisy's virtues as a wife, a friend, a businesswoman, a concerned citizen.

I wasn't sure yet why I needed to hear this, or why I was

sitting across from him, but I wasn't about to rush Cliff into telling me what favor he wanted. The iced cappuccino was refreshing and if all Cliff needed was someone to listen, I had no problem filling the role.

About fifteen minutes into the visit, I noticed our chief of police enter the café. Before I could put my cup down and raise my hand in greeting, she came up to our table. One might even say, stormed over to our table.

"Hey, Sunni," I said.

She nodded and looked at Cliff, then me, then back and forth one more time. "I hope this isn't what I think it might be," she said, a neutral expression on her face. "It will be much better for all of us if we stick to the jobs we're committed to do." She rapped her knuckles on the table and strode away, without the teasing smile or pat on my shoulder that I expected, leaving me agape.

"What was that about?" I asked Cliff, who seemed to know what Sunni was talking about, as evidenced by the dramatic nodding of his head while she issued her directive.

"It was a warning," he said. "I may have vented a little down at the station today, about how they're not doing much to find out who killed my wife."

"They've hardly known about it for a day," I reminded him.

"I know, but they're not exactly the NYPD, or even the BPD, are they?"

New York and Boston. Apparently, Cliff put more faith in big-city police forces. I couldn't blame him. Sunni had four officers, one admin, and a fleet of three patrol cars at her disposal. I didn't know the stats of the NYPD, but in my former job, I did interact with the BPD's postal needs and recalled that there were over two thousand officers and nearly one thousand civilians in the department, all together about the entire population of North Ashcot.

While I'd been doing the math, Cliff had continued. "When I went down there this morning, there was Ross—Officer Little, that is—playing solitaire or poker or something on his computer."

I felt a great urge to defend my friend and her staff. "They've all been working overtime since the storm on Monday. What if Ross worked all night and finally took a twenty-minute break?" I asked Cliff, tentatively, conscious of his vulnerability at the moment.

I knew this couldn't have been the first time Sunni had to deal with a distraught family member of a victim of crime, and I was sure she had the skills and temperament to handle the job, but a little support couldn't hurt.

"You're right, you're right, Cassie, but it's, like, I'd just convinced myself that Daisy was one of so many victims of storms and natural disasters over the years, and I was going to have to deal with it, and then I hear that she was"—he seemed to be holding his breath—"that someone deliberately . . . I'm sorry if I just lose it."

I put my hand on his, gave it a squeeze, and offered to get refills for both of us. While I waited at the counter in the sparsely populated café, Sunni's words came back to me.

"Do you know what Sunni meant when she said 'stick to our jobs'?" I asked when I returned to our table.

Cliff shrugged. "I guess she figured I was asking you to help with the investigation."

"But you're not."

"Well . . ."

Uh-oh. I realized Cliff still hadn't asked for that favor he'd mentioned on the phone. I shook my head before he could utter the words. "No, Cliff. I can't do that. I'm not a cop."

"But you've done this before. Everyone knows you helped Sunni last year in that murder investigation."

And almost lost Sunni as a friend, I remembered.

"I'm a postmaster; you're a security guard. That's certainly closer to being a cop than I am. Isn't investigation considered part of your job?"

"Not unless the school was set on fire, and even then, it's the local agencies that take the lead."

"My point exactly."

"This is Daisy we're talking about, Cassie. My wife. You can't ask me to sit around and watch. You know, the whole town knows, that I couldn't get into the police academy. My eyesight doesn't meet their standard"— he removed his eyeglasses and held them out, as if to prove his point, then wiped the lenses with his shirt while he was at it—"but I have good instincts. And security guards have high-quality training." He took a deep breath, then continued, this time pointing a finger at me, albeit unobtrusively. "Did you know that it was a private security guard who alerted the police to the break-in at Watergate in the seventies?"

"I didn't know that."

"Yeah, the guy was only twenty-four years old, making his rounds in the building, and he noticed a door had been rigged to stay open. He dug around a little, reported it to the local police, and they found out what was going on and eventually arrested five guys who weren't supposed to be there."

"And the rest is history," I said, fascinated.

"The guy was pretty famous for a while, even got a mention from one of those Watergate scandal reporters, either Robert Redford or Dustin Hoffman, I forget which, but then he came upon some hard times."

I felt his confusing of Woodward and Bernstein with the actors who played them in the movie was understandable, given the circumstances, and let the reference stand. I could tell that this tidbit of history was important to him, and probably in the annals of security firms and personnel everywhere.

"You're just making a case for going off on your own, Cliff. Not that I recommend that. But I have absolutely no training along those lines, except to hit an emergency button if an armed person comes into the post office."

"You're being modest. I know better. I think if we worked together, you and I, we could . . ."

I held up my hand. I was doing a lot of that lately. Cliff continued anyway.

"We could claim you're just helping me clean out the shop."

I'd already shaken my head so much my neck hurt. I stood to leave, which seemed to be the only way to end this conversation. But that didn't work, either. Cliff put his fingers on my wrist, and locked my hand in place. I was amazed that I felt no pain, just a steady, gentle pressure. But one that didn't leave much room for fleeing. His expression registered nothing but pleading.

"Please, Cassie. Will you at least let me tell you some of my ideas?"

I sat back down. I thought about the risks. That we'd

get nowhere, but Sunni would find out we were working on the case and cut me off her list of friends, thus shortening my list considerably. That Cliff and I would actually make progress in uncovering Daisy's killer and be killed ourselves. Either way it wasn't a good outcome. The chances that we would discover Daisy's killer and be alive and well at the end, in good standing with the police, were near zero.

"Okay," I said. "Let's hear it."

Cliff and I decided to move to more comfortable, private quarters, and drove separately toward my house. While he made a detour for ready-made chicken dinners, I ran around my rooms brushing crumbs off my chairs and stuffing stray clothing into closets or hampers.

My mind raced along with my body as I tried to organize what was known about Daisy's murder. That it was not premeditated was obvious—the convenience of a downed tree branch couldn't have been built into the crime scene ahead of time. It seemed most likely that, as the post office gossipers theorized, her murder was the result of an argument that went bad and got physical in the heat of the moment. I wondered if Cliff had come up with the same scenario, and could put a face to the other person.

I remembered the tale of antagonism between Daisy and several merchants along Main Street, especially Liv Patterson, the owner of the card shop next door to Daisy's Fabrics. I nearly laughed at the idea that a quilter could be a killer. But there was nothing funny about what had happened in the backyard of Daisy's Fabrics.

Once Cliff returned with dinner, we wasted no time putting the food on the table and getting to the matter at hand. Although Cliff had chosen top-of-the-line for a precooked meal, and the aroma was appealing, we picked at the servings, neither of us taking dinner too seriously. Somewhere in the last hour, my appetite had left the building.

"What if this was a complete fluke, like a stranger drifting through?" Cliff suggested, clearly struggling with the idea.

"It's possible," I said, though I figured we both knew the unlikelihood of a random killer passing through town during a severe storm, looking for a shop owner to attack, or, finding her hurt, shoving a tree limb across her body.

Cliff rested his forehead in a steeple formed by his arms. He looked defeated already. "Otherwise, I have to believe that someone in this town, someone I may have known for years, killed my wife. Deliberately. Someone who might have been to our home."

Someone whose packages I've processed, I added to myself. "We have to start somewhere," I said. "Is there anyone in particular that Daisy was upset with lately? Or vice versa?"

"Sure. If you deal with the public at all, there's bound to be someone unhappy with you at any given time."

"Absolutely," I said, remembering a few nasty notes I'd received in my career at all levels of postal service.

"I feel awful saying this, but my Daisy could rub a lot of people the wrong way." He blew out a breath, as if trying to gather the courage to say anything negative about his deceased wife. "A few months ago, she had it out with Pete at the hardware store. She said the lightbulbs he sold her didn't last as long as the package claimed they would. Pete tried to make her see that the package had some weasel words, like 'up to' a certain number of hours, not guaranteed. But she wouldn't quit until she got her money back." He smiled. "And if you know Pete, you know he was no match for someone looking for a fight."

I did know that about Pete, the contrast of his sister, Andrea, having been brought home during our quilting session when she showed herself to be the fighter in the family.

"Daisy was a strong person," I said, for lack of a better response.

"That she was. These days, as you know, it's Olivia Patterson she was having trouble with, but truthfully it was Liv who started this little feud."

"Over the greeting cards."

Cliff nodded. "Daisy's been over-the-top angry lately because Liv attacked her decision to branch out into cards and gift items in the shop. You simply can't run a one-item store in a small town. Unless it's auto parts, or bikes. Even then, Mike has started to carry a few toys in his shop. But Liv kept yelling how she wouldn't think of selling fabric in her card shop." He took another breath. "Then Daisy pointed out that Liv did sell fabric in a way—she had some tea towels for sale. And on it went."

"But Gigi carries greeting cards in her florist shop, too, which is not unusual," I noted. "Is Liv going to go after every merchant in town?" I asked.

"It wouldn't surprise me. Daisy tried to be a responsible merchant, you know. She purchased the cards we carried from an independent artist over in Springfield. But most of

Liv's card were from a huge chain. Sure, Liv made a bigger profit, but how is that helping the local economy?"

I saw that although it was now a moot point, it was important for Cliff to run through his defense of his wife's choices. I felt he was trying to rewind recent history to see what could have been done differently. I was no stranger to that mode of dealing with a highly charged emotional experience.

"Surely it wouldn't have been that hard for them to come to an agreement," I said. "Even if Daisy agreed to limit the number of cards she carried, or offered to maybe carry only cards with fabric themes."

"Yeah, that might have worked," Cliff said, brightening, as if it could still happen, as if it weren't too late.

I noted how easy it was in the abstract to settle a dispute that had cost two businesswomen their mutual support and friendship and, possibly, one of them her life.

As for me, I was almost ready to close the case. I pictured what might have started as a verbal confrontation between Daisy and Liv, and then the two women ending up, in the middle of the storm, pushing each other around. I could see Daisy falling, perhaps hitting her head, and Liv, frantic, seizing the chance to cover up the unfortunate result with a tree branch that had already fallen. Too easy a solution? It was not for me to say.

The business issue was so much more complicated than a cursory glance would indicate. I wondered, for example, if I'd ever parked in front of Liv's store and gone in to buy a card in Daisy's shop, thus keeping someone who wanted to shop at Liv's from easy access. My head hurt with the possibilities. There was also the impulse buy. I, for one, never bought just one greeting card. While I scanned the rack for something for Linda's nephew's graduation, I might remember another friend's upcoming birthday or the need for a get-well card. And so on. Almost as bad as my Internet shopping patterns—I'd go online to buy pads for my kitchen chairs and end up with a new flannel nightgown and surely a book or two.

Investigating the card-buying habits of North Ashcot citizens was one thing, but it was another entirely to link the local feud to the murder of Daisy Harmon, making Olivia Patterson the chief suspect. If that was all there was to police work, we probably wouldn't even need a chief.

I returned my focus to Cliff. "Maybe there was something else going on between Daisy and Liv, some issue bigger than greeting cards."

"If there was, I don't know," Cliff said.

I thought about the altercation at the quilters' meeting. "I heard about the farmers' market proposal and a hint that Daisy vocally opposed it."

Cliff nodded. "Right. That was Daisy's beef with the Harrises. Reggie and Andrea. Daisy went at it a few times with both of them. But it wasn't personal. It's not like they're farmers themselves who'll profit from the new business. They just want the produce readily available, I think."

It occurred to me that Daisy might have thought otherwise, with the interests of local businesses in mind.

I looked at our dinner plates, both still untouched. Roasted chicken, mashed potatoes, green beans, rolls—it had sounded like a good idea at the time, but all either of us had had for nourishment so far was a bite or two of a roll and an entire pitcher of ice water between us.

"Why don't I box this up again?" I said, already into the process. "You might want it later, or tomorrow."

Cliff looked doubtful, but he agreed to accept half of everything.

I stored my half in the fridge, already knowing what I'd have for dinner instead. I planned to dig into a box of candy Quinn had sent me from a specialty shop in Ogunquit, Maine. I tried to focus on the sweet message that accompanied it, pushing away all the nasty, vengeful thoughts that had filled the day and evening.

5

With no dishes to wash, and three truffles—one vanilla cream, one chocolate toffee, and one raspberry (they were small) under my belt—I settled down to work on my quilt. I started to sew together the pieces of my block depicting the 9/11 HEROES stamp, the most recent design the late Daisy Harmon had found for me in her efforts to help with my patriotic theme. She'd been thrilled when she tracked down the special fabric for me. When too many thoughts of her generosity as an instructor and her unthinkable end came to mind, I put the sewing aside.

I turned to my pile of local newspapers. The top story of the last couple of weeks was the controversy over the farmers' market proposal, submitted to the town governors for review, by Reggie Harris, quilter Andrea's husband and the town's biggest contractor. Cliff had made little of the animosity between the Harrises and Daisy, but I noted that

Daisy was not so dispassionate. Daisy's Fabrics had taken out an ad inviting everyone to come to the shop and sign a petition against Reggie's proposal. Not as trivial a difference of opinion as Cliff thought.

Here I was, not just reading the newspaper, but looking for suspects. Sunni would not be happy with me.

I read on. The pros for a market were clear: fresh fruit and vegetables for all, increased revenue for the town. And who could be against healthier North Ashcot citizens?

No one objected to organic veggies. The main problem seemed to be the proximity of the proposed location to the regular downtown merchants, and the redundancy of items already being sold by established shops. The farmers' market would carry products like honey, special teas, candles, and, as noted in a letter to the editor from our florist, Gigi, even plants and flowers. I imagined Gigi, a somewhat shy young woman, mustering the courage to put her thoughts in writing and air them to the public. Clearly, this was a sensitive issue for all concerned.

I saw the dilemma: On the one hand, the farmers wanted their stalls close to where people usually shopped; on the other, the local merchants had some rights to a buffer zone between them and the competition.

I sometimes journeyed to the farmers' markets in surrounding towns with somewhat larger populations than ours. They'd managed to find space far enough away from their main shopping area that no one complained. Not loudly, anyway. I wondered how they got their plan to work.

Figuring it out was a job for the selectmen of the town, I decided, and perhaps the Reggie Harrises of the area. I abandoned the issue for the night, doubly glad I had no political aspirations. Why anyone did was beyond me.

I adjusted my reading pillow and climbed into bed, hoping to lose myself in a thriller. But it was hard to focus when my mind was off on a tangent, replaying the real-life drama of Daisy Harmon's murder. No need for spies, international intrigue, or hijacked fictional vessels when North Ashcot itself was the center of captivating theater. Was it possible that what I saw as a minor problem—working out fair business practices in a small town—could have led to murder? It was difficult to accept, no matter how many similar stories fiction and history might provide.

At eleven o'clock, my computer, waiting on my bedside table, pinged. Quinn checking in. I put my book aside and replaced it with my laptop. Though we texted frequently during the day, we'd gotten into the habit of a voice-to-voice or electronic face-to-face good-night chat.

Tonight Quinn was staying in a suburb south of Boston. Behind his handsome, ruddy face was a typically drab motel bedroom in oranges and browns, long past their primes. I felt I could smell the dust mites nestled in the drapes and carpet. It occurred to me how challenging it must be to live with furniture put together from a kit while you were seeking out hand-carved pieces from master Philadelphia cabinetmakers. Poor Quinn.

"Did you find any hidden treasures for the shop today?" I asked him.

Big smile over the wires. "I got lost for a while in a cool

antiquarian bookstore in downtown Boston. It's huge, and offers all these special services."

Quinn spoke in excited tones, as he always did when talking about his passion. I often thought how much Aunt Tess would have enjoyed him. I urged him on. "What's a special service for books?"

"Glad you asked. Say you need eight feet of books bound in blue, for example; they'll put them together for you."

"That seems strange. Why would anyone buy books by color, or order them by length?"

"Lots of reasons. It could be for a theater set. Or some people like to use books for decoration and they want colors complementary to their living room. Or they want a certain theme in their summer rental. Or they're selling their house and they need to stage it. Or—"

"Okay, I get it." I ran my hand over the book at my side. The dust jacket pictured a large sea vessel, its front end in the water, its back end on fire. The image of red and yellow flames was raised from the glossy paper, an approximation to three dimensions and a promise of action to come. This cover hadn't been designed for any particular décor. "I can't imagine buying books for any reason other than to read, no matter what the cover looks like," I said.

He laughed. "That's why you're not in my business. I bought a couple of leather-bound sets, one in dark green and one in brown with gold trim. I have no idea what's inside."

"And you think someone will buy them?"

"Uh-huh. Especially if I display only one set at a time. And if you don't understand why I'll put out only one at a time, you have a lot to learn about the games we play in this business."

"Not my first clue. And speaking of business issues . . ."

I told Quinn about my meeting with Cliff, and the various town controversies as I understood them. I did my best to play down the part where Cliff had almost hooked me into playing detective or, at least, security guard.

Quinn let out a long breath and I knew I'd said too much. "Do I need to come home and make sure that doesn't happen?"

"No, no."

"As if I could stop you. Just—"

"I know. I'll be careful."

When we hung up, I realized that I'd unintentionally begun leaning toward a decision. One more plea from Cliff, or one tiny clue that might surface, and I'd end up helping him look into his wife's murder. The best I could hope for was that Cliff would forget he'd ever asked that favor.

As if I needed a prod in the opposite direction, my next call was from Chief of Police Sunni Smargon.

"Did you and Cliff have a good visit?"

"Uh, yes. He's having a tough time with Daisy's death, as to be expected." Clinical enough, I hoped.

"I noticed you extended the visit to your place."

I should have known that Sunni would have seen Cliff's car outside my house. She saw everything. She probably knew he'd stopped to pick up dinner, and what kinds of sides were included.

"Excuse me? Is this the NSA or CIA calling?" I asked. Humor was always worth a shot.

"Don't be cute. And don't tell me the incompetence of the North Ashcot PD didn't come up in your conversation."

"He needed consoling."

"And second-guessing us, I'll bet."

"Isn't it only natural that he'd be questioning everything and wondering how it happened that his wife was murdered? He hasn't said so directly, but I think he feels guilty that he wasn't home to protect her. He's a guard, after all. In the protection business." I left out "like you."

"He was at your house a long time."

"You really are the NSA." Still keeping a smile in my voice. "I suppose you won't believe that we talked about the parade next weekend and whether we'd wear costumes."

She shook her head. "All of a sudden you're both big fans of General Knox and his ox?"

Finally, a chuckle, at the rhyme. "Did you know that Knox and the load of cannons crossed the state line from New York into Massachusetts at Alford, and probably sledded right through what is now North Ashcot?"

"Fascinating," Sunni said. "Here's another thought. Maybe what happened tonight was that the widower Harmon has made a complete and swift recovery, and you've dumped the antiques dealer for the local security guard."

"You got it," I said. "Cliff and I are eloping at midnight. In fact, maybe you can help. Aren't you legally certified to perform a marriage ceremony?"

"Touché. Do you stay up thinking of ways to annoy me?"

"Are you still patrolling around town?"

"Yes, and I could use some coffee."

"How about some chicken and mashed potatoes?"

It was worth my getting out of bed to be able to give some comfort to my hardworking friend. Either Sunni was too tired to issue her usual warnings about my snooping (she called it "obstructing") or she was too hungry to care. After polishing off the chicken dinner in record time, she moved to the living room and leaned back in one of my glide rockers, feet up on the matching ottoman.

"I may be getting too old for this job," she said.

"What is it? Only another twenty-five years to retirement?"

She gave her forehead a slap. "Thanks for the reminder. The worst part is that I have to look at everyone as a suspect and every situation as a potential for crime. People I deal with every day. Last week, I walk into Andy's Dry Cleaners and I find myself looking more closely at the equipment. That hot, heavy press would make an effective weapon, I'm thinking. Poor Andy. He must have thought I was nuts looking at him suspiciously. And I wasn't even working a homicide at the time."

Sunni didn't usually share such feelings with me. I decided to move in while she was in a vulnerable position, having sought solace in my home, ingested my food, and stretched out on my furniture. Bad Cassie.

"Did Barry offer anything useful? Like a clue as to who might have been fighting with Daisy?"

"No hair or fibers, if that's what you mean. Who knows what the wind and rain that day might have washed away? He found a trace of a substance that at first he thought was blood, but of course most of it would have been washed away. Turned out not to be blood anyway. Possibly ink. How about that?"

"That's something, though. Where was the ink?"

"On Daisy's wrist, I believe."

"Can they tell what it's from? Like a marker or a regular ballpoint? Or would that even matter? Maybe it could be traced to a particular user, like a specific shop owner, something like that?"

Sunni shook her head, shrugged in a helpless gesture. "On TV maybe, before the next commercial. The only clear conclusion of our ME's exam is that Daisy struck or was struck by a hard object, like a rock, and that she put up quite a fight."

I shut my eyes against the image of bruises on Daisy's small body. From the look on Sunni's face, I thought she might be having the same reaction. I left the room and took a few minutes in the kitchen, refilling our mugs.

"It must be awful when you don't have much to start with," I said.

Sunni popped up in the seat. "Hey, enough."

Good intentions but bad judgment on my part. I gave Sunni an innocent look and held up my hands in surrender.

"What did you put in that coffee?" she asked.

"Truth serum," I said, getting a welcome laugh from her and relieving the tension.

She lumbered off the chair, looking only slightly better than when she had arrived. "I'd better get going."

"I can drive you home if you like," I offered. "And pick you up in the morning. No problem." Obliging Cassie.

"I'm fine. Thanks anyway."

Sunni departed on her own, assuring me she'd drunk enough coffee to keep her awake for the few miles to her house, and leaving me with nothing but a last-minute mention of a spot of red ink to think about.

6

To an outsider, it might have seemed like a normal Thursday morning at the post office, with customers lined up, glad to be out of the summer humidity, exchanging complaints ("The line isn't moving fast enough"; "The grocery store is out of lemon-flavored sparkling water") and pleasantries ("It's much cooler this week after the storm"; "Fall TV shows will be starting soon").

But my guess was that, like me, most of the residents felt a pall over the town, a heavy cloud bearing the weight of the drastic escalation of bad news that had shaken us, from a possible casualty of the small storm, to the accidental death of a member of the community, to the declared murder verdict in the case of Daisy Harmon. Aunt Tess always said you could smell a storm, even after it had passed, and I thought the observation was never more true than now.

I suspected it wasn't just Sunni who looked at everyone

with suspicion today. It was hard to trust any but our closest friends. I recognized a few people from South Ashcot who often came by when their post office lobby was even more crowded than ours. My immediate reaction when I saw the interlopers: Had Sunni thought of looking for motives among those nonresidents of North Ashcot? Maybe one of them was an unsatisfied fabric shop customer. Or someone who was part of an old feud that had resurfaced across town borders?

I had enough to do, with more than the usual number of money orders today and a couple of people who needed help wrapping unwieldy packages, but in between, my mind went to Daisy's unsolved murder. I longed to know how the investigation was proceeding. I was dismayed that my status as best friend of the chief of police gave me no insight into the progress, if any, she and her staff were making, or what they were focusing on.

Now and then I replayed sayings from Daisy in my head. One was embroidered on a T-shirt she had made up for each new member of the group: QUILTERS ARE PIECEMAKERS. Another was a sign above the door to the back room of her shop: BEFORE ANTIDEPRESSANTS THERE WAS QUILTING. And her most useful: WHEN LIFE GIVES YOU SCRAPS, MAKE A QUILT. It was hard to reconcile her playful outlook with the way she had died.

Cliff had texted me sometime during the night saying he'd like to come by with lunch "to firm up some plans." I imagined his list might include "break into the PD and copy police case notes" and "bring in all of Daisy's friends, acquaintances, and customers and line them up for questioning." Short of those tasks, I couldn't see what two regular citizens could accomplish. But I felt I owed Cliff a hearing, and when I was free enough to text back, I wrote sure.

I'd cleared the lobby line by ten minutes before noon, giving me a little time to look more carefully at the pile of questionable pieces that had been delivered this morning. Stuffing the post office boxes, my second duty after raising the flag every day, usually moved quickly. I inserted mail with correct addresses and tended to the problem pieces later, as time allowed. Generally, I could make up for mislabeled mail from memory. I knew that the Olsons rented box 457 and not 754, for example, and that the Carrolls lived in South Ashcot, not North Ashcot. But there were times when I had to do a little research before being able to take care of an incorrect label. I never liked writing RETURN TO SENDER unless I'd exhausted all other options.

This morning, I'd left a postcard from Quinn on top of the stack. I read the *wish you were here* message, then looked again at the beautiful photo. On the front was a shot of the Eastern Point Lighthouse in Gloucester, a center of the fishing industry, north of Boston on Cape Ann. The vista made me wistful not only for my boyfriend, but for the days I'd spent walking the beaches along the Atlantic Ocean.

I tucked the card in my desk drawer and worked my way down the pile of misfits. A letter addressed to David Rafferty, a name I didn't recognize at first, had me stumped until I remembered that he was the Raleys' nephew from Chicago, spending the month of August with them and their tiny animals. I placed the envelope in their box.

Another anomaly was an envelope addressed to a former

box holder who'd moved. I checked my register, added the forwarding address, and dropped the item in the bag for pickup tomorrow. If only every problem could be solved so simply.

The last letter was addressed to "Postmaster." I slit the plain white envelope open and read the handwritten note. I gulped and read it again, bringing on a shiver.

Do your job or go home.

My name wasn't on it, I reasoned, once my breath returned to normal. It wasn't a personal message. It could be meant for any postmaster, maybe Ben—though after a year on the job, I had to admit it probably wasn't for my predecessor, and the "go home" part was suspiciously pointed. The most positive spin I could put on it was that an ill-humored customer was unhappy with my job performance and unwilling to face me directly with his or her issue.

I tried to think of an altercation I'd had; nothing came to mind that would provoke this response. I'd opened the office a half hour late once this summer when a plumbing problem at home kept me longer than I'd expected. Ben had been away on vacation and I'd asked a neighbor on Main Street, two houses down, to post a sign on the post office door for me. She hadn't fastened it securely and the paper blew away. I'd returned to a small klatch of annoyed customers.

Was this note from one of them? Or from the woman whose five-hundred-dollar money order I wasn't able to cash until the end of the retail day? Or the man who was unhappy that I was out of medium-sized complimentary Priority Mail boxes? I guess it had been a less than perfect summer at the North Ashcot Post Office after all.

I hoped one of those complainers was responsible for the note in my hand. Anything more sinister would be hard to grasp.

Letters of complaint were not something new to me. There was no limit to the number of people who might have a gripe. The grievance could be about poor service, too few hours of operation, a package that arrived damaged. I'd done my best to make up for any inadequacies, perceived or otherwise, over the course of my fifteen-year career with the postal service in various parts of Massachusetts. I remembered a time when I was working in Boston—a spider found its way to the top of my counter, prompting a woman to go screaming from the lobby and later to put her angry thoughts in writing. I wasn't proud of the good laugh Linda and I had at the woman's expense. Later, of course.

I inspected the current letter again, this time more calmly. It wasn't really ominous, I decided. Probably someone whose birthday card was lost in the mail for a while, through no fault of mine; or someone with a package I hadn't taped securely enough, definitely a fault of my own.

I put the letter in a "Miscellaneous" file, just in time to greet Cliff as he walked through the front doors carrying a leather-flap briefcase.

The chief of police was the only exception I made to the NO UNAUTHORIZED PERSONS rule posted behind the retail counter. Cliff didn't measure up to that standard, so I took advantage of the adjoining community room where a group of volunteers was setting up for an evening meeting. With their permission, Cliff and I took our lunches to a table at the back, promising to leave it as clean as we'd found it.

I'd brought my usual peanut butter sandwich, but succumbed to an aromatic offering from Cliff, who'd stopped at a new seafood restaurant in South Ashcot. If he was trying to woo me with food, he was on the right track with an order of shrimp scampi.

Cliff showed no signs of being rested. Last evening's dark rings seemed more prominent, as did the lines around his mouth. I recognized the same polo shirt he'd worn yesterday and wondered if he'd even tried to rest. "Did you get any sleep?" I asked.

He shrugged. "I've got a lot to do. The police might release Daisy any minute and I'll be flying down to Miami where her parents are."

I remembered that Daisy's parents had started out as "snowbirds," the term we used to describe longtime residents of New England who spent the winter months in Florida as soon as they retired. Every year, with the first snow and the search for ice scrapers, I thought it was an idea worth considering, but never acted on it. Eventually, like other couples, Daisy's mom and dad sold their New Hampshire home and moved to Florida permanently.

Cliff pulled a folder from his briefcase. He had two copies of everything in the folder. One by one, he handed me sheets of paper, giving me a quick explanation for each. A list of friends ("Not suspects, but they may have some useful insights"). A list of customers who had a complaint in the last six months ("Nothing big, but you never know"). Assorted lists of tasks, possible motives for wanting Daisy out of someone's life, and photos of the backyard where Daisy had met her killer.

The last items he pulled out of his briefcase were copies of pages that seemed to be from a ledger.

"Here's what I have so far on the financial side," he said.

"I'm pretty hopeless when it comes to money matters," I said, truthfully. I'd rejoiced when I learned that it was no longer necessary for me to slave over balancing my checkbook every month as long as I kept up online, and even the post office accounting chores were more and more centralized and streamlined every year, thanks to the Internet.

"I'm not that great, either," Cliff said. "But we have to follow the money trail, as they say. Daisy handled the money herself, with Jules, our accountant, of course, but she talked about it a lot. In fact, she did her best to share the information with me. Now I wish I'd listened more."

Cliff reached for his container of shrimp, but only to push it farther from his spread-out papers. I hadn't had much to eat since a quick lunch yesterday, but I hated to be the first to do something as mundane as eat during this highly emotional meeting. Part of me hoped my stomach growls would reach Cliff's ear, and maybe serve as a reminder to him.

No such luck. He stayed on track, sips from his bottle of water his only gesture to nutrition.

"I've asked Jules for whatever else he has, and he's going to help me interpret everything. I'm hoping you'll be at that meeting."

"As I say—"

"We'll arrange it for your convenience. The more heads, the better, right?"

"Right." Though the saying wasn't necessarily true if the extra one was as uninformed as mine.

"Jules said that this"—he tapped the ledger sheets—"was just the beginning. It'll take him a while to get everything together, which is understandable. I made sure he knows I'm not auditing his work. I wouldn't know where to begin even if I wanted to. I'm just looking for something that might lead somewhere. Who knows? Maybe we owe somebody and they . . ." He stopped, unable to complete the thought.

We left it vague enough that I felt I could be at the meeting if only for moral support.

"Let me know when you need me," I said, hoping for so many reasons that the time would never come. First, because a swift solution of Daisy's case would be best all around. Preferably, today. Second, because I didn't want to annoy the chief of police by doing anything that resembled investigating. The third, fourth, and following reasons were the same as the second.

"Thanks," said Cliff, who wasn't privy to my mental reservations. He extracted his copies of the lists of Daisy's friends and customers. "I thought we could start by splitting up these names and talking to as many of her friends and acquaintances as we can."

"Don't you think the police are doing that already?"

Cliff grunted. "Maybe."

I didn't argue but simply agreed to take *A* through *M* and put the folder aside for later viewing.

Not a good sign. As Daisy used to say, "It takes a long time to finish a quilt you're not working on."

* * *

As soon as Cliff left, I put my container of shrimp scampi in the small fridge behind the post office boxes. Dinner, I hoped. For now, with no time even for my peanut butter sandwich, I unwrapped an energy bar and opened the doors for the retail afternoon.

The afternoon line was steady; no crowds, but I didn't have much downtime, either. Now and then I glanced at the folder on my desk and thought about what it would mean for me to act on its contents. I took a minute to reach over and place the manila folder in a drawer, out of sight. Although it was labeled only CASSIE, in Cliff's careful printing, I imagined if Sunni dropped by she'd be able to see through the cardstock to the notes on Daisy's murder, and I guessed that I was heading for an obstruction of justice charge. Or if Ben, my bored mentor and predecessor, dropped by, he might feel free to open it. Ben was having a hard time with retirement and was known to poke around and offer his assistance at random, but he'd never open my desk.

Midway through the afternoon, I noticed Molly Boyd in the lobby, wrestling with a couple of packages. She'd shed her crutches and was down to using a cane, a flashy pink paisley one. I heard an interchange between her and the young woman behind her in a UMass sweatshirt. I couldn't help eavesdropping while I waited for my current customer to complete a customs form for international shipping.

"I'm glad to see you're walking better," said the woman, whom I recognized as a barista from Mahican's café.

"Yes, thanks," Molly responded.

The barista pointed to Molly's bandaged ankle. "How did you do it?"

"In the storm last Monday. My cat got out and I was chasing her and tripped over the little wall around my garden." Molly gave a weak smile and shrugged. "Dumb accident."

"Aren't they all?" the barista asked.

Something clicked in my head and I flashed back to our quilting session on Tuesday evening. I could have sworn that at that time Molly had blamed her new Adirondack chair for the storm-related accident. Strange that she would tell the barista a different story two days later. The cat made me do it?

It was Liv who was unhappy with Daisy's decision to stock greeting cards, the mainstay of her own shop next door. I knew that Molly and Liv were friends, outside of the quilting circle. Was Molly also unhappy with Daisy? I asked myself now, faced with her suspicious alibi for a wounded ankle.

Any desire on my part to pursue the matter was cut off by my customer, who handed me her completed form.

"Daydreaming?" she asked me.

"Always," I said with a customer-friendly smile.

With no one in the lobby just before closing, I sat at my desk for end-of-day paperwork. As he sometimes did, Ben stopped by at this hour to take down the flag and ask, "Anything exciting today?" or a variation of that.

Today, I'd had more excitement than I needed, though not necessarily the kind I wanted to share with Ben. There was the *Do your job or go home* note, for one thing. I debated showing it to him. He might overreact and coax me to take it to the level of reporting it to the postal inspector, or underreact and leave me feeling foolish for giving it a second thought.

One thing I knew for sure—I wouldn't share Cliff's plans for me with Ben. What he didn't know wouldn't hurt our relationship.

"I see Cliff's been coming around a lot," Ben said.

I nearly laughed in his face. Ben gave me a questioning look and I recovered in time to say, "Uh-huh. It's a tough time for him."

Ben lifted his long, thin frame onto the counter (where children were forbidden to sit during his reign as postmaster). "I'd say so. The husband is always the number-one suspect, you know."

Another near laugh. "Not in this case. He was more than seventy miles away in Springfield."

"Maybe yes, maybe no."

"What does that mean?"

"He could have slipped away, driven like crazy, done the deed, and then gone back without anyone knowing."

"In a raging storm?" I asked, eyebrows raised.

Ben shrugged. "Or he could have hired someone here to do it."

I screwed up my nose against the unpleasant idea Ben was airing. "I see. He paid someone to wander around North Ashcot for a day or so, in case there was a storm that might tear a limb from a tree in his backyard, at exactly the time that Daisy would be outside?"

It was clear that Ben needed a life, and I feared my tone suggested as much.

"Anyway, you wouldn't be letting Cliff drag you into some edgy detective work, or anything like that, would you?"

From his perch (deliberate?) on the counter, Ben looked down at me. I could have sworn he could see through my desk to the folder marked CASSIE, with Cliff's notes for just that task.

"Why ever would you think that?" I asked.

Ben's turn to stifle a laugh. "I might be old," he said, and left me to finish the thought myself.

"I know you're not dumb, Ben."

"So that's a yes?" he asked.

"Yes what?"

"That's what I thought." He slid off the counter, his mouth twisted to the side, half grin, half frown. He draped his lanky body over the chair next to my desk, his face turning serious. "You know, they closed the post office over in Brookside."

"The small town down near Hinsdale. Yes, I heard."

"It's a pet-grooming place now."

I grimaced. "It's sad to lose facilities like ours," I said.

"The flagpole is still outside," he said. "Wonder if they're just going to keep it."

"There's no law against it, I guess."

His eyes took on a faraway look. "Brookside wasn't that much smaller than North Ashcot, you know. We could be next." Ben's tone was somber, as if he'd already received a memo with the bad news.

Post office closings were a fact of life these days. I often thought of the possibility of losing ours. What would I do? Go back to Boston? Just as I was getting settled and satisfied being back where I was born? And what about Quinn? I couldn't allow my mind to go there, though I knew I should be more practical and concerned about other uses for my skills in the future.

Meanwhile, I could convince myself that the North Ashcot Post Office was indispensable, a bustling place. I looked around at the piles of boxes and bags of mail ready to go out on Monday, and thought how we were thriving. People came from surrounding towns because we had a good track record and lots of parking, which mattered to a lot of busy people.

I thought it admirable of Ben that he still cared about the future of the office. He'd earned his pension, after all, and didn't have to bother anymore. I drew in my breath as a frightening thought entered my mind. Ben was still connected to administrators across the state. He chatted with higher-ups all the time. An unfailing old-boys network. What if . . . ?

"Do you know something I don't?" I asked him.

"Not yet. But I know we have to be on our best behavior."

I folded my hands around the placket at the top button of my shirt. "Clean uniform every day," I said.

"It's a lot more than that."

"Meaning?"

He shrugged. "You figure it out."

I didn't like the sound of Ben's comment. Was he warning me off, afraid I'd get hurt, or worried that nosing around a police investigation would earn bad marks for the North Ashcot Post Office? Or both? Was he uneasy about me or his legacy in the town? I studied his face and saw concern about both.

"There's nothing to worry about, Ben," I said, with nothing to back up my confidence.

He drew a loud, deep breath. "I'll walk you out," he said.

I retrieved my things, including my dinner from the fridge, hoping Ben wouldn't ask details about anything I was carrying.

7

I drove home with a fully occupied passenger seat—the take-out container with my aromatic shrimp dinner in a cooler, resting on the thick file of notes and to-do lists. Both legacies of my foodless lunch with Cliff Harmon.

The evening was clear, the roads nearly free of debris, but as I approached Daisy's Fabrics, I wondered if I'd ever again drive by without slowing down and remembering what had happened during a summer storm. I noticed that the yellow-and-black caution tape had been removed.

I had a strong urge to pull over. A short walk down the narrow alley between Daisy's shop and Liv's card shop would take me to the backyard. The scene of the crime. And there was plenty of parking at the curb.

Ben's thinly veiled warning to behave myself and do nothing that would bring negative attention to the post office rattled around my head. But Ben was an old man, I told myself. Old people were overly cautious. I knew he also cared about me, though he couldn't completely abandon his reputation of surliness to show it. But he loved his town, too, I reasoned, and would want me to take an interest in all that was going on, to be active in a way that he might not be able to.

By the time I made my decision, I'd arrived in front of the police department. Bad place to park, considering what I was about to do. I made a right turn down the next street and came around again on Main Street, parking before Mahican's, on the same side of the street as Daisy's. And the police station. But far enough away, I thought. I tapped my steering wheel. I still had a choice. Turn the key in the ignition and continue on home. Yes or no?

A minute later, I exited my car and walked toward Daisy's Fabrics. I wouldn't have been surprised to see Sunni. How likely was it that she'd choose this moment to take a stroll outside her building? Not very, I hoped. I made it to the alley between the shops and traipsed along the gravel path to the back lot where Daisy had died. I imagined her fighting until the end and choked back tears.

The area was half landscaped, with a lawn and a row of flowers toward the front, tapering off to more gravel and rocks for the few feet before the back fence. The enormous branch that had fallen from the maple hadn't been moved; its brown leaves extended into the untended section.

Although the sky was overcast, it was well before sunset and I saw shadows everywhere. There was nothing sluggish about my imagination. I stepped toward the branch, not sure what I expected to see. Blood? Signs of a struggle? An indentation where Daisy's body had lain? My eyes burned from my efforts to hold back tears. I imagined the police combing through the gravel for evidence, checking every rock of significant size.

I saw nothing unusual and questioned why I was here at all. To investigate as if I were a cop? To lose points from Sunni? To indulge a morbid curiosity? To win points from Cliff for brilliant scouting work and perhaps get a coupon for a free evening with a bodyguard? Or simply to mourn my friend. Whatever the reason, the fact was that I was standing where a killer had stood only a few days ago, and if I were smart, I'd beat it out of here.

As I started back down the narrow alley toward the street, I heard a loud, prolonged clatter, as if a cabinet had fallen over and emptied its contents. The noise was coming from inside the shop. I stopped short and leaned against the white clapboard building where Daisy's Fabrics was housed. More noise, this time of the thumping variety. I held my breath. What if Daisy's killer had returned to the scene of the crime? Didn't they always do that? Was that my real goal today—to meet the killer?

What was wrong with me?

Above my head was a window that I hoped was closed. The last thing I wanted was curious eyes peeking down and outing me. I hadn't thought to try the back door that led down a few steps to the spot where I'd been standing; I hadn't thought of entering the shop at all. Unlike the intruder. Was the intruder now planning to exit that way, or through the front door? Could it be Cliff roaming around inside? Maybe it was a crime scene tech back for further scrutiny? Or Jules, or a cleaning crew, or any number of people with a perfect right to be in the closed shop? Including the chief of police.

I determined with less than one hundred percent certainty that the series of noises—a clatter, a thump, followed by a scrape, then shuffling—was moving toward Main Street. I inched my way along, following the footsteps that were only a few inches above my head, on the first floor of the building.

A little farther down the alley, the noise stopped and so did I. I calculated that I was now next to the side wall of the store where the large cutting table sat.

Traffic whizzed by, if that can describe the way cars move in a small town on its main street at what passes for rush hour. Nothing like the many areas of Boston and vicinity where sometimes a dozen lanes were forced to merge into two to enter a tunnel or cross a bridge. It helped to remember that aspect of Boston when I became nostalgic about my life in the big city.

Since I arrived in the alley, there had been no foot traffic along Main Street. A good thing, since I had no idea how a pedestrian might have responded to a uniformed postal worker skulking in the shadows between downtown shops after hours.

The next sounds I heard could have been those of opening and closing the front door of the shop. I took a chance and moved farther along the side of the shop toward Main. I inhaled deeply before I ventured a look around the corner.

A figure was already walking away from the front door, away from the alley where I stood. He must have been inside for a while, I reasoned, since he hadn't passed me on Main.

A male, maybe, average size, though it was hard to tell. He wore a dark jacket, too bulky for a summer eve. His hood was over his head, his hands in his pockets. I'd already decided after hours of watching television crime dramas that, of all the trends in casual wear, the hood was the criminal's best friend. A large envelope or package was tucked under his arm. He moved swiftly to the traffic light just after Mike's Bike Shop. My wish came true and he had to stop again for a DON'T WALK sign at the corner. Did I dare come out of hiding and walk toward him?

Why not?

I headed out, put my own hands in the pockets of my sweater, wishing it had a hood, and tried to focus on what he was holding close to his body, something he might have taken from the shop. It looked like a Priority Mail envelope. Or was that my job talking?

The stiff-looking package was close enough to nine and a half by twelve and a half, the size of a Flat Rate envelope, in my view. The red, white, and blue trims on the envelope weren't showing, nor could I see the red stripes across the front and back of the top, long end. It seemed thin enough to be one of the complimentary items from the shipping supplies section of any post office. Mine? I felt an unwelcome shiver.

The traffic light turned green and I had a new decision to make. Push forward or retreat? There was only half a block before the police department building. If my stalkee discovered me, surely I wouldn't be in danger practically in earshot of law enforcement.

That scenario was comforting in theory, but when he turned before crossing the street, and I thought he spotted me, my cowardice came to the fore. I indulged in a bit of sleight of hand. I pulled a package of tissues from my pocket and dropped it on the ground. I bent over to pick it up, made a show (for anyone who might be watching) of dropping it in the trash can at the curb, then made an unobtrusive U-turn and headed back to my car. This time I was aware of a faint scent in the air, as if the (other) intruder had left a trail. The scent was sweet enough for me to consider that I'd been tailing a female, but I couldn't be sure one way or the other.

Strong feelings of inadequacy bugged me as I approached the front door of Daisy's Fabrics again, this time from the other direction. I needed to be braver, to take more risks. What were the chances that the door might be open? Good, I decided. It was unlikely that the intruder who preceded me had stopped to lock the door. I made another surreptitious, choreographed move, climbing the two steps from the sidewalk, and turned the doorknob. The door gave way and I found myself inside the shop, dark and slightly musty smelling. And empty, I hoped.

I looked around, distracted by the neat bolts of fabric, grouped in some displays by theme (Fourth of July patterns were on sale, I noted; Halloween designs half in, half out of shipping boxes); and in other setups by the kind of material (wools, silks, cottons lined up together), or color (who knew there were that many shades of green?).

Where had the clattering noise come from? Not from bolts of fabric. And not from the items on the wall of notions. I walked closer to the Peg-Board. I wasn't able to identify everything in the fading light, but I made out cutting tools, bags of batting, totes, packaged costumes, old-fashioned fabric-covered sewing baskets. I wondered if Daisy kept a supply of Flat Rate envelopes on hand. Maybe the man I saw availed himself of one. To put what in it? And escape with what? The police had been through the shop, and had to have confiscated anything that would help in their murder investigation. What did I expect to find? I needed to go home.

The area near the cash register was neat as always, with a few novelty items—pincushions shaped like fruit, cards with decorative buttons, small sewing kits for travel— and a large book for customers to sign up for an e-newsletter. A small bell was available to call a staff member if help was needed. I had a surreal moment where I hit the top of the call bell and Daisy appeared.

One more aisle, I decided; then I'd leave the shop and put this upsetting day behind me. I turned a corner toward the racks of magazines I often looked through. Daisy carried a line of quilting and crafts magazines and how-to books that included instructions for knitting, crocheting, needlepoint, and other fabric arts as well as sewing.

Paying too much attention to the array of covers promising quick results for holiday projects, I nearly tripped over an object in the aisle. I looked down. And saw a body.

More exactly, half a body. A woman cut off at her waist, with wild, overly blond hair, dressed in a crisp white tunic. I gasped, too loudly for a stealth operation, and felt my heartbeat everywhere but in my chest.

Just in time, before I collapsed in fright, I recognized one of Daisy's mannequins. One of the plastic women that lined a shelf in this aisle, showing off samples made from the patterns on sale. You, too, could whip up a robe or a fancy shirt that would look like this. Clearly, Madam Tunic's fall from the flat surface of the top of the magazine rack had been the source of the clattering noise I'd heard, and the reason her resin head was at an unnatural angle on her neck.

Plastic or not, the partial body unnerved me, and I turned quickly to make my exit, bumping into a set of filing cabinets on the way. *"Ouch!"* I groaned out loud as my sweater caught on a rough metal edge and at the same time I nicked my arm and dropped my purse. Some sleuth. One incapable of stealth. I held my breath until I was sure no one would come running at my outburst. Through the front window I saw a group of youngsters walking by. I crouched down until they passed.

As I rose from my squatting position, I saw a flash of light between the cabinets. Daisy had piggybacked a couple of white two-drawer cabinets, one on top of the other, to save space. She'd teased me that the main reason she accepted me into the quilting group was that I was the only one who could easily manipulate the files in the top drawer. It was hard to believe that she'd never tease me again about my height, how she could use a few of my extra inches.

The flash I'd seen had come from a newly turned-on streetlamp striking something that was stuck between the surfaces of the two filing cabinets. The cabinets had shifted from their vertically aligned position when I bumped into them. I reached to examine the object, hoping it wouldn't move on its own. In my mind, there was no end to the different kinds of insects that might live in stores at night. I pulled on the item and extracted a small notebook with a shiny magnetic closure.

The notebook was about two inches by four inches, the handy size I had in my car and at various spots around my office and home. Mine were filled mostly with to-do lists that I never looked at. Apparently, I carried some strange gene that allowed me to remember things I wrote down whether or not I referred to them later.

This notebook was Daisy's, as attested to by the small return address label she'd stuck on the cover, partially obscuring van Gogh's sunflowers. I wondered why the police hadn't taken it. Probably because no cop had been clumsy enough to crash into the filing cabinets and fall.

I flipped through the book and saw that it was partially full, though it was too dark to read the contents. I squinted at a page that had large letters, and thought I read JULES. It appeared to be a calendar page where JULES had been entered into several dates this month. Or some month, maybe even not this year. Who knew how long the book had been stuck between the cabinets? I flipped a few more pages, trying various angles to catch the dim light. A few more tries and I caught a couple of pages that were filled with short to-do lists, most of the items with check marks next to them. I deciphered phrases like *return library bks*, *pick up* (illegible), *and take* (illegible) *to S.A.*, which I took to be South Ashcot. I saw parts of words that could be *dentist* and *crafts fair*. My eyes and knees hurt as I squatted in the dark shadows of Daisy's Fabrics.

With no warning a small pointed light came on and startled me so much that I dropped the notebook-cum-calendar and felt my heartbeat leave my chest once more. I looked around, expecting to see a flashlight in the hands of a hooded man. With a gun. Or a large tree branch. Instead, I saw that a night-light in the shape of a thimble had responded to the growing darkness and had come on automatically in a corner near me. I half laughed, half gasped. Without thinking it through, I tossed the notebook on top of a small table as I ran from the shop.

I got to my car, my breath coming in short spurts, every muscle tense. For no reason. The shop had been empty while I was in it, and stayed empty. The so-called intruder had walked away, barely noticing me (I hoped). And even if we had met outside, we might simply have exchanged a pleasant greeting. I had no reason to assume otherwise. I was unhurt. Then why was my heart still beating wildly?

I wondered how Sunni and other law enforcers faced this kind of thing every day. Answering distress calls, walking into places where anything or anyone might be lurking, not shrinking at the sight of a retreating hoodie, rushing toward scenarios others were fleeing. Maybe it would be different with a badge and a gun?

I thought of Cliff, a security guard. In theory, he was standing watch, making sure no one broke in to a building in his charge or vandalized it in any way. In practice, how did he react if he came upon a threatening situation? Still in my postal uniform, I was more grateful than ever for a job where the most difficult scenario involved nothing more than a cranky customer or one trying to sneak disallowed items into a media mail package.

I was surprised to find my car door unlocked. Most of the time, I succumbed to OCD and hit the lock button twice, similar to the way I often worried about whether I'd closed my garage door, drove back, and found it closed. This time it hadn't worked that way with my car, though I was sure I'd heard the short burst of horn when I hit the button on leaving it.

Well, no problem. There were few safer places than Main Street, North Ashcot, to leave a car unlocked.

Except not this time. My passenger seat was bare. Someone had taken my shrimp dinner and my files on Daisy Harmon's murder case. A thief had broken into my car and stolen my property, within sight of the police department. He was either very dumb or very bold. Either way, I was distressed, unsure whether the violation was worth reporting. On any other summer evening, I might not have given it a second thought, but in the vicinity of a crime scene, where my friend had been murdered, it seemed a significant turn of events.

I did a quick inspection of the doorframe and saw no scratches that appeared fresh. My car had been over some rough terrain a few times, and the scars on its exterior attested to its history. I'd have to wait until daylight tomorrow to get a closer look. The inside hadn't been vandalized, as far as I could see. The upholstery was intact and any debris was mine. A few napkins from the coffee shop, crumbs on the floor from a quick snack in transit, an old blanket on the backseat for when I transported packages that might soil or tear up the seat covers. All mine.

I decided to think more about my loss before telling anyone. I drove home with a queasy stomach, running through possible scenarios. Had the thief been a poor person who'd seen the cooler and assumed correctly that it contained food? He might have been hungry enough to break in, the files being an inadvertent add-on. In my year back in town, I hadn't seen anyone who fit this profile, but it was a possibility.

I hated the alternative—the thought that someone had been following me, seen Cliff give me the file, and then taken the opportunity to steal it when I left my car on the street. The shrimp dinner was then the add-on, an extra perk.

By the time I reached my driveway, I'd almost settled on a prank theory. School wasn't in session yet and a couple of bored teenagers decided to cruise Main Street in search of a little mischief. In this scenario, I'd forgotten to lock my car and the kids were happy for the easy pickings, until they opened the box and found gourmet shrimp instead of pepperoni pizza.

Served them right.

I changed into jeans and a CAL BERKELEY T-shirt that Quinn had given me. Trying to balance all the UMass apparel I owned, he'd said. I wasn't happy about being robbed of my dinner—a continuation of my bad food karma this week—but I decided it wasn't worth reporting the petty theft. And though I didn't look forward to it, I could text Cliff and ask for another copy of the file.

I made the rounds of my house, checking windows and doors. Daisy's murder had affected me in ways that I couldn't explain.

Relieved that I was alone and safe, I dropped a bagel into my toaster, disappointed that I had to be satisfied with the aroma of cinnamon and raisins instead of shrimp and lemon. While I was waiting for the meager meal to pop up, I scrolled through my smartphone for messages.

How could the list be so long after only about an hour of neglect? Wasn't it just a short time ago that I'd had to wait until I was in the physical presence of a landline answering machine for this information? Longer ago than it seemed, I realized. Aunt Tess had given me my first cell phone, a flip style, as a high school graduation present, making it nearly twenty years ago. If I wanted to feel anything but old, I was probably better off not checking the timeline of cell phone development and use.

A text from Quinn said he'd be home Saturday or Sunday. *Good news.*

Linda still planned to visit for the General Knox parade next weekend. *More good news.*

Cliff wanted to hear my progress in the short time since I saw him. *Not so good news.* I had to gear up to telling him the file was gone, probably in some kid's wastebasket by now, smelling of fish.

Sunni called to cancel our plans to get together this evening. *Good and bad news.* Good, because she wouldn't be able to query me on how I was keeping Cliff happy; bad, because I wouldn't be able to query her on how her investigation was going.

My inner circle was accounted for.

Besides the real messages, I listened to offers for new carpeting and for cleaning my old ones; and to solicitations for community projects. A couple of hang-ups were also the norm, but one of those was different tonight, consisting in fifteen or twenty seconds of breathing. Or maybe I was hearing telephone noise on the line.

I thought of the *go home* note I'd received. And of the burglarizing of my car. Were they all connected? Was I someone's target? Overreacting, I decided, and proceeded to extract my bagel, smear it with a thick layer of cream cheese and a dab of grape jelly, and carry it and a mug of coffee to my rocker in the living room. Before settling in, I made another trip around my house, double-checking all windows and doors.

Not that I was worried about anything. But when my cell phone rang, I jumped and spilled coffee onto the napkin on my lap. I blew out a deep breath when I saw the caller ID. Martindale Qui, which was as close as my cell phone could come to spelling out my long-named boyfriend.

Before the first "Hey," I decided not to let Quinn in on the mini attacks I'd been through today.

"I'm doing fine," I said. "So happy you'll be home for the weekend."

"I can't wait to show you all the treasures I picked up. Though some of them will be arriving by truck next week."

"No business for the USPS?" I teased.

He laughed. "Maybe tomorrow I'll find something mailable."

We made plans for dinner on Sunday evening, which was the latest he expected to arrive. I chose an Italian place, since I had an unexplained (to Quinn) craving for shrimp scampi.

My phone alerted me to another call, from Cliff Harmon. I clicked over, happy for an excuse to tell Cliff I had to make it short.

"I'm on another call right now," I said, "but I wanted to let you know that I'm going to need another copy of the files."

"Why? What happened?" He sound flustered, as I expected.

"That's not important right now. Can you bring the copies by the post office tomorrow?"

"Sure, but—"

"Thanks. Sorry to rush off. See you then."

I clicked back to Quinn. "Okay. Everything's all set."

"Good," he said, though I knew he had no idea what I meant.

It was just as well. Soon enough, it would be almost impossible to keep a secret investigation secret from him also.

8

There was no use trying to sleep with my head swimming, full of confused thoughts. About Daisy, about tasks to keep Cliff happy without alerting Sunni, and about my own safety. Was that surly note addressed to "Postmaster" a one-off, or would there be more, sullying my mail? Was the looting of my car only a prank, as I wanted to portray it, or a warning message? If so, a message about what?

As if all that mental commotion wasn't enough, I missed Quinn and worried about my friendship with Sunni, given my near promise to play cop with Cliff. Not even a new thriller downloaded to my e-reader was enough to engage me tonight—a tall, handsome ex-SEAL (who graduated first in his class, of course) notwithstanding.

The sooner Daisy's murder case was solved, the better. I put aside complications with the chief of police and decided to proceed, working with what I had until I could obtain another copy of the file from Cliff.

I thought about the small notebook I'd pulled from the back of the file cabinet in Daisy's shop. Pillows propped behind me, I sat up in bed and tried to remember what I'd seen, berating myself for not taking it with me. At the time, I'd been startled by a night-light, of all silly things, and raced out of the shop. I'd flipped through the pages briefly and seen snippets of to-do lists and pages of a calendar, plus some sketches I took to be ideas for fabric patterns or quilts.

Maybe Cliff could go back and retrieve the book. I certainly wasn't about to. I made a note to ask him about it tomorrow.

Or right now, I thought, as I heard my ring tone and saw his name on the screen of my smartphone.

"Sorry if I'm waking you up, Cassie, but I got a little worried when you said you needed another copy of the file I gave you today."

What was I thinking? That I'd get away without an explanation? All I'd managed to do was put off the inevitable probing.

I gave Cliff an edited version of my trip home from work, including my vehicle break-in, which I labeled a prank, and excluding my own break-in of what was now his shop. (Was it breaking in even if the door was unlocked? Probably.)

"That's awful, Cassie. What makes you think the killer himself didn't take the file? He could have followed you and seen that I gave you stuff and—"

Way to go, security guard. "You're scaring me, Cliff," I said, even though that very thought had occurred to me.

"Sorry, sorry. Of course that's very unlikely. I would have noticed if anyone were watching us."

I considered mentioning that at least one person had been watching us. The chief of police, in fact, and we hadn't been aware of her, even though she was probably in a well-marked patrol car. I held back. No use stirring up already troubled waters.

"I have a question for you, Cliff."

"Shoot," he said, seeming pleased that I was involved.

"Did Daisy have regular meetings with Jules Edwards?"

"Our accountant? Sure, they met every Friday. But, as I say, I never knew the details."

"They wouldn't be likely to meet every day?"

"No, no reason I can think of. They were both very efficient and kept up to date during those weekly meetings. Unless it was tax season, which it isn't. He's extremely busy then. He has a lot of other clients, in other towns as well as here. Is this important, Cassie?"

I'd come to a point of reckoning. To tell Cliff about the multiple calendar entries in the notebook, I'd have to admit I'd found it while wandering around the shop, which would give rise to questions I wasn't ready to answer. Some other time, I decided. "Nothing special. I'm just trying to get a picture of what her business life was like."

"She gave it her all. I'll tell you that." Cliff's voice broke up and I could hear that, as clinical as he was trying to be about the investigation, and as eager as he was to find her killer, first and foremost, he loved and missed his wife.

My heart went out to him. I did my best with soothing words, and suggested we both get some rest.

Once we signed off, another reason for frequent meetings between Daisy and Jules popped into my head. What if they were having an affair? Wasn't that the number-one motive for murder? Surely on the top ten list. I shoved the thought aside. Who writes down times and dates of secret trysts? I was glad it hadn't come up when Cliff and I were talking. He had enough to worry about.

Since I was still fully awake and reluctant to turn off my lights and toss around in the dark, I figured I might as well do something useful. I pulled a notepad onto my lap and began to compile my own list of people to contact. The quilting group was a good start. But it was after ten o'clock, past the time when I'd feel comfortable calling most people.

I looked around my bedroom, tapping my pen while I thought, pausing now and then to doodle. Without consciously applying myself, I found I'd drawn what could pass for a tree branch and part of a quilt. It wasn't hard to figure out how my mind worked.

I was distracted by the dusty surfaces of my room and the pitiful state of the décor. It was past time to take down tattered posters that were from trips to Boston's MFA more than a year ago. Linda would have had her favorites matted and framed; I still acted as though I lived in a dorm room. I'd thought about removing Aunt Tess's old, busy lilac wallpaper and painting the room a fresh off-white or pale yellow for a change. Maybe I could talk Quinn into helping. As a woodworker, as well as an antiques dealer, he had a practiced eye for interior decorating. Or maybe I could just declutter and dust before committing to a bigger project.

When my glance landed on my purse, in its usual place on a chair next to my bed, I felt a plan taking shape.

I knew that Eileen Jackson, who'd hosted the quilting meeting the other night, was a night owl. She'd mentioned it in connection with an all-night radio talk show she listened to. I scrolled through my phone contacts and called her. To my relief, she sounded chipper, and ready to chat.

"No apology necessary. You know I was up," she said when I mentioned the late hour.

"I think I left my new sunglasses at your house," I said, after our greetings. "It was still sunny when we arrived at your house, but dark when we left, so I didn't notice."

"Do you remember where you might have left them?" Eileen asked, sounding eager to help, thus bringing about a sour taste in my lying mouth. I cleared my throat, now nervous about prolonging my fiction. I should have checked on whether it had rained on Tuesday evening, for example. "I'm pretty sure I put them on the table with that beautiful stained glass Tiffany-style lamp."

"Oh yes, I love that lamp. The shop where they made them is gone now. I guess I'm not the only one who's allowed to retire." She paused, possibly reflecting on all the cool shops that were no longer with us. "I think I would have seen your glasses, since that's my reading corner, but let me check. Maybe they fell behind the chair. Can you hold?"

"Sure."

I felt really bad sending Eileen on a wild-goose chase, since I knew for a fact that my sunglasses were in my purse. Did real cops rely on this kind of trick? Did Sunni ever pull something like this? Did she train Ross Little, the young officer I'd come to know, in these wily ways? Had she ever pulled a fast one on me? I didn't want to believe it.

Eileen was back. "Sorry, Cassie. I don't see them. I'll check again tomorrow, when it's light, and I'll also check with Buddy. He might have found them and moved them. I'll call you if I find them."

Great. Now Eileen's husband would be enlisted in this fool's errand. I thanked her for her trouble, thinking I should bring her some candy or flowers to make up for my deceit.

I realized I hadn't quite thought through the next step. I'd created a believable excuse to contact Eileen, but how was I supposed to get from her useful information for the murder investigation? I couldn't exactly ask her whereabouts during the storm. The category-zero storm that hit the town on Monday was already old news to most of North Ashcot's citizens. The wind and rain had done little damage, except to provide a fleeting cover for Daisy's murder.

Cliff's idea had been to ask Daisy's friends if they noticed anything unusual or if Daisy had fought with anyone recently. I had no idea how to approach that topic with Eileen. It was clearer than ever why someone with training in interrogation techniques should be left alone to do her job. I should go back to perfecting my skills at the job I already had. What had that note said? *Do your job.*

Contrarian that I was, I made a stab at prolonging the conversation with the accommodating Eileen.

"Thanks for checking, Eileen. I suppose I might have left them in another purse." She had no way of knowing that I never changed my large, roomy leather purse, unless it was to switch to a small clutch for a wedding or, in Boston, for clubbing with Linda (who changed purses with each outfit). "And thanks for hosting us the other night, by the way."

"It was the least I could do to honor Daisy and try to keep her passion alive. It's such a shame, what happened."

A nice thought from a nice lady. One who didn't deserve to be manipulated. "I wonder what will become of the shop," I said, as if I didn't have a direct line to its owner.

"That's a good question. Of course, I'm happy to have the group here on a regular basis," Eileen said.

"Or we could rotate so no one has the burden every week." In a record-breaking round of questionable connections, I thought of Molly and her lameness, how she'd told us a different story from the one she offered in the post office today. "We could give Molly a pass for a while, however, until her ankle heals."

"Oh, for sure," Eileen said.

"I saw her today at the post office," I said. "She's doing much better. Which reminds me. You wouldn't happen to know if she still has her cat, would you?"

"Not anymore. She swore last winter, when the last of her three tabbies died, that she wouldn't get another one. Why do you ask?"

"Mentioning her reminded me that my friend's cats passed on also, and she's looking for someone to give their toys to."

"Well, not Molly. And not me, I'm afraid. I'm a dog person. Bitsy is a very shy little chow chow, so I tucked her away in our bedroom the other night when the group was over, but I know you two would get along really well."

After a minute or two of pet talk, we were ready to end

the call. I thanked her again for searching for my sunglasses and for her great hospitality. I looked forward to meeting Bitsy, I told her, as my final fabrication.

By now I was upset with myself and a little frightened at the ease with which I'd come up with falsehoods. Would I ever be able to look Eileen straight in the eye again? Or myself in the mirror?

As if I'd conducted a real interview, I inserted a check mark next to Eileen's name on the Daisy page of my notepad.

And a question mark next to Molly's. Why had she lied to the curious barista in the post office? Did it mean anything in the larger scheme of things? Maybe Molly was a chronic teller of white lies, and both stories—blaming first the Adirondack chair and then the cat for her tripping— were fiction. I didn't know Molly very well; maybe she was a private person, not wanting to share her personal life with a casual acquaintance or a stranger as the barista might have been, and made it a practice to make things up as she went along.

Aunt Tess always said one reason not to tell lies was that you had to have a very good memory to keep them straight, whereas if you always told the truth, you had nothing to worry about. I felt a flush across my face as I thought of what she'd have to say of my dealings tonight.

Of course, Aunt Tess didn't have a murder to solve.

But then, technically, neither did I.

I made quick calls to Quinn and Linda, who'd texted me while I was on the phone with Eileen. I was glad I was able to end the evening with honest exchanges and a few smiles.

Quinn didn't press me for how I was handling Cliff's

recruitment efforts. Instead, he teased with news of something special he'd picked up for me. I made a few guesses, but he stuck to his plan. I'd have to wait till he returned to find out.

Linda kept me distracted for a while, talking about a possible career change. An opening had come up for a job as postal inspector. It would mean more travel and she'd miss the group she now supervised, but maybe she was ready for that change. What did I think?

"Do I really want to be the 'Postal Police'?" she asked.

"What's the best thing and the worst thing about the job?" I asked, pulling out the kind of question we always asked each other before a big decision.

"Best: An amazing variety of challenges. Mail fraud. Identity theft. Credit card fraud. Robberies that involve our employees or facilities. Mailing of contraband. The variety is endless."

"But you'd have to specialize."

"Right. And believe it or not, I'm attracted to the education programs, teaching kids especially how to use the Internet wisely—it's now considered a form of 'mail' and therefore falls under our mission."

"Wow. Do we even need to get to the worst part of the job?"

"A lot of new training, for one thing." I heard a partial yawn. "Maybe more tomorrow night?"

"Okay, if you must go."

Linda sensed my need for an upbeat ending and hit me with an old joke.

"Did you hear the one about the unstamped letter?" she

asked. Then gave me the punch line, though I'd already started to laugh. "Never mind. You wouldn't get it."

With two large doses of happy talk, I was ready to call it a night, grateful to have both Linda and Quinn in my life.

I inhaled deeply, turned out my light, and slid under the covers.

9

My commute to work should have been uneventful. The skies were clear, traffic normal. But my head ached, as it did when I was a kid and had a chocolate hangover the day after Halloween. And many other days in the year, I recalled.

Stopped at a light, I reached to massage my lower back. I'd twisted my spine somehow, possibly while rechecking the condition of my car in my driveway. I'd wanted to take advantage of the daylight to look for scratches or other marks, and to be sure I hadn't had any unwelcome visitors during the night.

I had a moment of embarrassment over the lies I'd told Eileen. Would a confession to her make it better or worse? Or was it enough that I promised myself I'd never carry out such a charade again? I blamed Cliff in part, for talking me into sleuthing. I blamed Quinn for not being here to stop me. And I blamed Sunni for not inviting me to share in the investigation in an open way.

As I drove I kept looking at the empty passenger seat, trying to picture how my property was stolen yesterday. Whose hands had snatched my dinner and my files from the gray cushion? A hungry homeless man? A masked man, a killer who was a stranger to the town? I doubted it as much as I doubted that such a drifter was responsible for Daisy's murder. I preferred to believe I'd been the victim of a couple of kids with sticky fingers from oversized soft drinks, or teenagers high on their parents' stash of something stronger.

I replayed my actions on parking the car yesterday evening. I wanted to convince myself that I had left the car unlocked in my agitated state at the time, from following the intruder into the fabric shop, and therefore, my car was easy pickings. It was nothing personal, I told myself over and over. Just as the nasty *do your job* note was nothing personal.

Still, as I parked in my spot today, I scanned the area in a way that was different from yesterday. Later, as I hoisted the flag, I glanced across the lawn at my car, the only one in the lot at this hour. I hurried into the building through the side door, locked it, and headed for the sorting area, my heart rate returning to normal only after a few minutes of routine stuffing of post office boxes.

I focused on filling the boxes with letters, flyers, and postcards, pausing a few times to fill out a form for pickup at the counter when an oversized piece came through. I resisted the temptation to stand at the window and keep watch over my car. I knew I'd be nervous until it was time to open the doors and get caught up in new activity in the building.

No personal (or not personal) hate mail today. That was

a break. As if to teach me a lesson ("you're not off the hook yet"), the universe sent me a person of interest in a homicide as my first customer. Jules Edwards was at the head of the line when I unlocked the front doors for business. Not that I had assigned a motive to him—I'd scrapped the idea of an affair between him and Daisy as soon as it formed—but they had seen a lot of each other during her last eight or ten days on earth.

Jules and I stood, eye-to-eye, across my counter. "Hey, Cassie," he said. "One good thing about having to do my own errands today since my assistant is out sick—I get to say hi to a lot of people I seldom see."

I greeted him with a weak smile, aware of his name in my suspect column. "How are you doing?" I asked, assuming he'd know what I meant: now that one of your clients is no longer with us.

Jules's face took on a sad expression. I'd estimated that he was middle-aged, possibly in his mid-fifties, Cliff's age, ten years older than Daisy. "It'll never be the same, will it?" he said.

I shook my head. "I hope the police are making headway in the investigation. Whoever did this needs to be caught," I said.

"For sure."

While we were talking, I weighed and stamped a dozen thick envelopes that were over the one-ounce limit for first class, all from Jules's accounting practice to businesses in Berkshire County. I wondered if the packets contained informational literature, solicitations offering his services, now that he had an opening for a new client.

"Have you been able to help them at all?" I asked, affixing an extra-weight stamp to an envelope headed to Pittsfield, Massachusetts.

"Excuse me?" Jules looked confused. "Help to . . . ?"

"The police. I just assumed they would have talked to all of Daisy's employees and business associates."

"Yeah, yeah, of course, they interviewed me," Jules said. "I'm sure they're doing their best."

I noticed his nervous twitch and wondered if there were any forensic studies linking criminal activities to peculiarities like twitching. On one of our more interesting lunch dates, Sunni had taught me about anthropological criminology, the early attempts to link physical appearance, like the shape of one's head and the distance between one's eyes, to criminal behavior. I wished I had time to examine Jules for some of the correlations made in those early days. Large sinuses, sloping shoulders, large chest, and small forehead with wrinkles were a few that I remembered—features that it seemed everyone in line today exhibited. And what exactly was a "large incisor"? No wonder the "criminals are born" theory hadn't made much headway.

As I responded to my own need to scratch my nose, Jules leaned a bony elbow on the counter. "I just remembered—Cliff wants to meet with me to go over some accounting points for the fabric shop, and he suggested that you be there, too, Cassie. Do you have any idea why?"

"I guess it's because Daisy handled the financial aspects of the business, and Cliff wants to get up to speed," I offered.

"Sure, sure. But I mean, why would he want you there?" His expression gave every indication that he thought it would be a dumb idea. Or that he thought I was dumb. Or both.

If I believed in vibes, I'd have called the one coming from

Jules chilly, as if he were daring me to defend my right to be at the meeting. A meeting I didn't want to go to in the first place. But Jules's challenge gave Cliff's invitation a new twist, and in my special perverseness, I made up my mind to be there.

"I guess we'll find out," I said. I took Jules's money, handed back his change and receipt, and addressed the woman behind him, who'd been showing signs of impatience. "I'm sorry to keep you waiting," I said to her, holding out my arms to receive her oversized package. Jules gave me a slight frown and a salute of some kind and left the counter.

I could hardly wait for our meeting.

I shouldn't have been surprised when Cliff came by at lunch with another copy of his files and another set of white take-out boxes, the latter oozing the aroma of cashew nut chicken.

"You don't always have to bring food," I said, thinking especially of the hard time I had holding on to it. Or ever tasting it. The earlier chicken dinner had gone to the starving chief of police, and the shrimp scampi went the way of stolen goods never to be recovered.

"I've been meaning to try the new Thai place at the other end of Main," Cliff said as we made our way to the community room. Once more we took advantage of volunteers setting up for an event and entered through the unlocked door from the outside. A large banner across the stage welcomed freshmen for orientation. Cliff addressed a high school student who seemed to be part of the team preparing for the program.

"We usually have lunch here at this back table," Cliff told him, setting down the now-familiar plastic boxes and folders he'd carried in.

The young man, who had my vote for Cutest Homecoming King, scratched his head through his blond buzz cut. He looked around, anxious, but apparently saw no one above his pay grade. "I don't know," he said.

Cliff continued to set our table, so to speak, oozing authority, an attitude probably linked to his training as a security guard. "Don't worry; you won't have to clean up after us. We always take care of it ourselves."

I wanted to come out to the cute guy and admit that we'd done this only one other time, that it was not the regularly scheduled event Cliff made it out to be, and that we had no more permission to use the room as a lunchroom than any other citizen of the town. Since our students shared one high school with students in South Ashcot, where the school was located, I guessed the cute guy was from there and didn't recognize either of us.

The boy slinked away. I hoped he wasn't on his way to find a legitimate authority figure.

"Aren't you a little ashamed of pulling rank like that, buffaloing a poor teenager?" I asked Cliff, half teasing.

"Shouldn't they be in school anyway?" he countered.

"It's summer. And anyway, I think schedules today are more flexible than when we were in school."

"You mean me. I guess I'm an old man. But"—he pointed to the young man, busily placing literature on the rows of chairs—"as long as I can make my muscle work for me . . ." He ended with a smile and a shrug.

Cliff opened the tabs on our containers, releasing even stronger aromas of whatever Thai sauces were made of. I felt a pang of guilt as I wished I were sharing it with Quinn, or even Sunni, rather than with a guy who might be leading me into an obstruction of justice charge.

"When is our meeting with Jules?" I asked, now almost eager to be in the condescending moneyman's presence again.

"Can you make it this evening?"

With Quinn away I had nothing better to do on a Friday night, and I wanted to get all the meetings and investigative tasks behind me and, given a miracle, the case solved, before he returned on Sunday. "As long as it's after five," I said.

"Great. I'll text him." He pulled out his smartphone and got to work. "I'm just getting used to this, but everybody these days sort of demands it," he said.

"E-mailing is so yesterday," I said with a smile.

Cliff struggled with his wide thumbs, switching now and then to his pinkie, while I sampled a tender, flaky chunk of chicken, followed by a perfectly coated cashew. Although his bulky appearance suggested he was the fast food, quick burger type, apparently the man was a foodie, as attested to by his choice of takeout.

"Any news?" he asked when he'd finished the text.

I wanted to tell him about Molly's fib just to impress him, assure him that I was on the job, so to speak, but I knew that wasn't a good idea. I had the feeling that he'd jump on any possible lead and take it to a sorry end. I couldn't do that to Molly, or anyone else, without more information.

"I'm following up with the quilters' group, but nothing stands out. How about you?"

Cliff opened his folder, his lunch still untouched. "I talked to Reggie Harris about the farmers' market proposal."

I'd almost forgotten about the second part of the altercation that had broken out at the quilters' meeting. Andrea, Reggie's wife, had been the object of Liv's ridicule. I had to smile as the image of fabric featuring an overly pink mermaid came to mind. Andrea had escalated the drama by accusing Liv of, at least, being happy about the death of her competitor in greeting cards, and at most, possibly causing it. What had followed was an escalation of insults, including one about Reggie's sponsorship of the farmers' market proposal.

Cliff had continued talking, not noticing that my attention had gone elsewhere. I picked up his thread as he was making a confession. ". . . have to admit I feel awful trying to capitalize on sympathy for me as I more or less interrogate my friends. I know I should be in seclusion or something, but I can't sleep"—or eat, I thought, looking at his full box of Thai chicken—"until I figure out what happened to my wife, the love of my life. And going through her things? I can't handle it right now."

His last words were barely audible. It was bound to happen. Cliff broke down, as I should have expected. His head fell to his chest, and his shoulders shook with his sobs. His body seemed to sway from side to side. The lucky thing was that the high school contingent had taken a break and made a picnic scene on the floor of the stage at the front of the room. The kids' talk and laughter bounced off the walls and drowned out any sounds coming from Cliff's grief. The last thing to interest them would be two old folks in the back, folks who had at one time been in school, which had started and ended at the same time every day.

I was at a loss for how to respond to Cliff. We'd been sitting across the back table from each other, on folding chairs. Not wanting to draw attention from anyone who happened to be glancing our way, I reached out and put my hands around Cliff's, which were clasped together. I uttered a word of sympathy—not useful, but I hoped he'd feel my support. At that moment, I wanted nothing more than to help him find Daisy's killer and promised myself to stop wavering.

After a couple of minutes, I handed him a napkin from the pile between us. "I'm so sorry, Cliff," I said again, and pushed his bottle of water toward him. "You should at least drink some water. You're not going to be any use to anyone unless you take care of yourself."

What a surprise. I found myself uttering words I'd heard over and over when my parents died. I wondered if anyone, anywhere, knew what words or actions would have an impact at times like this.

He lifted his head, dried his face with the napkin. I waved away his "Sorry," and he was ready to continue.

"Daisy was in deeper than I thought," he said. When I looked confused, he clarified. "The farmers' market issue?"

"Right," I said. "Your talk with Reggie Harris." Which seemed to have been mentioned hours, not minutes ago.

He pulled a printed sheet from his folder. He was back to work. The eight-and-a-half-by-eleven page showed marks that suggested it had been crumpled, then smoothed out for copying.

He placed the sheet in front of me. "Last week, Daisy

wrote this letter to the *Town Crier* for the Letters to the Editor page. There's pretty strong language here, singling out Reggie, calling him some kind of traitor, saying he didn't care about local merchants and on and on, even accusing him of profiting somehow if the farmers were allowed to move in."

"Profiting because it's his land that the farmers would be using?"

Cliff shrugged. "That and other things not as aboveboard as renting or leasing agreements. It was sort of veiled, you know? Implying that he'd be taking a cut if he got the zoning through."

Something didn't seem right. "What kind of payoff could Reggie expect from a group of farmers? Unless the price of beets has gone up astronomically, a cut, as you put it, wouldn't amount to much."

"Maybe it wasn't just beets for sale."

"Cliff, are you saying the farmers would be coming here selling—"

"I'm not saying anything." He folded his arms across his wide chest. "I'm just trying to cover all bases, like I told you."

I moved on, picking up the letter. "This is what Daisy wrote to the newspaper?" I asked.

"Uh-huh. Reggie gave it to me. It was never printed. Reggie and Gordon Brooks, the *Town Crier*'s editor, are golf buddies, so Gordon showed it to Reggie."

"And Reggie was obliging enough to offer you the letter Daisy wrote, disparaging him?"

"I might have bullied him a little," he said, biting his lip. Sheepish?

I doubted the "little" part. After all, Cliff was a big man, trained in physical confrontation; Reggie was short and small framed, a little chunky, like his wife, Andrea. Cliff had a badge and, on some jobs, carried a gun. Even a little bullying would be enough to intimidate an ordinary citizen. But Reggie himself had a lot of clout, big developer that he was. He probably had muscle of his own. Or at least a couple of junkyard dogs.

I expected Cliff to give me a minute to read the letter for myself, but Cliff went on. "I can't believe Daisy wrote it. She usually would show something like that to me first, but not this time." He scratched his head. "Never mind. I guess I can believe it. When she was passionate about something, she put everything into it." Cliff choked up and I was afraid he was going to lose it again, but he took a deep breath and continued. "You can keep that copy and read it later. As I said, it was never printed. Gordon showed it to Reggie to give him a chance to write a response for the same issue if he wanted to."

"Did Reggie respond?"

"He did write a letter, but then Daisy"—Cliff paused and swallowed—"died."

"So neither letter was printed," I finished.

"Right, but here's the problem. Reggie wouldn't show me his response letter."

"Understandable," I said. "It will never be printed anyway."

Cliff's head snapped up. "But it's evidence, don't you see? You have to realize the farmers' market is just part of Reggie's big plan for the city. He's been touting it forever."

I really did need to read local news before checking the

Boston scene, I realized. "What if he threatened to kill Daisy in that letter?" Cliff asked.

"He'd hardly advertise it to the public before the fact," I said.

"You never know. Killers do crazy things."

For some reason, I balked at the characterization of Daisy's killer as, well, a killer. Her murder seemed more of an accident, an argument gone very bad. Not part of the master plan of someone who'd done it before or would kill again. I was at least smart enough not to share this conjecture with Cliff.

The students were back to work now and I realized lunch hour was nearly over for me.

"I have to open the office, Cliff," I said. "Can we talk later?"

"Yeah, sorry. I kind of lose track of time." He gathered his things, stuffing papers into his folder. "I'm going to follow up on this letter, try to get at what Reggie's answer was. Maybe I'll go see Gordon at the paper."

And bully him? I wondered. "Have you thought of taking the issue to the police?"

He laughed, the first time this week in my presence. So what if it was close to a sneer? "If you don't think the letter is that important, how do you think your friend at the station will feel?"

I started to defend myself and Sunni: He'd misquoted me; mislabeled Sunni, as if she were my friend only, and not the chief law enforcer in the town, as fair and honest as anyone could want in the police department; and he'd more or less accused her of going by her feelings, not the facts of the case. He called Reggie's letter of response potential evidence; on the other hand, he wouldn't trust those whose job it was to process evidence. I looked at Cliff's face—sad, determined—and I saw that there was no point in further discussion.

I tucked Daisy's letter in my purse and stood to leave. I'd been picking at my lunch on and off, but most of it was left in the box. I closed the lid, planning to put the meal in the fridge. I wondered if the food would still be there at the end of the day.

"We need to talk about getting alibis from everyone," Cliff said, walking me to the door.

I took a deep breath, holding back frustration at Cliff's unwillingness to trust Sunni and her force to do their jobs.

"Good point," I said. "Let's check in later."

"I'll see you this evening, right? Jules texted that six o'clock will work for him. His office."

I took Jules's address from Cliff and let him out through the front lobby doors. I welcomed the customers already in line, accompanied by a cool breeze that had a whiff of the fall to come. I was happy to see people who needed me for what I was good at: post office business.

10

Traffic in the lobby was slow for a Friday afternoon. Many businesses had a regular Friday post office stop and people in general wanted to get mail out before the weekend. But today the weather was more conducive to an early get-away to a beach. When Ben stopped by after lunch and offered to take the counter, I felt comfortable abandoning my spot to him.

"You probably have a lot of paperwork to catch up on," he said, his blue eyes watery. His way of not admitting that he was bored and looking forward to some interaction of the postal service kind.

When I was first back in North Ashcot, I sometimes took Ben's frequent appearances in the office as a sign that he didn't trust me in the job. I soon realized that, while that might have been a small part of his motive, it was mostly about his need to be productive and useful. It didn't take long for me to acknowledge how lucky I was to have him. Our occasional disagreements about protocol weren't much of a price to pay for having such a great and willing resource on hand.

Today, I dragged my desk chair to a corner by the side door, out of sight and hearing of the activity as the line of customers moved along, tended to by their former postmaster and friend. I let Ben think what he wanted about my paperwork; I had some non-USPS business to take care of.

No sooner had I sat down, a mug of coffee at hand, than my cell phone rang.

Sunni. Perfect timing. *Not*. I'd hoped to have time to process the meeting I'd just finished with Cliff. I wanted to read Daisy's letter and to figure a way to be invited into the investigation by Sunni herself. I could let my phone ring. Sunni used my cell number when she knew I'd be at work and might not answer. She also sometimes used it when she was outside my door or across the street to get my attention. Better not take that chance.

I slid my phone on and accepted the call.

"How's it going?" Sunni asked.

"It's a little slow this afternoon. Ben stopped in for a retail fix, so I'm off the counter." *In case you're out there in my lobby, looking in. See, I'm telling the truth.*

"That's not what I meant, and you know it."

Uh-oh. She sounded only half teasing. Was she still following me? Had she seen me having lunch with Cliff? Probably. Maybe I could smooth things over by offering her Thai chicken.

"We should talk," I said.

"Definitely. I might actually get a dinner hour tonight. Are you free?"

"I have a meeting at six," I said, choosing not to share the details of my arrangement to accompany Cliff to his accountant's office.

"With whom?"

Of course she'd ask. "Is this an official interrogation?"

Big sigh. "Not yet. What if I meet you afterward? Give me a call when you're done with the meeting I can't know about."

"Okay," I said, but the chief of police had already clicked off.

I swiveled around and caught a look at Ben, moderately busy. I had time for one more interaction, one that would be hassle free. I texted Quinn.

Where are u?

Heading for Keene.

He was in New Hampshire. On his way home. Going well?

So well that I may have to rent small trailer. Anything new?

Waiting for you.

Me too. Heading home early as poss Sunday. Skype tonight?

Definitely.

I smiled, my thoughts on Quinn, my gaze at the wall in front of me, next to the side door. A new poster collage commemorating five celebrity chefs smiled back and I felt all was not dark and heavy in my world. I took another minute to go through personal mail for the first time since yesterday when the *do your job* edict had come through. At one point I'd considered Sunni might be the author of the note. It certainly represented her sentiments—except for the *go home* part, I hoped. But Sunni was not the kind of person to attack from the side. If she had something to tell me, she would. And did. Often.

When I finished the pile of mail on my lap without incident, I felt my shoulders relax.

I remembered another letter I'd received today. I fished the letter Cliff had given me from my purse. Daisy's unpublished Letter to the Editor for the *Town Crier*.

Cliff had summed it up correctly. Daisy hadn't pulled any punches in expressing her opinion. I zeroed in on the most pointed paragraph.

> *Does anyone really think that Mr. Harris is working for the good of the citizens of North Ashcot? Never mind the overwhelming competition especially the new crafters will present to us small business people. We should also be worried about how Mr. Harris is lining his own pockets with kickback. And think about it. Where could that kickback money come from? Are his farmers selling only Brussels sprouts and crab apples? I think not.*

Daisy had barely stopped short of accusing the farmers of selling illegal substances and Reggie Harris of sponsoring their activities. I couldn't help wondering if this was Daisy off on some wild imaginings, or if she had evidence to back up her claim.

Even more threatening was Daisy's closing.

Mr. Harris and Mrs. Harris have profited greatly from our town. They live on the most expensive property and enjoy the perks of the wealthy. They may seem invincible, but remember the old saying: The bigger they are, the harder they fall.

It hadn't occurred to me to think of Andrea Harris as more than a member of our quilt group and a hard worker. She helped her brother, Pete, in his hardware store and I'd heard she also managed affairs at the Harris construction offices. I remember being surprised to learn that the offices were a set of trailers on the outskirts of town, not exactly high-rises in the heart of a city, as Boston developers could boast.

Maybe Daisy knew something we didn't. Or she was wrong. Either way, Daisy was no longer with us and that made me sad.

When business started to pick up around two thirty, I left my desk to work the counter with Ben. Our conversation between customers shouldn't have surprised me.

"You're sure spending a lot of time with Cliff Harmon," Ben said, straightening the bills in the cash drawer.

Only a parent could get away with that kind of talk, I thought, and gave Ben temporary status as a dad.

"Not you, too," I answered, using my temporary status as a teenager. "How do you even know? We haven't gone to a restaurant or anything like that."

A customer arrived and we both put on smiles and carried out the transaction together, Ben lifting the heavy box onto a dolly.

Alone again, Ben spelled out for me the chain of communication that fed his need to keep tabs on his friends and neighbors.

"The kid who mows my lawn, Kevin, has been helping out in the community room for a few days," he explained. "I've known his mother for years. It turns out she picked him up a couple of times and saw you two back there. Then I met her at the gas station and she mentioned it." He paused for a smile. "Don't you love small towns?"

"Is that why you came by today, to quiz me?"

Ben grinned, continuing his self-imposed task of tidying the cash drawer. "It's just a side benefit."

With the ebb and flow of customers, Ben was able to sneak in a few gibes and a few probing questions, and I was able to skirt them all.

And yes, I did love small towns. Just not today.

Jules Edwards ran his accounting business from an office suite above the hardware store on Main Street, in the thick of things, or as thick as they got in downtown North Ashcot. A separate entrance led to a small, well-maintained lobby and a flight of stairs to the second floor of the two-story building. Jules shared the floor with a counseling group on one end of the hallway and a family trust lawyer on the other. All offices were dark at the moment.

Though I was ten minutes early, Cliff was waiting, sitting outside Jules's locked office. The nicely polished mahogany bench reminded me of the kind of furniture in Ashcot's Attic, Quinn's antiques shop. A few more hours, I told myself, and I'd see Quinn's face, if only on my laptop screen. Cliff had offered to pick me up for this meeting, but I wanted the freedom having my own car would bring. Besides, I didn't need another dozen or so of North Ashcot's citizens taking notes as they saw Cliff and me riding around town together.

Cliff stood when he saw me, his arms full of folders. He extracted a fresh pad of yellow lined paper from the stack and handed it to me with "In case you need to take notes." I thanked him, assured him I had a pen, and took a seat on the bench.

Cliff checked his watch. "It's not quite six yet," he said. "I thought he'd be here, though, you know, still putting in his day's work."

"Maybe he's meeting with clients in the field," I offered.

"True, he often came to the shop if Daisy couldn't get away." He shuffled through the folders on his lap. "I went to see Gordon at the *Crier*. He wouldn't give me any clue about how Reggie responded to Daisy's letter. The one I gave you a copy of."

I nodded. I knew which letter he'd meant.

"I feel like going back and searching his office," Cliff continued. "I'm sure he has a copy somewhere."

I imagined Cliff putting on his uniform, muscling his

way into the newspaper offices at night with a flashlight between his teeth, lock picks in his hands. He'd also probably be wearing a hoodie.

"Wait," he said. "Here's an idea." I shuddered, but let him go on. "I'll bet Sunni doesn't know about either Daisy's letter or Reggie's response, since nothing came of either one as far as the public is concerned. We could show her Daisy's letter. Then she could ask Reggie for his response and he'd have to produce it."

"Don't you think Reggie has destroyed that letter by now? I would have."

"I suppose. But he'd have to admit he wrote a response. He couldn't lie to a cop." He lowered his voice. "Can't you just give it a shot?"

"Me?" I asked, though I wasn't exactly shocked.

"I could tell her, but she already doesn't want to see me. You're her friend," he said.

For now, I thought.

About twenty minutes later, the three of us stood outside Jules's office. He'd been a few minutes late, dressed in what passed as business attire in our town—newish jeans and a sport coat—rattling off apologies as he unlocked his door.

"I was actually with Molly Boyd, going over accounts for her salon," he said. "She had some kind of setback with her foot and can't get around very well."

"I'm so sorry to hear that. And what a freak accident," I said, seizing the opportunity. "I heard she tripped over her cat during the storm?"

Jules shook his head, in the office now, headed for his

desk, his phone in his hand. One-fingered texting? Jules fit right in with a generation at least one behind him. Cliff and I followed close behind him as he took a seat. "Molly's cat . . ." He turned his sentence into a cough. "Right, excuse me. Yeah, she tripped over the cat. Bad news."

Too late, I thought; that's the peril of multitasking. I had no idea why Jules would cover for Molly, or why I continued to pursue the real cause of her injured ankle as if it mattered.

Jules took his seat behind an enormous, highly polished executive-style desk; we took chairs in front. I glanced at my reflection in the surface. Real cherrywood or a finish? Quinn would know, but I couldn't tell. Before meeting Quinn, I wouldn't even have thought of the question. I also wondered how they'd managed to get the desk up the narrow stairway and through the office door.

I marveled at how all of Jules's accessories matched, with cherrywood (real or faux) bases for his stapler, clips, tape, pencils, organizer, and bookends. None of my homes or office spaces had ever been so coordinated. I relied on the "messy desk, clear mind" saying and what Linda called my dorm room décor.

Except for the cherrywood, the office was furnished with what looked like the latest in high-tech equipment. The side wall was lined with electronics. Printer, scanner, copier, fax machine, and one fancy piece of equipment, cubical in shape, that I didn't recognize.

"That's a three-D printer," Jules said, following my gaze. "They'll probably come down in price, but you know me, early adopter and all."

"What's it good for?" Cliff asked.

Jules laughed, as if he'd expected just such a question. He picked up two chess pieces, a blue pawn and a yellow rook. "Here are my latest creations. I hope to graduate to something more useful soon."

Cliff shook his head, clearly not impressed.

"We should get started," Jules said, pulling a file from a drawer. He opened it, ready to get down to the meeting agenda. "As I told you, Cliff, there's no need for you to take on any additional burden for the financial workings of the shop. I'm assuming you're planning to keep it going?"

"For now, yes," Cliff said.

I hoped that Jules had already offered Cliff some measure of sympathy before this meeting, which was to be all business, apparently. He spread out an array of forms, facing us. "As you can see," he said, "the last reporting was at the end of July." He jabbed his finger at the bottom of each sheet. "And Daisy signed off. So we're good to go until the end of this month. In fact, if you need to take a couple of months to get adjusted, don't even worry about all this."

Jules picked up his phone, which he'd kept at his fingertips, suggesting that he was finished with the meeting, that in his mind, he'd explained whatever needed explaining, and was ready for the next interaction, via smartphone. I surprised Cliff and even myself by prolonging things.

"Actually, we can't see," I said, with a chuckle. I pointed to the corner of the office where there was a small round conference table and chairs. "Can we sit over there so we can all get a good look? I'm not that used to spreadsheets."

Jules looked at his watch, then his phone, and grimaced. "I suppose we can do that."

A short while ago I hadn't wanted anything to do with Jules Edwards or the finances of Daisy's Fabrics. Now here I was, making sure we got what we needed from him. In for a penny, I guessed.

We headed for the corner where a large matted, framed print dominated the wall space over a low credenza. SUCCESS IS was in large type. I couldn't read the tiny lettering that followed on the next line, which seemed to defeat the purpose of displaying the message, but perhaps the sepia image of a footbridge cutting through rather swampy land was meant to prevail over the words.

As I passed the two large windows, it occurred to me that this was the first time I'd been above the first floor of the town since I returned a year ago. I had everything I needed on the ground floor. I stopped for a moment to gaze across Main Street to Daisy's Fabrics to the right, and to the police station a block down to the left. As far as I could tell, Cliff had walked right by the views, not looking over at what was now solely his shop.

I wondered if the chief knew where I was right now. I'd find out soon enough, I was sure.

Jules spread his files across the conference table. Though a trolley against the back wall had the makings of coffee or tea, Jules offered neither. "Now, what would you like to know?" he asked, almost as a dare.

I'd expected Cliff to be a master interrogator. Hadn't he referred often to his training, so close to that of police officers? At the moment, faced with his accountant and a windstorm of financial data, he seemed dumbstruck, slunk low in his chair. Without his stiff uniform, in a loose cardigan (and no badge), he looked much older than his fifty-something years. No wonder he'd asked me to sit in. My only choice was to step up.

"I imagine Cliff would like to know the bottom line, first," I said. "Is the shop doing well, as far as its financial health goes?"

Cliff gave a pitiful nod. Jules laughed, an intimidating chuckle, as if my question was silly. "Define 'healthy,'" he said.

As luck would have it, I was in one of my rare moods of Don't Tread on Me, from the days of the American Revolution. "I thought that would be your job," I answered.

I felt Cliff's nervousness in the seat next to me, whether for my well-being or Jules's I couldn't have said.

"I suppose it is my job," Jules said. "Let's just say that Daisy sometimes let her reach exceed her grasp and we have some debts to clear up."

Cliff sat up straight. "Debts? What kind? To whom?"

A big, reassuring smile from Jules. "I told you, I'm taking care of everything, buddy. You have to give me a little time to sort things out."

"But Daisy always assured me that we were doing well. We paid our bills and were mostly living off my salary. She was putting the profits from the shop into an account for our retirement."

"Is that what she told you?"

Cliff shifted his body, nearly standing, then sitting down again. I thought he was going to speak, but he simply swallowed, cleared his throat, and glanced at me. A cue, I supposed.

"What are you telling us?" I asked.

Jules waved his hand at me, as if a gnat had spoken up midflight. He pulled on his long, thin chin and addressed Cliff. "Hey, I told you, don't worry, buddy. I'm handling it."

Why didn't that ease my mind? I could tell by Cliff's fidgeting and his murmured "We were looking at a condo in Miami near Daisy's parents" that Jules's hand-waving, both literal and figurative, didn't help him much, either.

"You'll tell me if we're in trouble, right?" Cliff asked.

Jules reached across the table and patted Cliff's arm with the hand that was not resting on his phone. "Of course, of course. Trust me—I'm on top of it." He checked his watch. "Listen, I'm expected at a dinner meeting with a big South Ashcot client. But hey, don't hesitate to give me a call if you have any further questions."

Before we could respond, Jules was on his feet at the door. "You have my number, too, don't you, Cassie?"

"I do, and I promise to use it soon," I said, with a smile that wasn't returned.

I nearly asked for the number of the nearest auditor.

Outside, Cliff blew out a big breath. He walked me to my car, in my usual downtown spot in the lot in front of the bank, which generously allowed public parking after hours, both in front and in its back lot. We stood talking, leaning on my fender. In the shadow of the police department.

"What do you think?" he asked me, jerking his head toward the second floor of the building we'd just exited.

"I think you need to get copies of everything and show them to another accountant."

Another loud breath as Cliff's eyes widened, making me wish I hadn't been so blunt. "It's always a good idea to have a second opinion," I said. "Let's sleep on it, okay? We can talk tomorrow."

I couldn't think of a nicer way to separate myself from Cliff. I'd planned to walk over to Sunni's office, but I didn't want Cliff to know that. I didn't need any more prompting from him.

"You're probably right," he said. "I feel like my head is going to explode with all there is to do."

I knew what he meant. As careful as Aunt Tess had been to set her affairs in order before she died, I was still left with mountains of paperwork, phone calls, sorting, and transfers of this and that to deal with. At the time, I told myself I wanted to simply hide and grieve without letting anyone know where I was, but, in reality, the chores were distractions that were probably good for my mental health.

"I thought everything would be easier since we're going to have the service in Florida, but it's almost worse," Cliff continued. "People keep calling, wanting to send flowers, or attend a service here. I know I should be grateful."

Cliff's voice was choked and I felt another meltdown coming on.

"Why don't we have a simple memorial for Daisy in a couple of weeks? I'll take care of it, if you want. Just a gathering to honor what she meant to us and our town."

"Would you do that?" he asked.

I nodded. "Now will you try to get some rest? I'll check

in with you soon," I said. I took Cliff's arm, nudged him toward his car, three or four down from where we stood.

"Thanks, Cassie. I'm so lucky to have you on my side."

I wasn't sure about that, but I smiled anyway and wondered if it was truly my voice I'd heard, offering to arrange a memorial service. It was something aboveboard, and well within my abilities, I told myself. I stayed by my car and watched as Cliff walked down the street to his black, official-looking SUV.

I needed some downtime before I was ready to face Sunni, so I walked across the street to Mahican's. I placed my cappuccino order, took a seat, and called Sunni to say I'd be at the station in a half hour. For all I knew she'd been tracking me since I left work, but I couldn't worry about that.

In fact, I was tired of sneaking around, always concerned about what she would think of what I was doing with respect to the investigation of Daisy's murder, always questioning whether or not I should tell her about what might be a lead or a clue or who might be a suspect, or even strange things that had come my way this week. That wasn't how friends should be with each other, I told myself.

It might have been the rich espresso and the frothy steamed-milk foam that gave me clarity. Or it might have been the sugary morning bun I couldn't resist, though I couldn't get the barista to tell me if it was this morning's or tomorrow morning's fare.

Then and there I came up with a proposal. I packed up my things and headed out the door. As I crossed the street to my car, I noticed the lights were out on the second floor.

I thought of the arrogant moneyman who worked there. I hoped Cliff would take my advice and get a second opinion on his finances.

I put that aside and focused on how to present my proposal to the chief of police. Would she think it was crazy? Or that I was crazy?

It was time to find out.

11

In the bank's parking lot once more, I heard a low-level commotion—an overlapping of adult voices. I stepped back to the sidewalk to check out the source of the noise.

Next door to the bank was Molly Boyd's beauty salon, From Head to Toe. WE CAN DYE YOUR HAIR AND PAINT YOUR TOES AT THE SAME TIME, a sign in the window boasted. The door to the salon opened and I saw Molly greet a group of eight or nine people who'd been waiting on the sidewalk, chatting but somewhat subdued. Hard as I tried, I couldn't make out what they were saying.

I thought it strange that the salon would be reopening, then noticed that the salon's front lights were out, but lights in the back were on. I recognized quilters Fran Rogers and Molly Boyd. Andrea Harris was there with her pro–farmers' market husband, Reggie, in a baseball cap. Others who joined the group included several men I didn't recognize and a few more I did: Andrea's brother, Pete, whose hardware store was next to the salon; Jules (not surprising, holding a phone to his ear); and Fred Bateman, Quinn's boss at the antiques store.

The sight reminded me of brainteasers I'd seen: What do these people have in common? Or, who doesn't belong in this picture?

"Hey, Cassie." Fred had stepped out of the group and greeted me.

"Looks like a high-level meeting is about to start," I said.

Fred, in his sixties, I guessed, and usually as laid-back as you would expect of someone for whom a hundred-year-old hutch was "nearly new," glanced over his shoulder at a couple of new arrivals and let out a skittish laugh. "Nah, we'll just be shooting the bull in the back room. Looks like your boyfriend is having quite a successful trip. I'm sure you've been in touch."

Smooth transition, I thought, and played along, telling Fred that, yes, Quinn and I had Skyped often, and yes, I'd be glad when he was home.

More people straggled in, exiting cars in twos and threes; others came from both directions on Main Street. I saw Mike Forbes, who owned Mike's Bike Shop, and Dan Fuller, another bank worker. Curious as I was, I didn't know Fred well enough to make a point of querying him about the gathering. We said good-bye, the reason for the meeting in the salon having been buried under small talk.

I was left with my imagination, and came up with an illegal poker game on one end of the spectrum and a surprise party planning session for a milestone birthday on the other. It was a strange collection of townsfolk, including some quilters, excluding others. Maybe they were designing a memorial service for Daisy. I hoped not, not without Cliff. Or me. But I had enough to worry about and focused on meeting Sunni.

The police department building was a redbrick Colonial, similar to the post office, except that it was two stories high, with a basement, and the interior hadn't been renovated for some time. The white trim on the exterior was badly in need of a touch-up also and the landscaping left much to be desired. I wondered if Sunni's no-nonsense political style and lack of wiles had anything to do with her quarters being low priority for the town budget.

Sunni was alone in the building when I knocked on her office door around seven thirty Friday evening.

"I hope you brought food," she said, not raising her head from the files on her old oak desk.

"How does Thai chicken with cashew sauce sound?" I asked, lifting the container over my shoulder, waitress-style.

She looked up and I noticed dark circles under her eyes, her red hair falling out of her usually neat bun, her face almost as gray as her uniform shirt. "You wouldn't tease me about something like that, would you?"

I lowered the bag that contained my lunch, waving it slightly to release the aroma, proud that at the last minute before heading over here, I'd remembered that it was in my fridge and made a detour to my office. "It's the real thing," I said, not bothering to mention that the meal came courtesy of Cliff Harmon.

"Hand it over. I can't talk until I've had something to eat."

"That kind of day, huh?"

"Instant oatmeal goes only so far."

I followed Sunni to the small, windowless break room at the other end of the building and set the round table with plastic utensils and napkins while she nuked the plate.

It wasn't like Sunni to whine at such length. She continued. "As if there weren't enough on my plate"—she pointed to the container spinning in the microwave—"and I don't mean this kind of plate. Ross will be leaving us in about a week."

Reason enough to be cranky. "I'm sorry to hear that." Officer Ross Little was a capable, likable young man and I knew Sunni would miss him. His departure would also reduce her staff to four officers, including herself. "Why is he leaving?"

"He got a better offer from the Springfield PD. I can't blame him. He's not really a small-town guy." She smiled. "Maybe the last straw was his assignment to Girls' Hockey Day two years in a row."

I wanted to ask why a murder investigation, now in progress, wasn't enough to hold the interest of a sworn officer of the law, but I thought it was too soon to bring up the Daisy Harmon case. The success of the idea I would be presenting depended a great deal on proper timing.

We took bottles of water from the fridge and sat with our dinner, most of which I dished out to my hardworking friend.

"This is delicious," she said. "I'm really not in the mood for a restaurant. In fact, I hate stepping out of the office these days."

I knew Sunni was referring to the press corps, small but

persistent, who followed her around at times like this. Even worse, the murder in North Ashcot had drawn reporters from surrounding towns as well. We gave thumbs-up to the Thai sauce and decided to visit the restaurant in person when things were more settled, whatever that meant.

I let Sunni go on about how she and her soon-to-be-reduced force of officers were stretched to the limit. She ticked off the issues. Bullying in the elementary school yard, requiring a new program of seminars and training for the teachers, as well as talks with the student body. A string of smash-and-grab robberies at a strip mall on the border with South Ashcot. A rash of Peeping Tom incidents in a neighborhood in the southeast corner of town.

"And, not that I don't love our citizens," she said, "but our building is the go-to place for any kind of complaint. Your neighbor sprays your dog when he waters his lawn? A passerby left a candy wrapper on the sidewalk in front of your house? The parking meters are too close together? Tell the police."

"People actually report these things?"

She nodded. "Sometimes they file a report, sometimes they just want to vent. We try to steer this kind of thing to a civilian volunteer, but most want someone in uniform to listen to them, taking up an officer's time."

I tsk-tsked in sympathy, figuring that every problem she listed was an argument for my idea as the most logical course of action. Help was on the way, in the form of Cassie Miller, Postmaster and Sometime Sleuth, I thought, as Sunni went on.

"We also had a request from Brookside to help with their security. The storm ravaged their shopping district, landing on them minutes after skirting our own Main Street. The storm hit them so much harder than it hit us." She paused. "Well, not as hard in some ways. No one died there."

Although Sunni seemed to give all items on her to-do list equal emphasis, it was clear from her drawn face and shaky voice that Daisy's death and its aftermath were weighing on her. "And, as if we needed one more little project, we have two Brookside men in custody in our jail, since the perimeter of their facility was compromised during the storm."

I was ready to move in, convinced that the litany of Sunni's overload was the ideal setup for me to make my case. Especially since she opened the door, as the lawyers on TV said, to talking about Brookside.

"You know, they've closed the post office there," I said. Casually, of course.

"I saw that as I drove by the other day. I thought I was on the wrong block for a minute. Then I figured they were remodeling. It's really gone?"

"It's a pet-grooming place now." I tried to imbue the statement with as much of a heavy, dramatic tone as Ben had given it earlier.

"Sad," Sunni said.

"Makes me realize I need to keep my options open and my résumé polished," I said.

"Don't say that. They'd never close North Ashcot." Said with such authority I decided to let it stand. "What's for dessert?" she asked, causing me to lose my nerve.

"Coming up," I said, clearing away the trash from our meal.

"You're kidding." Her eyes widened. "I was kidding."

"No kidding. It's not much but"—I pulled out a package of two chocolate cupcakes that had been included with lunch—"better than fortune cookies, which would require our presence in a restaurant."

Sunni seemed overly pleased by the poor excuse for dessert, and led the way to the more comfortable chairs in her office, around a small conference table. I quashed unpleasant memories of a similar arrangement in Jules's office earlier this evening. The packaged cupcakes were no match for those from our bakery, but washed down with excellent coffee from Sunni's superb top-of-the-line equipment, they weren't too bad.

"This is nice, Cassie. You know, I've never had a close friend. I mean, as an adult." She took a bite of cupcake, a swig of coffee. "There's the quilting group, and I love that, but it's not the same as one-on-one."

"With a job like this, you don't have a lot of free time. You're practically on call all the time," I said.

"It's not only that, but also no one ever wants to hear what I do all day." She chuckled. "I'm starting to sound like my undertaker brother-in-law in Maine."

What did it say about me that I loved hearing what cops did? And undertakers. I didn't know one personally, but I had a feeling I'd find her or him fascinating. Much more exciting than the time I uncovered mail fraud when I found a teddy bear in a media-mail-only package.

"I'm surprised," I said. "Don't people always want to hear cops talk about their adventures?"

"Like whose cat was in the tree and why did it take all day to get it down? Or, worse, as I just poured out all my woes on you?" She shook her head. "Nuh-uh. Sometimes a case will capture their attention, but then I'm not at liberty to talk about it, am I?"

"Like with a murder," I said.

"Exactly. I remember when I was working in a big-city department. Hartford PD. And at the end of the day one of my girlfriends would be complaining that the copy machine in her office was on the fritz. And I'd be thinking how I'd nearly gotten shot, stranded in an alley with a guy high out of his mind."

"Wow," I said, to keep her going.

"Yeah, this one time, my partner and I were stranded in the worst part of town. This was before GPS, and the bad guys knew we depended on street signs to call in our location. What they'd do is remove the signs in the neighborhood to make it almost impossible to get backup in the middle of a war zone."

"Clever, when you think about it. But how awful for you."

"You said it. But who's going to let me whine about how tough a cop's job is, like I'm doing now? Except you just did, so thanks."

Another opening? If not now, when? It was the first I'd heard that she'd once worked in Connecticut and that she had a brother-in-law. Sunni was in a sharing, perhaps vulnerable mood. As her friend, I owed it to myself to take advantage of the situation and offer to help.

"My pleasure," I said. I gazed up at the large framed portrait hanging on the wall over a file cabinet, of North Ashcot's first chief of police, one Joseph Lemuel Tanner. He seemed pleasant enough, encouraging me. "I have an idea," I said. More like *croaked*.

"Oh?" Sunni sounded curious enough but didn't pause

in her nibbling at the edges of the decorative cupcake frosting. "Is this going to ruin a nice evening?"

Maybe she wasn't that vulnerable. I shook my head, though I wasn't sure. "What if I could help you?"

She spread her arms to encompass the table and the evidence of a meal shared. "You are helping. That's my point."

"I mean really help. You have so much going on, and Ross is leaving in the middle of it," I said, my palms sweating.

She smiled. So far, so good. "You want to replace Ross?"

"No, no, I'm just saying that there must be some way you can use me, temporarily, to help with the biggest case you have to deal with right now. You wouldn't have to pay me, of course."

She ran her hand across her brow in a mock gesture of relief. "Whew."

"I have a few things to offer," I said, buoyed by the fact that she hadn't cut me off yet. Or pulled her gun on me. "Did you know that the postal service has an extensive investigative branch? Much of our inspectors' work is like police work. They have to sort through communications from all kinds of people. It could be a report from a supervisor, a lead from a suspicious customer or coworker—or a tip from a man on the street." I threw up my hands, as if to surrender to a great truth. "It's truly detective work."

"Did you work for that department? As an inspector?"

I cleared my throat. Why did I think Sunni might have let that little attempt at deception slip by? She was no longer hungry and she wasn't *that* tired. "No, but I've heard postal inspectors speak, and seen them in action." Sunni laughed out loud this time, and I couldn't blame her. But I forged ahead. "I've been called to take over a post more than once when an inspector has come to arrest a supervisor. I even had to testify a couple of times. I can't tell you the details of the cases, but—"

"Not exactly frontline action," Sunni said.

"Sorry—I wasn't trying to put something over on you. Not completely, anyway. But I do believe I have the skills and at one time I thought of applying. And in the job I have, I have to know a lot about postal rules and regulations, and a law is a law, right?"

"A lot of homicides in the Boston postal system, were there?"

Since Sunni was still in a relaxed frame of mind—maybe it was the low-end cupcakes—I chose to chuckle at her comment and continue, sticking closer to current reality this time. "I'm close to this case," I said. "And even though I'm in the quilting group only because of you, there are some members who might be intimidated when they have to deal with you professionally, whereas I'm just another fellow gossiper."

"So you've decided that Daisy's killer was a member of the quilting group?"

I blew out a breath, my stress level having caught up with me. "Sunni, you know that's not what I mean. I have a feeling you know exactly what I'm proposing." I took another breath and went all out. "Yes or no?"

The silence nearly strangled me. Sunni took her time. Another bite of cupcake. Another sip of coffee. At least she still hadn't gone for her handcuffs, I reminded myself. Her face gave nothing away, which I chose to interpret as her giving my words serious consideration.

"You know," she finally began, "I have to give you credit

for not throwing it in my face that you helped immensely on a case last year."

"I didn't do all that much," I said, softly, recalling with reluctance an upsetting time when I'd been back only a couple of months.

"Tell you what," she said, replacing her mug on the table. "I could use a serious brainstorming session. Why don't we start with that and see where it gets us?"

"Great," I said, feeling better than I had all week. "Maybe I'll be deputized before the night's over."

"Don't push your luck."

I was glad Sunni had suggested a break before we got down to the details of the investigation. She needed to make some calls and agreed to meet me at my house in an hour, at nine o'clock.

"It's about time I got out of this office," she'd said.

I sent a quick text to Quinn before starting my car.

1 mtg over, another starting. Skype later?

I turned my key and got on the road for home, glad I'd have time to get my thoughts organized. So far this week, I'd scribbled things in my notebook as they'd occurred to me, intending to put them in order. Now was the time. I didn't want to ruin the chance I had to work with Sunni by appearing amateurish. Never mind that I was, in fact, an amateur.

There was still light left to the day as I pulled into my driveway, excited to be on this new path of cooperation. I'd climbed three or four steps before I saw a piece of white paper sticking out from under my door. More ads, I thought. I played a guessing game with myself. The opening of a new Japanese restaurant. A discount on dry cleaning. A coupon for breakfast cereal. An offer for housekeeping service.

I reached the landing, unlocked my door, and entered, dodging the rest of the eight-and-a-half-by-eleven sheet. I continued my internal guessing. A lost kitty, a kid looking to mow my lawn at a reasonable rate.

I bent down and picked up the sheet.

And the winner was: another handwritten note, with only a few words.

One last warning. Back off.

I slammed the door shut and turned the key in the lock. I hoped I hadn't locked myself in with a madman.

12

I leaned against my front door, breathing hard, clutching the second note. With a stab of fear, I realized I couldn't presume that the messenger had left the note and disappeared. He might be in my house right now.

I pushed myself away from my door, opened it, and stepped outside. I took a breath. Should I call Sunni? Was I becoming one of those frantic, pesty-citizen stories she'd be relating to someone next month? I tried to override my fright and think.

The first note, the *do your job* admonition, had been sent through the postal system—addressed to Postmaster, stamped, and delivered to my office via the usual route by the mail truck. It could have come from anywhere. This second warning was not in an envelope. This time, the sender, assuming it was the same person, had made a brazen move—a sheet of paper stuck under my door. It was just now turning dark, so the culprit must have marched up my front steps in the daylight. He was telling me he knew where I lived and didn't care who saw him. But if he'd broken in, the note wouldn't have been sticking out the door; it would have been inside.

Now that I'd settled that, I reentered my living room, treading softly, and carrying Aunt Tess's old cast-iron frying pan. Confidence and bravery aside, I crept through my rooms, holding my breath at each new threshold, checking corners, looking for anything out of place.

Not that I had a clue what I would do if a person with a knife or gun leaped out of my closet, or pulled my feet out from under me from a hiding place under my bed. I couldn't shake the creepy thoughts. All I could do was make sure my windows and doors were locked. I made the rounds, doing a three-sixty spin now and then to be sure there was no one over my shoulder. The fact that locks were in place and that nothing seemed disturbed didn't calm me as much as it should have.

Back in the living room, I took my phone from my purse and sat on my rocker, tempted to call Sunni and ask her to rush over. I wished I'd told her about the first note. At the time, I believed the note had nothing to do with the investigation of Daisy's murder. Now I wasn't so sure.

Still, I resisted sounding the alarm. No need to overreact. I was safe; my house was locked up, and I could use the next forty-five minutes before she was due, to pull my thoughts together. So what if I was jittery and jumped at each shadow created by the lights of a passing car, at every old-house creak and refrigerator noise? Suddenly, the ice cube maker had all the crashing sound effects of a B&E and the ticking of Aunt Tess's grandfather clock was louder than a Boston club on a Friday night.

It took a few minutes to adjust to the fact that I was now operating with permission from Sunni. There was nothing I had to hold back from the chief of police. I knew there would be caveats and limits attached to what she could tell me, but I felt I'd finally made the team. I waited for the feeling of safety that should give me. It wasn't speeding toward me.

By eight forty-five, with the help of a large mug of coffee, I'd almost finished a list of people I had reason to suspect in Daisy's death. I couldn't bring myself to call any of them murderers or even potential murderers; they were citizens of my hometown. Friends, acquaintances, customers; not killers. I jotted down names and what I called their suspicious behavior.

First, there was the note writer. The words and phrases themselves should not instill fear in a typical reader of thrillers like me. *Do your job, go home, warning, back off.* These were phrases associated with mild outbursts, not ransom notes or bomb threats. But in the context of my snooping around, being seen with the victim's husband, entertaining the chief of police in my home (and feeding her), the note writer, Anonymous, had to be considered at least a person of interest. Thus, my first entry listed a specific suspicious behavior, but no name. Not the best start.

Next was Jules Edwards. Because I didn't like him? I couldn't think of another motive for suspecting Cliff and Daisy's accountant. He'd hand-waved over the numbers at our meeting earlier, but maybe that was par for the course for accountants. I had little experience to call on. I found myself almost wishing that a financial audit would show him guilty of doing something illegal. No need to share that line of fuzzy thinking with Sunni. My second entry had a name but no really suspicious behavior.

I moved on to the quilting group, hoping for more useful entries. I started with the widow Molly Boyd. She'd shown up at Tuesday's quilters' meeting, the day after the storm and Daisy's death, with a broken ankle, and I'd witnessed her telling two different stories about how she'd hurt herself. Wasn't it obvious: A black eye or a scratched fist or a broken ankle was a dead giveaway that the person had been in a fight with the victim. How simple things were when you didn't have to prove theories or substantiate common myths and fictional devices.

Molly, a short woman in her early sixties, ran the beauty salon across the street from Daisy's Fabrics, the salon that hosted the meeting I'd come upon earlier this evening. I couldn't think of what Molly would have against Daisy from a business point of view. It wasn't as if Daisy had competed, offering to do her customers' hair or nails while they chose their bolts of fabric. I knew little of Molly's life outside of our quilting sessions, only what she'd shared over tea and stitching—that she was a widow, a grandmother, and a lover of reality-television shows. And I couldn't help knowing what she sent and received through the post office—packages shared with a daughter in Maine, orders she placed with a plus-sized clothing store, requests for donations to a political party.

Whatever personal motive Molly might have had to dislike Daisy wasn't evident. Neither was there an obvious reason why she'd lied about her injury. Needing a full entry, I wrote "lying" and "hosting after-hours meeting" as her suspicious behaviors.

Olivia (Liv) Patterson, on the other hand, held more promise, with one of the clearest motives I could think of. Competition with Daisy for greeting card–buying customers, the lifeblood of her business.

I thought back to the last time I saw Liv in the post office. I remembered letting her enter just under the wire on Monday, before Ben and I closed up as the storm swooped in. Liv had atypically refused to engage in a conversation on a Western-themed quilt she'd spent hours and hours on. Now I manufactured a reason: She didn't want to support Daisy's Fabrics, the only brick-and-mortar fabric shop in the area, by admitting that Daisy had helped her find appropriate designs. I congratulated myself on coming up with that idea, then quickly chided myself for creating a story well beyond the bounds of plausibility and evidence. Liz was entitled to an off day, a cranky hour or two, without being suspected of murder. Detective work was harder than I thought.

Andrea Harris and her husband, Reggie, were also prime candidates for violence against Daisy. Daisy was single-handedly trying to undermine their campaign for the farmers' market proposal, which it seemed was a big part of their overall business plan. They'd both been headed for the meeting in the salon this evening. Acting like American citizens, with the right to assemble, I reminded myself, and moved on.

I couldn't come up with anything suspicious for Terry Thornton, our young bride-to-be, who was probably too wrapped up in her wedding planning to care about much else; nor for Eileen Jackson, our hostess this week. If lying were suspicious behavior, I was the one who should go on the list, for fabricating a reason to call Eileen and draw her into giving me information useful to the investigation. I only hoped she and Buddy weren't still looking for my sunglasses.

Fran Rogers was the last of the quilters on my list. She'd been part of the group, with Andrea and Liv, who were at the gathering in the salon. Fran was a pretty quiet woman, closer to my age, short and wiry, and always working on a quilt for a cause. One month she'd be talking about the children's wing of the hospital, and their need for baby quilts; another month she'd have on her lap a quilt meant for a military unit in a country I'd barely heard of. Hard to imagine her fighting or arguing with anyone, let alone killing someone.

That was it for the quilt group.

I needed to broaden my scope. I jumped to Fred Bateman, Quinn's boss, also an attendee of the alleged (by me) secret meeting. Such a nice guy. Quinn liked and respected him. I hated to put him on the list. But he was at the meeting. I snapped to attention. Quinn's boss. Finally, I had a source to tap for more information about a potential suspect. My boyfriend. Why hadn't I thought of him right away?

Sunni was due in a few minutes, but I figured I could squeeze in a call to Quinn. I was thrilled when he accepted on the second ring.

"I'm surprised you're available," I said, before I thought about it.

He chuckled. "And yet you phoned."

"I was excited to talk to you."

His pause was telling. "Something on your mind?"

Could he know me that well after less than a year of dating? That was both good and worrisome, but I didn't need to decide that now. "I ran into your boss this evening."

"Okay." A questioning tone.

"He misses you."

Another chuckle. "I talk to him every day. Sometimes twice a day. And I send photos of potential buys." Another telling pause. "What's up, Cassie?"

Busted. He was on a business trip, looking for merchandise; of course he'd be communicating regularly with his boss.

I heard a noise that could be a car pulling into my driveway. I carried the phone to the window and peeked out to see Sunni in the driver's seat. Of all times for her to be early. No time to beat around the bush. "Fred was going into a meeting at Molly Boyd's salon," I said.

"Why does that matter?" Quinn asked. "Maybe he thinks it's time to cover up his gray. Though he keeps telling me that people like a little gray in their antique dealers. It gives them an air of authenticity."

My turn to chuckle. "This meeting was after hours." I named the people he'd been with. "I'm just curious. Do you have any idea what he might be doing with them?"

I heard a warning throat-clearing. "Does this have to do with Daisy's murder case? Are you still snooping around?"

"You sound like Ben."

"Who also cares about your well-being."

It was a good thing I hadn't shared my special "Postmaster beware" notes with Ben or Quinn. I was about to inform Quinn that Sunni had backed down and welcomed me into her investigation, but it was just as well that the doorbell rang. Some things are better addressed face-to-face.

"Company?" Quinn asked.

"The chief of police." An exasperated sigh floated over the wires. "She's my friend, Quinn."

"Please be careful, Cassie."

"Always. I have to go now."

"Skype later?" he asked.

"Can't wait."

I never did get an answer from Quinn about what Fred Bateman might have been doing hanging around with my suspects. Were all detectives so easily distracted? I doubted it.

I'd cleared my dining room table for work space and in a few minutes we were seated in front of a deep mahogany surface covered with papers, folders, and two laptops. I couldn't help remembering a time when Aunt Tess would cover the same table with a lovely lace cloth on top of protective pads, and set out a fine-china tea service. What a change in entertaining style in just one generation.

"You first," Sunni said.

"Me first?" I asked. A stall while I prepared myself for an orderly presentation.

Sunni nodded. "Show me what you've got."

If Sunni meant to be intimidating, it was working. This wasn't the atmosphere of working together that I'd hoped for. I took her attitude as a sign that we were suspending our friendship for the moment while we got down to business, and that I'd better prove myself worthy of the new partnership.

I plunged in. I turned my laptop and placed it in the middle of the table where we could both see my document. I'd cleaned up my notes so they were arranged in two columns: Suspect and Motive. I'd left out "Anonymous" and his notes for the time being.

My mouth went sour as I realized how pitiful my efforts looked. A half dozen people. I'd eliminated the other three thousand or so citizens of North Ashcot without so much as a glance. And as for the rest of the state, it might as well not exist. I could hardly wait for the comparison with Sunni's list.

I swallowed my misgivings and talked Sunni through my reasoning for each pairing: Molly—lies and meeting; Liv—card competition; and so on. Now I wished I'd added: Others—unknown motives.

The chief of police sat through my report, with an occasional question and a few uh-huhs.

When I was finished, she sat back and folded her arms across her chest. "Where's Cliff?" she asked.

"I don't know. I left him around quarter to seven."

She straightened and tapped the edge of the laptop, its screen still glowing with my neat arrangement of suspects. "I mean, on your list."

"Why would Cliff be—?" A dull moment.

"The husband. Always the first suspect. And where's Tony? The guy who found Daisy's body. The second favorite."

What? I'd written down everyone in Daisy's inner circle but those two. I flashed back to a conversation with Ben.

He'd reminded me about husbands being prime suspects and it still never occurred to me to consider that possibility in this case. I'd been hanging around with Cliff Harmon, the husband, trusting him, presuming his innocence. I'd left him off the list for the same reason I put Jules on it—based on whether I liked them. Either I was a good judge of character with keen instincts or I was truly a babe in the woods.

And Tony? I wasn't that well acquainted with the young man who worked at Mike's Bike Shop, didn't even know his last name, but I had no excuse for not factoring in the person who had been first on the scene. I had a lot to learn about solving homicides. Maybe I should have begun my law enforcement career with traffic violations, or abandoned vehicle citations, which were handled by civilian volunteers with more training than I'd had.

For now, I felt I had to defend the husband. "Cliff was miles away, at a training conference, probably seen by dozens of people, most of whom would be in law enforcement and security."

"And maybe a few chiefs of police giving seminars," Sunni added.

"The good guys," I said.

"And wouldn't that be handy?"

I searched Sunni's face. Was she seriously considering Cliff a suspect? The Cliff I'd been consoling, helping, accepting food from? The supplier of this evening's meal for both Sunni and me? "You think he hired someone? What possible motive could he have?"

"Cassie," she said, using a grade school teacher tone. "There's a reason spouses, boyfriends, girlfriends, and the exes of all of the above top the list. Whenever you have the capacity for love, you also have the potential for hatred and greed."

"And the rest of the deadly sins," I added, feeling my shoulders sag and my spirits hit bottom.

"A ripe environment for violence."

"Depressing," I whispered. Was there no possibility of romance? A happy marriage? Was it necessary to hold this worldview to succeed as a cop?

I thought of my ex-fiancé, Adam Robinson, who'd called it quits last year, by way of three text messages. My *do your job* warning letters paled in comparison with the hurt inflicted by Adam's curt memos. We lived in the same city at the time, within walking distance, and saw each other regularly, but he chose to inflict his wound not face-to-face, but remotely and electronically.

Sunni knew about Adam and now seemed sorry for inadvertently reminding me of him. "I apologize, Cassie. I didn't mean to dredge up old memories."

I shook my head. "Not a problem. I only hope Adam is alive and well. I wouldn't want the Boston Police Department banging on my door asking for my alibi if they find him otherwise."

"I guess you're over him," Sunni said, her first smile of the evening.

On the whole, I was over Adam, happy I'd returned to my roots over one hundred miles away, and happy with Quinn Martindale, so I was surprised at my reaction to Sunni's negative view of relationships. I found myself wondering about the chief of police herself, who shared little of her personal life. I knew that she'd been married briefly, divorced—ostensibly because each was married to a job (cop for her; defense lawyer for him), and had one daughter. As for the present, I didn't see that she had much time for dating.

Sunni followed up on the question of Cliff Harmon's status. "Granted, the details of Daisy's murder don't support a hired gun. It seems more spontaneous, an argument gone bad, and a handy opportunity for cover-up."

"The storm," I said, a bit relieved. I could no more imagine Cliff hiring a hit man than I could his wielding the blow himself.

"But I must tell you, there was motive there."

I started. "Cliff had a motive to kill Daisy?"

"More on that later."

I almost screamed how unfair it was of Sunni to withhold that information from me. Shouldn't I be alerted since I was hanging around with the man, sharing meals? But the chief and I were just beginning our alleged collaboration, and I didn't dare.

"Maybe we should go back to Tony," I said.

"Tony Masters. Claims he was surveying the damage in the back of the bike shop. He saw that the tree branch was down in Daisy's yard next door, thought he heard shuffling noises, and climbed partway up the fence to see what was going on, and, yada yada, I think you've heard this story."

"I have. Does this mean we can pinpoint Daisy's time of death? If he heard noises, it might have been the killer. Tony might have just missed him."

"It's not that cut-and-dried. Tony couldn't say for sure that it wasn't the wind he was hearing, or something else falling in the yard. It's close, though, according to the medical examiner. Daisy died about one o'clock, give or take, about a half hour before Tony found her."

I wished I'd known that part of the timeline while I was compiling my list. I'd have to go over it again with that in mind. Liv had finished in the post office just before noon, which neither incriminated nor eliminated her. I couldn't account for anyone else. "Do we need to consider Tony a suspect?"

"I doubt it. He's clean. No record, has a wife and a new baby, goes to school nights to get his mechanic's license, saving up to open a body shop eventually. His boss and his neighbors say only good things about all the Masters family."

At least there'd been no harm done in my leaving Tony Masters off my list, no matter that I hadn't thought of him in the first place. "Where do we go from here?"

"I hesitate to even say this, but it would be good to have you involved with the quilting group, see if there's anything to this feud with Liv Patterson, or anything else that might be going on where ladies gather."

"I can do that."

"As for the farmers' market thing—I'm glad for the tip about the letters to the editor. I'll see if I can get Reggie Harris to cop to writing a response to Daisy's letter. I'm sure he's deleted it, if there ever was one, but I can ask nicely if he'll let us have his computer, and his answer will tell us a lot."

"Wouldn't he be within his rights to refuse to surrender his computer without you thinking that makes him look guilty?"

"Right," Sunni said with a wink in her voice.

I was beginning to appreciate my own job more and more. When someone entered my post office lobby, I had only the most pleasant expectations for our interaction. I made an assumption, mostly justified, that my role was to bring people together for mutual greetings and presents. And the occasional breakup letter.

Sunni continued. "Can you find an excuse to talk to Liv and Molly and the others privately and see if anything pops? Try to get their alibis, for one thing, and we'll compare them with what they told me."

"You don't believe them?"

"You'd be surprised at what people don't tell the police."

"Okay, I'm to go undercover. I like the sound of that."

"Don't push it. Can I count on you to stay within the bounds of what I'm asking you to do?"

"Absolutely."

"I mean it."

"So do I."

She added a couple more notes to whatever document she'd been working on, sat back, and closed her laptop. I did the same.

"Is there anything else before we call it a night?" she asked.

A moment of truth. To show her my recent threatening mail or not? "Uh—"

"So that's a yes?"

Apparently, my face had answered for me. I retrieved the sheet of paper that I'd found shoved under my door. She took it from me and immediately focused on the content.

"And there's a reason you didn't show this to me right away?"

"This is number two," I said, getting it over with. "The first one came yesterday morning. It's in my desk at the office."

"Again, you weren't planning to show these to me because . . . ?" Her eyes were questioning, her tone bordering on scolding.

"Because—"

She held up her hand. "Never mind struggling for an excuse. You didn't show this to me right away because you thought I'd try to curtail your snooping even more. Or you just couldn't see that it was anything but a prank." She paused for a breath. "I'm taking this one and I expect the first one in my hands tomorrow morning. I'll send Ross to get it."

I gulped. Duly scolded. "I'll have it ready for him. Or I could bring it to the station before work?"

She shook her head. "Ross needs a boring errand to convince him he's making the right move out of a small town."

"You want him to leave?"

"I don't want to hold him back. He'll only resent me and I don't want that. This way there's a chance he'll be back."

Smart thinking. I forgave the fact that she'd named me part of a boring errand and focused on the positive. "Then I'm still on the case, so to speak?"

She nodded. "I figure it's better that I know what your assignment is rather than worrying that you're out of control." She cleared her throat. "You will stay in control?"

I gave my head a vigorous nod. "Deal."

* * *

No sooner was Sunni out the door than I realized I'd forgotten to expand on my theory about the group of suspects—that is, ordinary people—I'd seen entering Molly Boyd's salon together earlier this evening. I maintained my strong suspicion that their agenda had to do with the farmers' market proposal. I doubted that Daisy would have been invited to the meeting and I wouldn't have been surprised to find out that there was something shady going on.

I told myself I could add "farmers' market research" to my newly approved duties without getting specific permission. Surely that wouldn't be violating my deal with Sunni. A girl needs fresh produce, after all.

As if the letters hadn't been enough of an omission, I'd also forgotten to tell her about the theft of my property, files, and food from my car: either a bad sign that I was in denial, especially in light of two nasty notes, or a good sign, that I wasn't stressed-out over the theft or the notes. I chose the glass-half-full version and decided I'd tell Sunni later, when I was ready to report on my new missions.

For a nanosecond, I considered asking Ben to cover for me for a few days while I sleuthed, but I came to my senses and ironed my uniform shirt.

13

My nightly Skype call to Quinn was brief, since we'd both had a long day, his very likely more productive than mine. As I feared, he started right in with "How was your evening with the chief of police?"

"Sunni's fine. We always enjoy our time together."

"Any murder talk? Did you make any promises?"

I heard a challenge in his voice, which was unusual. Maybe absence was making the heart snarky. He was wearing the UMass sweatshirt I'd given him. I was relieved that he wasn't so upset with me that he'd abandoned the shirt.

Quinn faced me, a typical inexpensive motel bedroom in the background. Dull brown and orange décor. Small table holding a lamp with a tipsy shade. Even the framed picture of autumn leaves looked listless. I could only imagine the covering of dust and sticky stains on all surfaces.

I noticed several brown carton boxes of various sizes piled

on the bed behind him. I could make out the label LAMP on the side of one of them, DESK SET on another. "Looks like it was a rewarding treasure hunt for you today," I said, not the least bit snarkily. "Did you pick up some cool stuff?"

"Yeah, and this neighborhood is a little sketchy, so I thought I'd better take the smaller pieces inside."

"I hope you're locked in," I said, and immediately wished I could take it back. Why in the world would I want to remind him of the necessity to keep safe? Too late now. I heard it practically before he said it.

"You're the one who needs to be careful. You didn't answer my question. Did Sunni set you straight on what an ordinary citizen should not be doing with regard to a murder investigation? Emphasis on 'not.' And on 'murder.'"

"You think I'm ordinary?" One more attempt at diversion. I could tell by his face and posture, by the way he frowned and ran his fingers through his hair, that it hadn't worked. I almost wished we were limited to voice contact. Or, for that matter, Pony Express, considered speedy communication during the Civil War. The men on horses covered more than two thousand miles; Quinn was little more than one hundred miles away. The distance would give us time to process each other's reactions. "I'm sorry," I said to Quinn's frowning countenance. "I know you're serious, but everything's fine here, really. When are you coming back?"

His face turned grim, his square jaw pulled up, thinning his lips. "Bad news, sort of. Fred wants me to check out a big estate sale on Sunday, so I had to double back to Manchester. Then, depending on how long it takes, I'll head out late Sunday evening or Monday morning."

I should have been more disappointed, but the delay

bought me some needed time. I tried not to sound too up-beat. "Can we leave the topic of investigating, or not, till then?" I asked. By which time, I figured, we'd have solved the case.

I was amazed that Quinn agreed and guessed that he didn't want unpleasantness at a distance any more than I did. At least, face-to-face in the same room, I might have a chance to explain myself and what seemed like rash be-havior. He was probably thinking the same thing about his position.

"I wish you could have seen the nine-thousand-dollar mirror at the last dealer I visited today," he said, the change of topic bringing a smile to his face and a sigh of relief from me. "From the sixties, with an illuminated frame, made in Germany. And another one from 1950s Italy with a leafy ceramic frame. About a dozen small lights stuck between green leaves. Too bad the guy wouldn't let me take a picture of them."

"But aren't they all on the Internet anyway?"

"Sure, and that's what I told him, but apparently he doesn't trust cameras in the shop, period. Maybe he thinks some crook is really using the camera to case the joint"—Quinn laughed at his forties noir talk—"and the guy will come back in the dark with a truck."

"I'd be afraid to own even one piece like that. If breaking a small, inexpensive compact mirror brings seven years' bad luck, how many gruesome years could we expect if we broke a nine-thousand-dollar version?"

We had a good time over the math, deciding we couldn't live long enough to fulfill the prophecy.

Quinn and I signed off, "I miss you" from both of us not

less fervent because of our disagreement. The usual closing blips poured out of my computer speaker and I closed the cover of my laptop.

I'd planned to call Linda in Boston next, but couldn't face the possibility of another prickly scolding about my new project involving police work, low-level as it was. Maybe this was what Sunni meant when she said her job precluded close friendships. Was I so unusual in my desire to help solve a serious puzzle? Didn't everyone want to be part of the job of setting matters right when an innocent person, who was also a friend, had been struck down?

I fell asleep hoping I wouldn't lose all the contacts in my smartphone, all my friends near and far.

Saturday morning I stopped at the post office to pick up Nasty Letter Number One for delivery to Sunni via Ross. I let myself in through the side door. With all the shades in the building pulled down, as I'd left them at closing yesterday, the area was dark, only a small amount of early sunlight peeking through. I had the same creepy feeling I'd had in my home last night at the arrival of Nasty Letter Number Two. I didn't like this at all. My home and my post office had always been havens for me, places where I felt connected to the world, yet comfortable and safe.

Ignoring the creaking sounds of hundred-year-old floors in my Colonial-style building, I headed straight for my desk. I wanted in and out as quickly as possible.

I opened the middle drawer. I'd slipped the note in it yesterday morning and hadn't looked at it since. I searched and felt around now and couldn't locate the letter. I sat in my chair and bent over until I was at eye level with the drawer. I pushed aside clips, pens, rubber bands, adhesive notes, highlighters, cough drops. No letter. I ran my hand under the desk blotter in case I'd somehow missed the opening yesterday. Nothing. I checked the drawer again, this time removing larger items and placing them on top of the desk— a hand paper punch, a fifteen-inch ruler, two pairs of scissors, a roll of red, white, and blue tape I'd been looking everywhere for, and a cardboard box of oversized binder clips. I pulled the drawer out as far as it would go and rummaged once more. Still nothing. All I had for my trouble was a small splinter from the back end of the drawer and lint-rich fingernails.

To stem a rising panic, I sat back and took some breaths. What was I missing? The wastebasket, of course. I dragged the round metal container from under the desk and started to plow through it. Brenda, my occasional cleaning help, hadn't been in for almost two weeks, but I emptied the trash myself every other day or so, depending on how many smelly lunch remnants I'd tossed in it. I remembered dumping the contents on Wednesday evening, so two days' worth of scrap had accumulated.

I knew even before I started digging that it was hopeless. The basket held only small scraps—bits of tape, hand wipes, and (busted!) a candy wrapper or two. Something as large as an eight-and-a-half-by-eleven sheet, even folded, would have stuck out in the rubble. Besides, unnerving as it was, I knew for sure that I'd slid the letter and the envelope, separated, into my middle drawer.

I was stumped. And worried. If I hadn't taken it home, which I was sure of, or thrown it away, the inevitable conclusion was that someone had stolen it. Or taken it back. Had Anonymous found a way to retrieve the letter? Why? Out of regret? To further rattle me? How would anyone have gotten into the building? I had no extra key in a planter or under a mat outside. Only Ben had a key of his own. Not even Brenda, who worked only when I was present, had a way to walk into an unattended building.

Eight thirty on a Saturday morning and, instead of relaxing on my sofa with a cup of coffee and a good book, I was already on course for a bad day. I'd made arrangements to meet Ross, Sunni's soon-to-be ex-officer, at Mahican's for the transfer of the now-missing letter. I made one final round of possible locations, then pulled out my phone and texted him.

Handoff cancelled. Misplaced letter.

And received an immediate response.

Back to bed.

Was everyone under thirty thumb-ready with a phone, twenty-four/seven? This was one time when I was grateful for the trend.

I knew I should call Sunni right away and report the missing note, but I talked my way around it. She needed her rest, and shouldn't be disturbed this early, I reasoned. Magnanimous, that was me.

I had the strongest urge to follow Ross's example and

retreat to my own bed for extra sleep. I remembered weekends in Boston, when Saturday morning meant staying in bed as late as I wanted, sometimes dragging a couple of books over and beginning the day with juicy fiction. This would be after Friday evenings that usually involved a quick change out of work clothes and a show or concert with Adam, Linda, and however many of our friends we could round up.

For the rest of the weekend, if our bank accounts were in good health, girlfriends and I would hit the chic shops on Newbury Street. If they were a little low, we'd browse Quincy Market or downtown Boston. I was completely unaware at the time of how the officers of the Boston PD spent their weekends—working hard while I was playing.

Annoyance crept in as I realized I couldn't even count on my home now for an atmosphere of peace. What if Anonymous was at this moment skulking around my door delivering Nasty Letter Number Three? I might as well keep to my plan and stay in the field like any good agent of the law.

I changed my mind about a quick in-and-out, and decided to do a bit of research in my office. Why should Anonymous intimidate me to the level of being afraid in my own domain? I swept my supplies back into my desk drawer, pulled my laptop from my briefcase, and set it on the desktop.

Like with every other business enterprise these days, big or small, I expected farmers' markets to have an Internet presence. I searched for locations within thirty miles of North Ashcot and found ten markets that had their own websites and their own social media pages. Each site listed the number of participating vendors (up to fifty in some cases), the products sold, and directions to the originating farm or orchard (which generally also offered an amusement such as a hayride or pumpkin picking). I felt a field trip coming on.

Farmers' markets had come a long way since I shopped with my parents years ago. Then, a few local farmers drove their battered trucks to a vacant lot on the outskirts of town and sold seasonal vegetables and fruits, using their tailgates as counters, often literally weighing the items by hand.

"This feels like exactly one pound," a farmer would say, tossing green and yellow bell peppers from one hand to the other.

"Wow," I'd say in my little girl voice, believing the old man's hands were magically calibrated. I usually earned a wink and a smile for my eager involvement.

I remembered dipping my fingers into paper cups holding cherries and pieces of apple to sample. There might have been a cooler with soft drinks for sale, but certainly no line of food trucks as pictured at today's venues. By the time I was in high school, the farmers had disappeared, and I wondered if those same farmers had joined the more formal cooperatives whose wares were now spread over the Internet. Were those farmers the ones Reggie had in mind in his proposal for North Ashcot? Or did his all have MBAs?

I clicked through mouthwatering photos of ears of yellow and white corn; white and green heads of cauliflower; lettuce in many shades of green and red; deep purple eggplants; three kinds of carrots (Yellow carrots? Who knew?); blue green beans (another eye-opener); jars of orange and strawberry jam; jugs of maple syrup; and racks of candied apples, the smooth caramel syrup seeming to drip onto my desktop.

For my destination today, I chose the market with the

most attractive website, thus confirming the wisdom of advertisers everywhere. I clicked on directions for the Knox Valley Market, located in the newly gentrified civic center of a town twenty miles from North Ashcot. My choice might also have been influenced by the name of the venue—the same as that of my current hero, Henry Knox, of Revolutionary War and commemorative stamp fame.

The trip seemed like an ideal way to turn the day around from its bad start. I could buy fresh produce, and while I was taste-testing the plums, I could chat with the help about the proposed market a few miles north and be on the lookout for . . . for what, exactly? Merchandise being passed between the flatbeds of trucks or the trunks of two cars? A ten-dollar bill offered under the table (literally) for a few extra blueberries in a basket? The plastic bag franchise?

The truth was that I was hoping to come upon dramatic, incontrovertible evidence pointing to Reggie Harris as Daisy's killer. I still had strong suspicions about Jules, the moneyman, and even Liv, the card seller, but the stakes might be even greater for a business enterprise like a farmers' market. Close-up photos on the website showed credit card transactions, indicating that a serious, professional business was on-site. I wouldn't have been surprised to learn that liability insurance had become a must, not to mention the challenges of organizational structures and tax issues.

So much had changed since I carried cucumbers and long celery stalks to our car as a child.

Maybe I could unearth something bigger than a baker's dozen of zucchini as Reggie's payoff for bringing one of these highly photogenic markets to our town.

The more I thought about it, the less likely it seemed that

I'd find anything of value. But I had to try. I was in favor of anything that even hinted of progress toward making me and every North Ashcot citizen feel safe again, to say nothing of honoring Daisy's memory.

I left my office, tempted one last time to tear it apart, inside and out, in case Nasty Letter Number One had mysteriously reappeared, having landed in a dusty corner far from my desk. I figured I'd had enough fruitless searching for one day, and left the building.

I bought a coffee to go at Mahican's, resisting the pastries, since I'd seen photos of mouthwatering turnovers at Knox Valley. I headed out, hoping for answers. I figured at least I'd come home with a bunch of fresh asparagus and a bag of kettle corn for my trouble. More rewards than other ventures of the last week.

14

My forty-five-minute trip over two-lane country roads was well worth it. The Knox Valley Farmers' Market lived up to its Internet presence. I stepped out of my car to be greeted by a wandering accordion player, an old man squeezing out, of all things, a tune about big fun on the bayou. I estimated that we were a thousand miles from the nearest bayou, but that didn't keep me and other patrons in the parking lot, especially the large number of toddlers, from clapping (me) and dancing (not me) along with the music.

I laughed at a large sign at the entrance to the market, warning: DON'T EAT VEGGIES THAT HAVE JET LAG.

Only five minutes into my field trip and I was already in a better mood.

The market was more like an outdoor mall, combined with an amusement park and a crafts show, all in full swing at ten o'clock. Was this what Reggie Harris envisioned for North Ashcot? I tried to picture the rows of colorful canopies lined up along our Main Street or close by. Too crowded, so I moved the scene in my mind to the school parking lot along Second Street. The proposal was gaining ground in my imaginary, reconstructed debate between Reggie and Daisy.

The accordion man launched into "America the Beautiful." Appropriate, considering the aromas of apple cider and buttery popcorn. The smell of hot dogs sizzling on a grill near a food truck was a little over-the-top for my taste in the middle of the morning, but I could hardly object.

I started down the aisle that began with small samples of homemade fruit drinks (better than the bottled variety sold at our local grocery store) and led me on to the table of yet more turnovers and scones (fresher looking even than those served at A Hole in the Wall, plus the option of gluten-free treats); the flower tent (with more square feet than Gigi had at her disposal); baskets of fragrant herbs (not in sealed plastic bags); and enough jewelry, cards, knitted caps, woven scarves, and handmade soap to give every specialty shop on Main Street a run for its money.

Farmers' markets: not just for farmers anymore.

And a clear threat to the likes of Daisy Harmon's small business.

Even as I enjoyed the feast for my senses and the purchases I'd already made (including, but not limited to, kale, cheese, and fudge, for a well-balanced meal later), I worried about how the small businesses in North Ashcot could survive the influx of such competition. The warnings in Daisy's letter shouted at me, as if she herself, with her high-energy passion, were still alive in my head. I thought about her accusation that, besides the fruits and veggies that were on the table, something more lucrative was under the table. I sniffed the air as if I were an expert at discerning the presence of contraband or controlled substances.

I stopped for a minute to adjust my purse and bags of raspberry squares and jars of jam. It had been difficult, but I'd managed to eat half a strawberry rhubarb turnover on the way. Out of the corner of my eye, I saw a man I could have sworn was Reggie Harris. The same short, muscular build and cowboy walk. A baseball cap, which he always wore, proclaiming one or another sports team, and a windbreaker that I'd seen on him as he headed for the meeting last night. I wished he would turn around so I could be sure, but he continued walking away from me. Of course, the man might have been Reggie only in my imagination, since Daisy was on my mind. I pressed forward, slowed down by a family with a stroller, and whoever it was had gotten lost in the crowd.

I noted the proliferation of electronic scales in the tents and felt a wave of nostalgia for the farmers who tossed veggies in the air and came up with a fair price. A long way from the current professionally printed signs welcoming cash, check, or credit card with logos for all.

Spiffy banners on the vendors' tented structures identified farms and orchards from Massachusetts towns like Montague, Colrain, and Shelburne Falls, and from as far away as southern Vermont.

A young boy, surely too young to have a work permit,

lured me to his family's tent, holding up an elaborately painted hair clip.

"Wouldn't this be great to go with your pretty hair?" he said, a salesman already. "My mom makes these."

Not for me, but I spied a pair of earrings that would be perfect for Linda and her long neck. Here was a chance to show my city friend what a small-town craftsperson could do. I bought them, thus encouraging the boy, who followed me out of the tent for a few yards, pitching a matching bracelet and a greatly discounted pinkie ring, before giving up.

A few minutes later, I realized I'd passed up a great opportunity for questioning a vendor. Two adults, who were probably the boy's parents, sat behind the table, ripe for an interview. Another failure as a pretend sleuth, getting wrapped up in the moment and forgetting that my mission wasn't shopping, but investigating.

I looked around for another likely candidate for a little quiz and spotted a beekeeping family. A middle-aged woman stood behind a table full of jars of honey in large and small attractive jars. Better yet, there was a man in farmer's clothes on a seat behind her, and a young girl focused on a smartphone close by, but no customers at the table.

"Do you keep bees?" I asked, approaching the woman, hoping I was using the correct verb.

"I do indeed," she said, looping strands of long, straight gray hair over one ear. "Josie," she called to the girl, "bring that phone over here."

There followed a multimedia lesson that included a one-minute video on Josie's smartphone, outlining all I'd need to prepare my first hive. I accepted a FAQ sheet and a form to send in for a free kit that contained all the starter equipment I'd need plus a subscription to a newsletter. I listened to an ecology lesson from Josie—about a fourth grader, I guessed—on how important bees are in our food chain and how they're disappearing because of our nasty pesticides.

I nodded and asked one or two relatively intelligent questions, then addressed the woman.

"By the way, do you know Reggie Harris?" I asked, in what might have been the world's most blatant non sequitur.

She abandoned her smooth pitch and stuttered. "Well, we, uh, why are you asking?"

I shrugged. Casual. "I'm just wondering if you'd be among those planning to sell at a future farmers' market in North Ashcot."

"Yeah, everybody's talking about it," Josie said. "I heard them say it's going to work out for us to be up there on Sundays. I—"

"Enough, Josie."

The man, who'd been silent until now, leafing through a magazine, stood, towering over the woman. Only a little above eye level with me, but considerably heavier. He grabbed Josie by the arm, too roughly, I thought. Nothing brutal, I surmised, but enough to send a message. Josie winced but didn't seem surprised.

"You don't know what you're talking about, Josie. Leave the lady alone." He glanced at me with anything but concern for my well-being.

"But she—" Josie began.

"I said, leave the lady alone." The man took the jars of honey I was about to pay for and set them back in their place on the stand. "She's done here anyway."

He was right. I turned and walked away, before I got Josie, and myself, in further trouble. Making progress, I thought. Someone is worried about what I'll turn up. So what if my palms were sweating and my heart was beating a little faster than usual?

I could do this. I'd just have to find a booth with shorter staff members.

To catch my breath, I stood for a few minutes before a bulletin board perched on an easel at the end of an aisle. I glanced through typical notices of events in other parts of town. A summer theater production of *Guys and Dolls* (Really? In this century?), a fact sheet about farmers' markets, extolling their virtues as local job creators as well as an opportunity for a better social life (people who shopped there had fifteen to twenty interactions per visit, as opposed to only two or three in a grocery store).

A hastily written memo stuck over more colorful, professional-looking flyers caught my eye. In thick black-marker letters, the announcement was a reminder of the meeting of vendors at one thirty, just after the market closed. Was that why Reggie was here today? If that was Reggie I'd spotted.

"I hear you've been asking around for me." A deep, rough voice took away any doubt. I turned to see Reggie Harris in his Red Sox cap and windbreaker. It was at times like these that I was happy to be on a par with the average height of a U.S. male, especially since Reggie was a couple of inches below it.

I straightened up, taking advantage of every inch of my height to fend off feelings of intimidation. "I'm impressed by the communication system on this site," I said.

He held up his cell phone. "Faster than service at the post office," he said.

I laughed, as I thought I was supposed to. "Nice to see you, too, Reggie," I said. "We could have carpooled."

"Funny. What brings you all the way to Knox Valley, Cassie?"

"Where else can I go before we have our own market?"

He shook his head. "More funny." Reggie pointed to a set of tables with attached benches and umbrellas where people had brought their food truck treats, including hot dogs. "Sit?" he asked.

Since he was asking nicely, I nodded and joined him at a round wooden table, evidently today's tree trunk surrogate, with hearts and initials carved into the surface. Reggie offered to get me a drink or snack, but I found the food truck aromas less appealing than when I'd first arrived. Maybe because my stomach felt a little queasy in the face of one of the prime suspects on my murder list.

"Look," Reggie said, "I know you've been working with Cliff Harmon. I know you know about the letter Daisy wrote that never got printed."

"And the one you wrote back that no one other than the newspaper staff has seen."

"Funny you should mention that," he said. He reached into his light jacket and pulled out a sheet of paper, folded twice, and spread it out in front of me. "Here. Read it for yourself."

I took the page. "You just happened to have this with you?"

"In case I run into people like you and Cliff."

"Or the police?"

"The police don't need to be involved in this particular debate. There's nothing to be involved in, really. Read it," he said, pointing at the letter, his face flushed. He seemed not so much angry as frustrated.

I glanced down and saw that the letter Reggie gave me was very short, addressed to the editor of the *Town Crier*.

To the Editor:

Allow me to remind your readers of the great advantages a farmers' market can bring to our town. Besides the obvious fresh fruits and veggies, we'll have an opportunity for our own local craftspeople to sell their wares. That means quilts, for example, which means more fabric and thread will be sold in our fabric shop. Also, handmade knitted goods and local honey, and tons more products. There will be something for everyone, both low-income families and foodies. And think of the savings on gas. Please, people, don't dis this project without knowing all the facts. For more information, go to our website.

A website address followed. Nothing in the letter was a threat to Daisy in any way, and in fact, it singled out her shop as one of the beneficiaries. Coincidence? Hard to swallow.

I thought of challenging Reggie, asking how I could be sure this was the actual letter he wrote to Gordon at the *Town Crier*. He'd had plenty of time to write six variations through the course of the week. He could also make and print and keep multiple and different copies with him. One copy to sway Gigi by using flowers as an example, one for Liv's card shop, and one to appeal to the bank tellers, probably. The wonders of the computer age. A twelve-year-old had the equipment to pull off any number of cons.

"Your letter seems innocuous to me," I said, seeing no value in continuing a debate between two people, one of whom was no longer around to participate. I put the letter in my purse. I'd let Sunni decide its merits. Good deputy that I was.

"Darn right, it's innocuous," Reggie said. "Maybe you can help me out and tell Cliff Harmon to back off. I know he wasn't happy with his wife's stirring up trouble in the first place. Let the police do their job. He can do his job and you can do yours, and everything will be solved in the end."

Probably Reggie didn't know why I shrank back and bristled at his warning to *do my job*.

It took a minute to turn some phrases in my head, trying to find the best wording for the big question. "I'm curious," I said. "What motivates you to work so hard to get this project through?"

"You mean what's in it for me?"

So much for roundabout wording. "I know you're a contractor. But there's nothing that will need to be built if the market comes to town."

Reggie leaned in, too close for my comfort. His upper arm muscles strained the sleeves of his jacket and seemed to ripple before my eyes; I felt his breath on my neck. "Are you implying something crooked is going on?"

I gulped. "Is it?"

"Listen, Madam Postmistress, I don't have to report to you, but because I'm such a nice guy, I'm going to anyway. North Ashcot is growing, Cassie. Do you know our population is expected to reach five thousand in just a couple of years, and probably twice that in ten years? Yet we have no large market, just that convenience store that pretends to sell foodstuffs. Just to show you, they're not complaining about the influx of real food that a farmers' market would bring."

Reggie was right about the quality of food in the convenience store—just the basic packaged supplies that would take you through an emergency. The nearest fresh foods were well past the central Main Street district.

"And that's not all." Reggie appeared to be waiting for my attention to return to him before continuing. "There are also no office buildings, very limited medical facilities, and only a handful of apartments. I have plans for our town. 'Plan North Ashcot,' I'm calling it. New developments everywhere, with housing, office space, specialty shops. A little bit of something for everybody."

He seemed satisfied. But all I could think of was what a motive for murder, with so much at stake. I was relieved that at least he'd sat back and wasn't breathing on me anymore.

The last thing I wanted was to show that I was nervous, that his intimidation techniques were working. I had only one move to prove otherwise. I stood and straightened my shoulders, leaving all five feet five of him hunched over the wooden table.

I had no second move, so I was relieved when a vendor came up to us.

"Excuse me," the young man said. "I need to borrow Reggie for a minute."

"He's all yours," I said, as if I were in charge of Reggie's schedule.

The look in Reggie's eyes, under the Red Sox cap, could have melted an umpire's mask.

I abandoned the idea of hanging around for the vendors' meeting. Some other Saturday, maybe. I beat it back to my car and headed home, leaving the old accordion man playing "Roll Out the Barrel" and the man who might be Anonymous in my rearview mirror.

15

On my trip home, I tried to focus on the lush environment on either side of the road. Rolling lawns with stately white houses set back and, now and then, a stone-based wishing well or Civil War cannons guarding the estate.

I opened my window and breathed in fresh air, listening to the swish of the tall, noble evergreens, remembering trips to Tanglewood, the summer home of the Boston Symphony Orchestra. One of the last outings I'd taken with my parents had been to a Friday-morning rehearsal on the great lawn. We'd brought a large thermos of coffee for them, a cooler of soft drinks for me, and the makings of a picnic lunch.

Had I expressed my appreciation at the time, or had I been a surly teenager, whining, talking about missing my friends back home? Telling my parents I wished I'd gone to the mall with Jamie and Ashley. Over the years, I'd gotten better about this kind of morose thinking—wishing for a redo of every holiday, every weekend, every breakfast with the parents I'd lost so early.

I shifted my attention to what I'd learned at the market, other than the fact that Reggie Harris deserved his spot on my suspect list.

Farmers' markets had become significant sources of retail trade in the community. It now made sense to me that kickbacks, if they existed, might involve substantial sums of money or other favors, not simply a twenty-dollar bill slipped under a rickety picnic table. Even the vehicles that carried the goods had been upgraded from when I was a kid—no longer rattling trucks with wooden frames to keep crates of produce secured, but instead, shiny vans with fancy logos on the sides. In Knox Valley, the tent covers were new and multicolored, bringing the beautifully landscaped civic center, with its modern brick buildings, to life.

None of these observations, not even Reggie's rudeness, was enough to take to Sunni as the work of an (almost) legitimate investigator. But there was still a lot left of Saturday. I needed to plot my next move and tackle the next suspects.

The obvious choice? The ladies of the quilting group. And, even better, they were my assignment from the chief of police.

I made a quick stop at my house to pick up a project that had been sitting on a shelf in my spare bedroom, waiting to be quilted. I'd finished the top layer, a simple nine-patch design, as recommended by Sunni and the others as a good quilt for first-timers.

"Just do squares. You're not ready for triangles," Sunni had said, sounding like my old geometry teacher.

She'd accompanied me to Daisy's shop and helped me pick out novelty fabric with sepia photos of antique lamps and small furniture in browns and rust. Suitable for a lap quilt meant for Quinn.

"Do you think it's too soon for a gift like this?" I'd asked her and Daisy.

"Do you mean, is there a list for dating, like for anniversaries? Twenty-fifth, silver; fiftieth, gold?" Sunni asked.

The three of us had a good time coming up with a parallel list for dating.

"First month, paper," Daisy had offered. "Like a 'Thanks for being a friend' card."

"Second month, food," said Sunni, who, despite her small frame and trim figure, seemed always to be hungry. "How many months has it been for you and Quinn, anyway?"

"We met about a year ago. It's hard to say when our first date was."

"Okay, one year is good for a quilt," Daisy had said. "But only a small one, a lap quilt for the living room, not one for a king-sized bed."

"Got it," I'd said, and we all had a good laugh.

Tears welled as I thought of that conversation and of a time when Daisy was so full of life. I imagined Cliff, less than a week after her death, reminiscing constantly, overwhelmed by good memories and a sense of loss.

I stopped in front of my house, not bothering to pull into the driveway. I squeezed between my neighbor's new truck and a beige sedan I hadn't seen before. I walked by the car and saw the driver. Officer Ross Little, in his dusty blue uniform, holding a map. Strange. Especially since I was pretty sure any car less than ten years old would have a GPS.

I bent down and addressed him through the open window. "What's up, Ross? You got my message about the cancelled pickup this morning, right?"

His response—stuttering, fumbling with the map—indicated that he'd been napping.

"Oh yeah, yeah, yeah," he said, straightening his posture, crinkling the map. "I'm just checking something out here."

Again, strange. It looked like a street map of North Ashcot, the freebie at all our fast food and convenience stops. How often would anyone have to look at that map before having it memorized?

I shrugged, told him to have a nice day, and climbed the steps to my house.

Inside, I cast a longing glance at my rocker and stack of books and magazines. Wouldn't it be nice to settle back with a newly acquired McIntosh—the apple, not the laptop—and read for a while? But a cop's work is never done. I took a deep breath and made my way to the back bedroom. I packed up the quilt top, the bamboo batting I'd bought, and a few yards of a mottled-cream-and-gold piece of fabric for the back. My plan was to take the bundle to Fran Rogers, who was one of the quilters in the group who owned a long-arm sewing machine. The other was Eileen Jackson, but I'd already bothered her enough, sending her on a fruitless mission to find my nonmissing sunglasses.

The first thing I'd learned when I joined the group was

that, no! Sewing squares of fabric together by hand or on my basic machine was not quilting. It was just that, sewing, or as the experts in my group called it, "piecing." Technically, quilting referred to stitching together three layers: a top layer, which could consist of any number of patched-together pieces of fabric or appliquéd blocks; a middle layer of batting; and a final layer or back of the quilt, often one solid piece, though some overachieving quilters in our group created backs as elaborate and complicated as the fronts.

This final step in the quilting process went so much more smoothly with a long-arm machine. Fran's model included a twelve-by-four-foot table with long railings, variable needle positions, a stitch regulator, and a host of other features she was always glad to talk about at our meetings.

I called Fran to be sure it was okay to stop by and take her my project. She agreed to take it on, and said she could have it done in a week to ten days.

"Were you hoping to have it for the display next week?" she asked.

"Oh no. Not hanging next to yours," I said, thinking of the beautiful quilts, works of art, that she and other members of our group and quilters in neighboring towns turned out. "Maybe a few years from now."

I didn't bother explaining that I didn't care how long the quilting took; my true motive for the visit was to talk about Daisy's murder. Besides, though I didn't admit it to Fran, it was unlikely that I'd be ready to hand over such a present to Quinn very soon whether it was finished or not.

I'd already stalled with the project, telling myself I didn't have time to work on it, but Linda had gotten me to face the real reason: I wasn't sure the time was right for such an elaborate (for me) personal gift.

"Didn't you say his birthday was coming up?" she'd asked recently.

"Right after Labor Day. Way too soon."

So far, Quinn and I had exchanged sweatshirts from our respective alma maters, UMass from me to him, CAL from him to me; and not much else of significance. My birthday had come and gone with no acknowledgment. I'd managed to hide it from everyone in North Ashcot except Ben, who had access to my employment records, but agreed to keep it to himself and claimed it was just a coincidence that he'd brought a strawberry shortcake into work that day.

Was a birthday quilt over-the-top for this point in my relationship with Quinn? Maybe a store-bought scarf was more appropriate. Or a basket of goodies from the farmers' market. Good thing I didn't have to decide on the spot.

I stuffed my fabric into a large tote and carried it to my car. I noted that Ross was still parked out front and gave him a wave.

Fran's home was on the western side of town, well past the post office. On the way, I passed Ashcot's Attic, where Quinn worked. I tried to shut out the image of my quilt one day flung over an old sofa, with CLEARANCE SALE signs on both.

Fran welcomed me into her home and into her quilt room. She'd turned what might have been meant as a TV or family room into an enviable sewing room, dominated by the elaborate machine/table combination, and lined with shelves containing well-organized storage boxes for fabric and notions. The skylights were the perfect source of light for close work.

"Daisy Harmon helped me set up this space," she said, her tone subdued.

"We all miss her," I said, feeling a little guilty that I was thinking about seizing the moment for data gathering. "I remember I closed the post office around noon on that day, just last Monday, and went home to wait out the storm. And then I learned that not too long after I drove by her shop, poor Daisy . . ." I trailed off.

Fran shook her head. "It's hard to believe." She sat on her sewing chair and motioned that I should sit beside her and hand over my project pieces.

"Cliff was all the way down in Springfield for a conference when it happened," I said. "Isn't it ironic that the seminars were all about security?" A second shot at alibi talk.

"I hope he's doing okay," she said, separating the three layers of my soon-to-be quilt. It seemed Fran was not about to give up her own alibi for the time Daisy was killed. "Cliff is one of our subs for security at the bank now and then, as you probably know. A very nice guy, not one to start trouble. I'm sure he regrets all the tension between them this last month or so."

Tension? This wasn't the first time I'd heard a reference to a less than perfect home life for Cliff and Daisy.

"I heard about that," I said, tsk-tsking, straining to remember where and from whom the subject had come up. "I thought things were getting better, though." A fake, and with it came a sour taste in my mouth. I tried to keep it at bay. I wasn't built for deception at this level.

"That's not how I understand it," Fran said. "Daisy didn't really care where or when she spoke her mind. She even got into a brouhaha with her accountant, right on the floor of the bank." When my eyes widened, Fran clarified, "I mean in the middle of the open area, not literally on the floor. The point is, lately Daisy had been stepping it up. Her community involvement was getting out of hand and Cliff was upset. It's never good for businesspeople to be too vocal about political matters."

Stepping it up? Involvement? Now I remembered. Random suspicions about Cliff. First from Ben, but only on general principles and murder lore. And then again from Sunni. During our suspect brainstorming, she'd implied that Cliff should have been on my list, and more than simply for his position as spouse. Once more from Reggie, this morning. He'd brought up Cliff's displeasure at his wife's activism with regard to the farmers' market. And now Fran.

I felt my loyalty to Cliff taking over. "Right now he's a grieving widower and wants nothing more than to find who killed Daisy." When Fran didn't respond, I pushed further. "I guess you're in favor of Reggie Harris's proposal. I noticed you were at the meeting last evening." Pulling out all the stops.

I'd only guessed at the nature of the meeting—another fake that worked. Fran nearly dropped my bamboo batting, which she'd taken from the dryer after a few minutes of fluffing. "You're very observant," she said, meaning, I surmised, nosy.

"I'm just an interested citizen," I said, worried that in her nervous state she'd stick herself—or me—with one of the nearly two-inch, large-head quilting pins on the table between us.

"I'm sure you are," Fran said. It was the first time I'd seen any sign of anger in the mild-mannered bank teller. Her wiry frame seemed to have come unglued. She took a long, loud breath and held up the top layer of my lap quilt. "We probably should talk about this instead. These seams are very well done, Cassie."

"Thanks," I said.

"I see you've followed the common wisdom of using dark colors for the corners and the center and lighter colors on alternating interior squares."

"I had advice from the chief of police," I said, but Fran simply smiled, already safely back in her neutral persona. The investigative moment had passed.

"This is for Quinn, right?" Fran asked, arranging the front and back of my quilt on a hanger, then on a rack with other to-be-quilted projects.

"Yes, but there's no rush," I said.

"Would you like me to quilt some hearts in the center? I can use red thread. Maybe with your initials and his inside? Or some other sentiment?"

I gasped. "Uh, no, thanks. No sentiment, okay?"

Fran gave a short wave to indicate understanding. "Too soon?"

"Uh-huh. Just some of your usual graceful swirls will do."

"I can do some small items like lamps or clocks. Would that be more appropriate?"

"Much better."

We both laughed and I was glad we were on good terms

before she attacked my project. I had visions of an angry Fran tearing into my layers of fabric with shredding scissors.

In lieu of a fee for her work, Fran usually asked her customers to make a donation to whatever cause was at the top of her list that week. In the recent past she'd solicited support for a neonatal IC unit, a community food bank, a girls' soccer team, and a homeless shelter. I took my checkbook from my purse and asked her preference.

She spelled out the name of an organization of hospital volunteers. "I'm going to ask our group to help me make at least six wheelchair quilts this fall. I have a special pattern that calls for usable scraps."

"I think I have a few of those," I said, already planning to weed them out of my stash.

We chatted for a few minutes about the upcoming Henry Knox Parade and other festivities, which had been taking a backseat to a murder investigation in the minds of our citizens. It was a lot for a little town to handle. The parade was scheduled for Saturday, a week from today. Would the selectmen cancel it? Would we go ahead with the plans but have a moment of silence for Daisy? Would there be another storm, as predicted? We were both looking forward to the display of quilts (Fran's included) that would be part of the weekend celebration.

Much to my relief, Fran and I parted friends. I wondered how soon I could come back and assume the role of investigator again.

I used my hands-free link in my car to answer a call from Cliff on the way home. Of course, he wanted an update on my progress, and I regretted that all I had were innuendoes that he himself had motive to kill his wife. Was it my place to tell him that? I decided against it. I did want to ask what he really thought of Daisy's aggressive interaction with the farmers' market proposal, but having to yell at my dashboard to be heard on the car's system wasn't the ideal setup for that conversation.

"I just heard from Dr. Wilson," Cliff said. "He's ready to release Daisy's body, so there's nothing standing in the way now. I can finally take her to her parents in Miami."

"I'm sure they're very relieved," I said. "When are you leaving?" It was up to Sunni to let him know if she felt she needed him in town until Daisy's killer was found. Or for more questioning.

"As soon as I can get the funds together. In a day or so, I hope. You wouldn't believe what it costs to transport a . . ." Cliff paused. I thought I'd lost him, then heard him whisper, "A person who's deceased. You have mortuary costs at both ends, plus the airlines. It turns out, like, about ten times the amount for an ordinary flight. I need to talk to Jules to see what's the best way to get the money together, but I can't reach him. He's not answering either of his phones. I hope I don't have to wait until Monday till someone's in his office. I'll let you know."

A call from Sunni to me interrupted us and Cliff rang off with a promise to touch base with me before he left for Florida. I clicked over to Sunni, feeling as if I'd been caught not doing the homework assigned by two teachers. It didn't help when I heard her first question.

"How come you cancelled the pickup from Ross this morning?"

I hated to admit to her that I couldn't find Nasty Letter Number One. "It's probably because I was in a hurry. I'm going back to check again," I said, coming up with the idea on the spot. It was possible that I had missed it, I told myself. Strictly speaking, I wasn't lying.

"How about I stop by this evening and get a report on your day?" she asked.

"And you show me yours," I said, a weak chuckle following my inane remark.

"See you around seven," she said, and hung up.

I realized what a mess my so-called investigation was. I couldn't even keep the terms of the reasonable deal Sunni had made with me. I'd lost a threatening note; I'd neglected to tell her about my car break-in, as well as my theory about the premeeting crowd that I'd witnessed in front of Molly's salon. So what if none of these things was in a direct line with the investigation? I remembered hearing someone— probably a TV cop, but they were smart, too—say that, in a homicide, everything matters.

I hadn't even talked to all the quilting ladies.

I checked my watch. Barely midafternoon. There was still time to pull the day out of the loss column. I could start with Liv in the card shop, and move on to Molly, who was sure to be in the salon today. The worst that could happen would be that I'd stock up on birthday cards for the year and, so that Linda would be proud of me, spring for a mani-pedi.

I turned onto Hawthorne Street and realized I made a wrong turn somewhere between Fran's house and a construction detour I'd been forced to take. Talking while driving, even on a hands-free link, had its disadvantages. After my mental ridiculing of Ross, it turned out I wasn't above using a North Ashcot street map.

I pulled over to the curb and reached into my glove compartment. Out of the corner of my eye, I noticed a car slow down, then pass me. I could have sworn it was Ross. In fact, I knew it was Ross. Another coincidence, or was he following me? I made a mental note to take Quinn up on his offer to install an updated GPS in my old car.

What if Sunni considered me a suspect in Daisy's murder and had set me loose while ordering her deputy to keep track of me? I could think of nothing more uncool. Or maybe Ross was acting on his own. He might even be leaving the NAPD because of me, preferring to work for a police department that did its own homicide investigations and didn't engage personal friends of his boss.

My perspiration level rose by the minute as I considered these possibilities, finally settling on the most convenient choice: coincidence. I had work to do.

I checked the map and made a U-turn that would ultimately bring me to the business district on Main Street. I drove off. No more wild ideas about being stalked or tailed, I told myself. There was nothing to worry about. Unless Officer Ross Little showed up for a dye job at Molly's salon.

16

I parked in the lot behind the bank again, in part to avoid walking in front of Daisy's Fabrics. From the steady stream of pedestrian shoppers in the area, all seeming indifferent to their surroundings, no one would know that the small house-turned-shop had been a crime scene earlier in the week. I knew it would take me a long time to achieve that level of detachment.

I crossed Main Street and entered Liv Patterson's card shop on the corner, which was comfortably air-conditioned and not very crowded for a Saturday afternoon. It was still pool weather, typically hot and humid for late August, and I imagined families gathered at various public and private watering holes in town. I'd gotten used to being near the ocean all those years living in Boston and, as a result, had passed on swimming during my year back inland. It wasn't the same without the tides and the waves and sandy beaches.

I waved to Liv, who was helping a customer choose an engagement book among the colorful options, and started down one of the card aisles. It had been a while since I'd bought a formal card for any occasion. I still drew from my large supply of note cards from Boston's many museum shops.

I was amazed at the different headings on the racks; many categories had been added since my last look. Now you could buy cards for pets; for all members of blended families; in foreign languages; and with a range of religious messages. I opened cards that played music, and cards for holidays I'd never heard of. National Hug Day, National Newspaper Carrier Day, National Cookie Day. And I was just in time for National Trail Mix Day at the end of the month.

I wondered why Liv was so upset that the fabric shop next door was carrying a few handmade cards from local crafters; surely Daisy wasn't trying to compete with this array.

Since there was no card labeled "From Mid-Thirties Woman to Boyfriend, Dating for About a Year," I chose an innocuous birthday card for Quinn, one very masculine with just the items Fran had offered to quilt for me. On the cover, an antique lamp with a bronze base and a dark green shade sat on a stack of old books, each volume with illegible but attractive gold lettering. Inside, a simple birthday greeting was spelled out in plain font.

On the way to the counter, where Liv was now alone straightening packages of tissue paper, I passed an aisle of small gift books, most of which offered inspiration or quick solutions—ten ways to do this or seven ways to stop doing that. On display behind Liv was one of her own quilted wall hangings. A colorful four-by-six-foot piece featuring images of summer, fall, winter, and spring. Meant to remind customers that there were cards and gifts for all seasons, I presumed.

"I remember when you were putting the finishing touches on that beautiful hanging," I said, stepping up to the register with my purchases. I'd picked up a small ceramic replica of the Duxbury Pier Light for Linda, who collected lighthouse tchotchkes.

"Hi, Cassie," Liv said, coolly, I thought. "It's been a while since I've seen you in here."

"I don't have much of a list for card giving," I said. I held back on assuring her that it wasn't because I'd been buying my cards at Daisy's.

"And you just happen to have a need today?"

I told her about Quinn's birthday and handed her the card I'd chosen.

Liv shifted her short, stocky body to reach the scanner and ran the card, and then the lighthouse, under its red beam. "For your information, by the way, on the day that Daisy died I was in South Ashcot, checking on my mom. She lives alone and I needed to be sure she was okay in the storm. I also stopped in at her next-door neighbor's, another widow, and helped with her shutters. I'm sure she, too, would be glad to vouch for my whereabouts."

Uh-oh. Apparently, word had gotten out. I felt my law enforcement career slipping away before it started.

"Okay, I—" I stammered, catching my breath.

"If you want, I can call Molly over here right now and make it easier on you. You won't have to cross the street to the salon. You can quiz her on that broken ankle. Oh, and did you plan to interrogate Pete in the hardware store also? I could ask him to come join us. Or is it just quilters whom you suspect of murder?"

"Liv, will you let me explain?"

"No need. It's all pretty clear. You come back to town and feel like your big-city life entitles you to lord it over those of us who have stuck it out and tried to make something of this town. You think you're smarter, so righteous. Doing us all a favor by coming back."

"That's not true, Liv. I wish—"

"Would you like your receipt in the bag?" she asked, cutting me off again, dropping my lighthouse and card in a bag. The *thunk* they made as they hit the counter told me she was finished with me. No room for discussion.

"Thank you. That will be fine," I said.

I turned and walked out the door, red-faced, figuratively if not literally. Another bust. I hadn't even gotten to the part where I'd ask simply if Liv had any insight into who might have been upset enough with Daisy to have killed her. The only tidbit I'd gotten was a reminder to look into Molly's broken ankle. Unless Molly was ready for me, too.

I hurried to my car, parked behind the bank, now next to a beige sedan with a driver asleep at the wheel. It couldn't be. But it was. Ross's forehead touched the top of the shiny brown steering wheel, his breath coming out in soft snores.

For some reason, I decided to wake him. Maybe because I needed to put someone else through an embarrassing moment like the one I'd just had. Perverse, I admitted, and not my proudest moment. I touched Ross on the shoulder. He jumped, his elbow landing on the horn. A quick blast, in case anyone else in the vicinity was trying to catch a few z's.

"Cassie. Wow. I guess I was asleep."

"Ross, what are you doing here? Is there some reason you've been shadowing me?"

Ross rubbed his eyes, shook his head. All the motions I went through at six in the morning. "Sunni asked me to," he blurted out.

I congratulated myself on choosing just the right moment to confront him, between sleep and wakefulness, catching him off guard. "She sent you to follow me around?"

He nodded, cleared his throat. "We heard about how stuff was stolen from your car and you didn't tell us."

"How did you hear about that?" As soon as I asked, I realized who had to have been the leak. The only one I'd told. "Cliff," I said.

He shrugged and I took it as a yes. "So Sunni figured the first threatening note must have been stolen also, and that's why you cancelled my pickup," he said.

"That's it? That calls for a police escort?"

"Plus, Cliff's going to be leaving town for Florida and he was worried about you being here alone. You know, security guards, they like to think they're police."

Which meant that Cliff had also been following me around? Which meant that instead of an aide to this investigation, I'd been a burden on several people. And insulted the others.

"Thanks, Ross, but I don't think I'm in any danger."

"Still have to do my job." He sat up straighter, scratched his head. "Say, Cassie, do me a favor?"

"Sure."

"About the nodding off."

"Don't worry; I won't tell your boss."

Ross let out an appreciative sigh. "The chief doesn't know this, but my captain-to-be in Springfield asked me to start a little early and take a couple of night shifts for him. I guess he's running a couple of guys low."

"That's a pretty long commute."

"Yeah, over an hour, even in the middle of the night with no traffic, but I felt I had to do it. Good first impression, you know. I've leased an apartment there, starting the first of the month, but until then, I'm putting on the miles." He let out an exhausted sigh, bordering on a groan. "I'm beat."

Poor Ross. I promised I wouldn't rat on him, as he'd put it. And he promised that though he had no intention of leaving me on my own, he wouldn't intrude on my personal life. I figured, in an emergency, a sleeping Ross was better than no Ross at all.

I was left with the fact that even sleep-deprived, short-timer Ross was more use to the North Ashcot chief of police than I was.

In spite of Liv's mockery, I decided to take my chances with Molly Boyd. Maybe Liv was only faking it when she implied that Molly (and the whole town) knew what I was about. I crossed the street and entered Molly's salon.

My nostrils were accosted by chemicals. It had been a while since I'd visited, as anyone with a keen eye for coiffure could tell you, and I'd forgotten what goes into the simple act of covering one's gray or trying a different color.

"Yeah, that's what I said. Red, white, and blue," I heard a young woman say to the beautician standing behind her.

"For the parade," the beautician said. "Great idea. Let's see what we can do."

Molly was in the middle of a serious project, tending to a woman whom I might have recognized if her head hadn't been covered with small pieces of foil and a host of hair clips, all nestled in foam. When Molly looked up and caught my eye, I expected to be ushered out without ceremony. Instead, I saw a smile, as if she were glad to see me. Could that be?

I stood in the center of the salon, surrounded by larger-than-life posters of the world's most beautiful hair, accompanied by the faces of women of all ages, while Molly removed her black apron and called out for assistance.

"I'll take it from here." A woman much younger than Molly's fifty-plus years stepped from behind a partition, part cloth, part plastic.

I hoped she was up to the major overhaul in process.

Molly thanked her and addressed me. "Cassie, come in back with me for a minute."

I walked down a short hallway, passing noisy blow dryers, a row of sinks, and a washer and dryer set, both in operation. Behind the curtain was a small area that served as a break room. I noticed their coffee equipment was nothing like the high-end brewing system I'd enjoyed in Sunni's office.

Molly pointed to an orange molded plastic chair, like the ones in front of the sinks that lined the hallway. "Have a seat." I followed her direction while she lowered her wide body onto a green chair of the same style. "I've been wanting to talk to you, Cassie."

Really? Was this a trap? Had Liv warned her and cooked up a way to trick me? Or worse? The break room had nothing more lethal than a few butter knives, but out there in the salon were enough instruments of torture for an army. I could be sprayed with a poisonous hair product or held down while my head was shaved with an efficient electric razor. I had a wild vision where all the women with black aprons were lined up for a curling-iron-burning contest with me as target.

"Cassie?" Molly repeated.

My hands clutched my purse under the table and I half stood to leave, the victim of my imagination. "I can see how busy you are," I stammered, forgetting that I was the one who came into her shop with a mission.

"No, no, don't worry about it. Everything's under control. I have my whole staff here on Saturdays. A bridal party is coming in later for an evening wedding, but we're all ready for them. Six girls and six boys. Gosh, isn't that a lot of attendants? We're doing the boys, too. And I've known the bride since she was in grade school. Sure makes me feel old."

Molly was even better at stalling than I was. I was sure she didn't intend to have this catch-up session, but I was too anxious, wondering what was up, to mess with the peaceful conversation. I stayed silent, except for nuh-uhs ("Can you imagine such a huge wedding party?") and uh-huhs ("Doesn't time fly?"), until Molly took a big breath, expanding her bosom, and got to her agenda.

"Cassie, I know you're helping Chief Smargon with the

case. With Daisy's case. And I want her killer found as much as anyone and I've been so afraid to approach the chief."

Molly got up, still limping slightly, and poured herself a cup of coffee, holding it up in a silent offer to serve me a drink.

I shook my head. The coffee smelled almost as bad as the chemicals in the next room. "Do you have information that will be useful in the investigation?"

"Not really. Well, maybe." She took her seat again. The green chair creaked. "The fact is that Daisy and I had a bad fight that day. The day of the storm." Molly pulled threads from a white towel that was stained with what I hoped was red hair dye and not anything more organic.

I thought back to our last quilting session on Tuesday night and the argument that had started when Liv insulted Andrea Harris's taste in fabric. A pink hippopotamus came to mind. Andrea had countered by accusing Liv of having a motive to eliminate Daisy, her competitor in greeting card sales, and Liv had shot back with references to the public discord between Daisy and the Harrises' farmers' market proposal.

As far as I recalled, Molly had stayed neutral, serving up her special raspberry-bedecked cheesecake. She'd also come up with her first story about her broken ankle.

"Your broken ankle was from the fight with Daisy," I said now. "Not from tripping over your Adirondack chair or your cat." I felt more confident now that things were falling into place, although on a very small scale.

"I feel awful about those ankle stories." She leaned over and ran her finger around the top of the blue brace that ended low on her calf, as if to loosen it. "I don't know what got into me. I'm really not a liar. That's what I wanted to tell the chief. Not about the ankle, but about that morning. Liv asked me to talk to Daisy, to try to get her to see Liv's point of view, how it looked like Daisy was encroaching on her turf. Daisy and I were close, you know. She was almost like my daughter, and Liv's my friend, too. I thought I could bring them together."

"You were trying to be a good friend to both. So you went to Daisy's shop . . ." I showed my palm, inviting more.

I got an enthusiastic nod from Molly and an eagerness to explain. "It was raining really hard, and the wind was out of control, as you must remember. But I didn't want to put it off. I left my girls to close up shop and ran across the street. Daisy wasn't out front or inside, and there were no customers, of course, so I checked out back. She was practically being blown away by the wind, she was so tiny. She was trying to move that heavy metal furniture she has out there and pull in the outside plants. I started to help her."

"What time was that?"

She shrugged. "I know I hadn't had lunch yet, but, you know, I don't have a regular lunchtime. I think I went over a little before eleven, and I didn't stay more than about twenty minutes."

I'd seen Daisy taking in the displays from the front of the shop around noon, after Molly left. If I hadn't been so self-conscious about being an interrogator, I would have dug out my notepad and taken notes. I tried to keep the time sequence straight in my head. Molly leaves; I drive by; the killer arrives and leaves; Tony finds Daisy's body—all between about eleven thirty and one thirty.

Molly was breathing heavily, a worry to me. She'd stopped talking and stared into the space over my shoulder, which happened to be the direction of Daisy's shop. She'd become more and more agitated, probably from finally sharing the details of what had to have been one of the worst moments of her life, and one she'd had to keep to herself.

"Let me get you some water," I said, already on the way to the small refrigerator. I pulled out a bottle of water and opened it. When I touched her hand, intending to call her attention to the water, I released another flood of emotion.

"Then I brought up Liv and the card issue, trying to be all casual, and Daisy went ballistic. She yanked a chair from me, so hard that I fell over, and she didn't even seem to care that I was hurt." Molly shook her head. "I'd never seen her that way. I knew I'd better get out of there before something worse happened." She gasped, realizing again that something much worse had happened.

I closed my eyes, as if to focus on the timeline taking shape in my head. Another data point came to me. "Did you report back to Liv after your fight with Daisy?"

"Oh, you bet. I gave her a call immediately. She wasn't happy, and"—Molly squinted, and jerked her neck forward, scrutinizing me—"wait a minute, Cassie, you're not thinking that Liv went over there and—"

I held up my hand, stopping her before she lost her breath again. "I'm trying to put things in order, Molly. It's important to have a clear picture."

I didn't elaborate about another piece of the picture that had fallen into place. I thought back to Liv's appearance as my last customer before Ben and I closed up on the morning of the storm. It had been before noon and, now I knew, after Molly called her and gave her the bad news about Daisy's aggressive behavior.

Even Ben had noticed the foul mood Liv was in at the time. I hoped Molly couldn't see the image taking shape in my mind, of Liv finishing her post office errand and storming over to confront Daisy.

One of Molly's employees came to the doorway, but left immediately. I guessed it was clear that a private meeting was going on. Molly and I sat in silence for a minute or so. I hated to bring her back to my reason for being there, but I knew I had to. "Is that it?" I asked, trying to keep my tone neutral.

"You don't believe me. And now you think Liv killed Daisy."

I'd failed again. "That's not it," I assured her. "I'm just asking if there's anything more that you remember. Is there some reason why you didn't talk to the chief immediately, once you knew she was dead? If nothing else, your story would have helped pinpoint a time when Daisy was alive."

Molly strained to recapture her powers of reason. "I would have called her, but I was hurting, in more ways than one, kinda shocked at Daisy's reaction. Then Tony stepped up right away with his information and I felt I had nothing to add."

I was stuck. I knew it would do no good to emphasize, again, that any tidbit could have been helpful.

Molly's eyes teared up. "I haven't been able to get the whole thing out of my mind. I console myself with the idea that Tony saw her not long after I left, so she couldn't have suffered very long. Someone just rushed in there and . . ."

I didn't like the image, either. We lapsed back into our inert state, staring past each other, the buzz of beauticians and clients in the next room incongruously cheerful.

"Are you going to tell the chief?" Molly asked in a hoarse whisper.

"It would be better if you told her yourself."

"Do you think she'll hit me with an obstruction of justice charge?"

"I don't know, Molly. But I know it's the right thing for you to do."

She nodded. "You're right." A loud sigh followed.

"Can we talk about one more thing?" I asked.

She screwed up her face, curious but wary. "I guess so."

"I saw that there was a gathering in here last night."

"So?"

"Anything I should know about?"

Wrong question. Molly bristled. "It's not my place to say, really."

"Because Reggie Harris was in charge?"

Molly leaned on the table and hoisted herself up. "I think I should get back to work," she said, limping away.

Though I smiled at everyone who caught my eye on my way out, I felt drained of energy. I couldn't help thinking that the result of my alleged helping with an investigation might be that I'd end up with no friends. Which was exactly my status when I first came back to town a year ago. Everyone I'd known in high school was on a path that didn't include me. I'd worked hard to be accepted and now I was headed back to square one. I passed a row of black sinks and I considered signing up for a complete redo of my untamed locks—its main appeal was that I'd be able to hide for a while under one of the sleek plastic drying hoods.

As I walked to my car, my purse rang. The old-fashioned ring tone signaled a text from Quinn. I leaned against the bank building and read it.

Home for Skype later?

Yes!!! I wrote, disregarding my old English teacher's firm direction never to use more than one exclamation point. "These are extraordinary times," I would have told her now.

·

17

Molly Boyd was out of my hands. She'd apparently taken a blood oath, like everyone else at the meeting in her salon. I hoped I'd at least convinced her to report to Sunni. If so, then I'd made one small contribution to the Daisy Harmon case file.

I still had items on my list to complete. Sunni had asked me to talk to the quilters and that was what I'd do. But not before I downed a good cup of coffee. I crossed Main Street and entered Mahican's coffee shop. I used my sweater to stake a claim to a chair at the back, away from a baseball game on TV, then placed my usual order at the counter.

On the way back to the place I'd saved, I saw that a woman had taken a seat at my table, opposite my sweater. No problem. Customers often doubled up when the café was busy.

The closer I got, the clearer it became that I knew the

woman and her cascading blond hair. I arrived at the table and greeted Terry Thornton, who'd settled in with a coffee and a brownie.

"Hey, Cassie. I was sitting over there"—Terry pointed to a long communal table along the street side of the shop—"and I saw you come in, so I figured I'd join you. Is that okay?"

"Of course," I said, thrilled that at least one person in North Ashcot appeared eager to talk to me. So what if Terry wasn't high on my list of suspects? She was a quilter and, therefore, on my assignment sheet. And she'd handed herself to me. That, and there was an excellent cappuccino in front of me. Maybe my luck was changing.

Terry reached down to a shopping bag on the floor and pulled out a white, semicircular headband, a narrow crown of sorts. "What do you think?" she asked. "I just picked it up. The trend these days seems to be minimalist."

"Minimalist?" I echoed, giving myself time to adjust to the issue on Terry's mind: her own wedding, not Daisy's murder. Without preamble, we were into wedding talk. I realized it might take a while to transition to homicide. I took in the sequins, tiny crystals, and pieces of shiny ribbon wrapped around the band. "Lovely," I said.

"So simple, right? No more wreaths or spikes sticking out of your hair or long, complicated veils. Most brides don't wear veils at all now. Course, styles change, which is why I'm not settling on a dress yet."

To my chagrin, I was on my second cappuccino, this time accompanied by a few small biscotti, and we were still discussing bridal issues. The cake (in fact, she was considering cupcakes, arranged like a multitiered cake), the attendants (there was some unfortunate tension, since one of her best girlfriends was on the chubby side and balked at wearing a sleeveless dress even though it was a summer wedding), the caterer (tastings with three companies were scheduled, with her mom and sister as advisers), and the rehearsal dinner (it was hard to choose between a casual, youth-oriented, fun place, and a fancy restaurant in one of Boston's finest hotels).

"Don't you have almost a year to get all this together?" I asked.

Terry's eyes widened, as if I'd said her crown was ugly or that she ought to elope. "Ten months and two weeks. It's closer than you think," she said. "We already have the church and the hall, naturally. It's going to be in Boston, where we both come from, down by the waterfront, and you wouldn't believe how everything gets booked even two years in advance."

I assured her I believed it, and sipped through one more wedding topic—shoes. Terry showed me transparent strips she'd bought to put on the soles of her wedding shoes. She wiggled the strips to show me how flexible they were. "They're for walking on the lawn, which we'll have to do, you know, for pictures. I've heard horror stories of brides slipping on the grass."

I tried to be suitably horrified, but I'd reached my limit and had to make an attempt to derail the wedding talk. I excused myself to get a refill, with an extra shot, and when I got back to the table, I was ready.

"I ran into Molly Boyd earlier today," I said. "We were talking about how we miss Daisy Harmon, how much help she was at our quilting meetings."

"Absolutely. Daisy was a cool old gal."

I cleared my throat, and kept silent, approaching cool old galhood myself.

Terry nibbled on her brownie, then shook her head, eyes toward the ceiling, as if recalling a scene from the past. "That is, unless she'd had a fight with her husband right before."

I leaned in toward Terry and assumed a do-tell position. "I haven't heard about that," I said, and decided immediately afterward that I was officially a bad person, capitalizing on Terry's immaturity and gossipy tendencies to get information. I hoped the result would be useful enough to justify my questionable means.

Terry waved her hand. "Well, you're sort of new to the group, you know, so you may not have heard as much. But she was always complaining about Cliff and his lack of ambition."

"I thought he had a pretty secure job."

Terry failed my private test—she didn't seem to get the pun. "Yes, but, as I'm sure you know, he tried out for the police force and didn't make it."

"That's nothing to be ashamed of." There I was, defending Cliff again. I had to be careful not to dissuade my companion from sharing further tidbits. "It was his eyesight, I think."

"I didn't mean that he's a loser or anything. It's just that there's not much opportunity for advancement in a private security firm. Justin, my fiancé, is in marketing, for example, and he's going for his master's in business administration. Really, you can go almost anywhere from there if you apply yourself." She paused for a sip of coffee. "Which he does. He's going for a promotion as soon as we're settled."

"What about you, Terry? What are your career goals?"

"Me? Oh, I'm happy in the school office, right now. There's always something new to learn, like new policies and procedures in the district. Maybe after all this is over"— she pointed to the bag at her feet, and I assumed she meant wedding prep—"I'll go back and finish my degree. It all depends." Terry had a slightly pained expression on her face, as if it hurt to think too far ahead.

Before we took a complete detour to a conversation about careers, I inserted a little gossip as a distraction. "I heard that Cliff wasn't happy with Daisy's activism," I said, cringing inwardly.

Terry rose to the bait. "Oh, no kidding? I heard Daisy say once—I think it was to Eileen at a quilting meeting— that Cliff was trying to get her to pull back on being so outspoken. 'It's not good for business,' he'd told her over and over."

Now I was absorbing not only hearsay, but tales with at least three degrees of separation from the source. "Really?" was my only contribution. I knew that was all it would take for Terry to continue.

"Daisy's point was that if it wasn't for her, always pushing to grow the business and work to make the conditions in town favorable to small merchants, their shop would have folded long ago. That's what she said to Eileen; she didn't talk about it with me directly."

I could see why Daisy might not have used Terry as a confidante. But I had to admit that for a young woman, Terry seemed to have her pulse on the community. Her vantage point was the office in the town's only school, K through six, where she interacted with the teachers, parents, and staff. Ripe for information. And she knew how to spin a good tale.

I'd thought about asking Eileen if she'd had any direct information about the tension between Cliff and Daisy, but Eileen was not the type to gossip. I gulped. Unlike me. When had I become the Queen of Scuttlebutt? Was it still gossiping if you'd been charged with uncovering chatter that might help the police in a homicide investigation? I could only hope.

Before I could intervene, Terry switched back to talk of her impending nuptials. I let her go on for about ten minutes, listening to reviews of the various bridal magazines Terry subscribed to, the catering catalogues she'd picked up this afternoon, and the choices of designer wedding apparel. When she took a break for a sip of coffee, I looked at my watch.

"I can't believe it's this late," I said, barely noting the actual time. "I'd better get going."

"Oh, me, too. I'm supposed to be going over all the samples of favors I've collected. Big decisions coming up."

I wished her good luck with the high-stakes verdicts and left Mahican's, wondering how I could manage to be left off Terry's guest list.

When I finally did check my watch, I saw that it was only four forty. A little more than thirty minutes since I'd met Terry. I could have sworn I'd spent a couple of hours with her. I sat in my car behind the bank and thought about Andrea, whom I hadn't spoken to since quilting night. Main Street was still busy with shoppers. Should I wander into the hardware store where she worked part-time, on the off chance I'd meet her? I tried to think of some use I might have for nails or a soldering gun and came up empty. An unplanned meeting had worked with Terry, but it was unlikely to happen a second time.

I pulled out my phone and checked my contacts, where all the quilters were listed. My finger was in midair over Andrea Harris's number when my phone rang. I said hello to Cliff.

"I'm really worried about Jules," he said. "I've been calling him ever since I heard I could take Daisy to Miami and he hasn't answered."

I felt compelled to remind Cliff again that it was Saturday. "Maybe he has a date," I suggested.

"Yeah, but he's never off the clock this long, you know. I'm outside his house now. I was thinking, what if he's sick or he fell or something?"

I realized I didn't know much about Jules's personal life, whether he had a family, lived alone, who his close friends were.

Cliff clearly knew where he lived at least. "I knocked and rang the bell and looked in all the windows I could. Then I checked the garage. His car isn't there, so he must be holed up in his office, not wanting to be disturbed. I'm going to check."

Thus thwarting Jules's plans to hole up. Didn't Cliff hear me the first six times? "It's the weekend, Cliff." I knew I sounded like a scolding parent. "Hard as it will be, you might have to wait until Monday. Don't you have access to other funds?"

"Not as much as I'll need for the trip and all the logistics. The shop's account is in Daisy's name only. I have the paperwork I need to access it, but I can't do that until the banks open on Monday."

"I wish I could help you, Cliff, but I'm not in a position—"

"No, no, Cassie. I'm not asking for that. I'm going to Jules's office. I'll call you from there."

The "there" Cliff referred to was two doorways from where I sat in my car. The lot covered the whole block from First Street to Second Street, encompassing the back properties of the bank, Molly's salon, and the hardware store above which Jules had his office. If I were a good friend, I'd offer to check the accountant's office myself. I took a deep breath and allowed my better self to come forward. "I'm in the neighborhood already. I can run up and check."

"Would you? Thanks, Cassie. I owe you."

"One question first, Cliff. Did you tell Chief Smargon about my car's break-in?"

"Uh, yes, I did. I'd never be able to live with myself if anything happened to you just because you were helping me out. Never. The chief said she was glad to know."

"I'm sure she was."

"I'm sorry. I knew you wouldn't do it yourself, and, like I said, it would kill me if I'd put you in danger. Whatever nutcase killed Daisy, I don't want him after you."

I should have been more grateful than annoyed, but it was neck and neck. Cliff had set himself up as protector, perhaps for Jules, too. I believed him when he said he was concerned for Jules's welfare as well as for accessing the money he needed. There was nothing like a murder in town to set a security guard to high alert.

I clicked off with Cliff, regretting that I hadn't found a way to ask him about the rumored tension between him and his late wife. As I climbed out of my car, parked directly behind the bank, I glanced at the salon windows next to it, into Molly's back room, and couldn't help thinking of the secret (to me) meeting held there last evening, one that Jules had attended.

There were few cars left here this evening, since stores were closing. The parking lot, devoid of people, was unpaved, a mixture of gravel, dirt, and puddles, with a few large rocks in the mix, plus debris that still hadn't been cleared from Monday's storm. Just like the lot across the street, behind Daisy's shop. The yard where Daisy met her death.

The shortest route to Jules's office was across the lot and into the back entrance to the hardware store, and up the stairs. Though it was still daylight, the lone walk through the rubble was unappealing and instead I took the long way around, over to First Street, then down Main; past the front of the bank, all closed up now; past the salon, still bustling inside; and into the front of the hardware store. I welcomed the coolness of the air-conditioning. It would be a couple of hours before the temperature dropped enough to be comfortable outside.

I opened the door to the building just as Pete, the manager, exited the side door of his store, pushing a broom, corralling sawdust, a few nails, and tiny pieces of wood. We nearly bumped into each other in the small lobby. A short, middle-aged man, but very muscular, Pete would have come out on top in any such collision.

"Hi, Cassie. Good to see you. But another minute and you wouldn't have gotten in. I came to lock that door." He tucked the broom handle under his arm and showed me a ring of keys as an offer of proof. "If you're headed upstairs, you won't find anyone. Dr. Hotte came down with her last client of the day a few minutes ago."

Did Pete think I needed a therapy session with Dr. Hotte? I ran my fingers through my hair, as if it weren't too late to make a more put-together impression. "I thought Jules might be up there," I said. "I've been trying to reach him all day." Close enough to the truth.

Pete shook his head. "I don't think you'll be seeing him for a while."

"Oh?"

"I was in real early this morning and he came bounding down the stairs in back with one of those rolling suitcases behind him."

I frowned, disappointed. "Did he say where he was going, or how long he'd be away?"

Pete scratched his nearly bald head. "Now that I think of it, not really. Andrea was here—you know, my sister helps me out part-time, though she certainly doesn't need the money. Andrea asked Jules if he was going somewhere for a little getaway, and Jules just answered her vaguely, like 'Yeah, right,' or something like that. Then later I noticed he'd already put next month's rent in my box."

I thanked Pete for his help and was almost out the door when I stopped and turned, Columbo-style, and addressed him. "Is Andrea in the store now? There's something I wanted to talk to her about."

"No, she comes in mornings."

I jumped on it. "So you were both working during the awful storm? I know a lot of shops closed up early. I hope you kept safe."

"I sent everyone home and hung out in the back, actually. Figured it was better to be on the spot, protect my investment, in case anything happened."

"That was brave of you," I said. Pete sounded oblivious of the irony of his statement. Something had happened, right across the street, but he seemed to have forgotten. I felt I'd get nothing of value from him without a too-direct question, like "Where were you and your sister at the time of Daisy's murder?"

"Is there something I can do for you? Do you want to leave a message for Andrea?" Pete asked, perhaps noticing my distraction.

I shook my head. "Thanks, anyway, Pete. I wanted to find out about that meeting you were all at last night in Molly's back room, but it can wait."

Pete blew out a breath and leaned on his broom. "Believe me—you're better off keeping out of things."

I uttered my usual, brilliant, "Oh?" and put on my best expression of casual interest.

"That brother-in-law of mine, you know, Reggie. Things are heating up, getting out of control, if you ask me. Not in a physical way, but more political, if you know what I mean." He shook his head. "Reggie's getting greedy. But you didn't hear it from me." He held the outside door open, a signal for me to be on my way. I took the hint. I zipped my lip and exited the lobby.

"Thanks, Pete," I said, knowing neither what I was keeping secret nor what I was thanking him for.

I headed back to my car, scrolling for Cliff's cell phone number on the way. Jules's departure was bad news for him, and maybe even more serious than a small delay in gathering his travel funds. I bumped into a newspaper vending box, and felt as if I'd joined the Z generation (or had we circled back to Gen A?), with my eyes on my smartphone screen and not on where I was going.

Cliff answered right away. I pictured him waiting by his phone, though that had a different meaning these days when phones could be with you at all times.

"Is he there, Cassie? Did you find Jules?" Cliff asked.

I briefed Cliff, trying at the same time to soften the blow, that his source of funding was not available, and might not be for a while, at least not for the rest of this month. Then I had a thought. "Did you happen to tell Jules that we'd talked about having the books audited?" *The way you talked to Sunni,* I meant, *unable to keep much to yourself.*

"Yeah, I did." He paused. "Are you thinking he skipped town because he's stolen from us and he's afraid it would come out?" Before I could reply, Cliff went on. "I don't think he'd do that. He didn't say he'd be gone long, right? I mean, Andrea didn't actually get an answer from him."

I understood why Cliff couldn't let his mind go to a place where he'd been cheated out of his investment.

"No," I said, "but he had a suitcase and—"

"And, besides, why pay a month's rent if you're never coming back?"

"That's a good point, Cliff," I said, though I didn't believe it. Jules was smart enough to know how to cover his tracks, to make it look as though he'd be back. A way to delay a search for him. I marveled at my new ability to come up so readily with something nefarious. "Does he have family?" I asked.

"Not that I know of, but I never paid any attention, really. He's always been a loner, works all the time. I just figured he's a numbers guy, you know, not that social."

I didn't voice the thought that it wouldn't hurt to have one of Sunni's officers check out Jules's home and office, to see if there were any signs that he'd gone for good, on a trip to a different future, financed by his unwitting clients.

"I'm sorry you're being held up on your plans," I said.

"It's okay. Thanks for checking, Cassie. There's always plan B. I'll just have to stick around until Monday when the bank opens."

And Officer Ross Little might get the rest of the weekend off from following me.

On the way home, I wondered if it had occurred to Cliff that Jules might have more than one reason for skipping town.

I arranged it so that my evening check-ins with Linda and Quinn would be early, and all about them. The day had brought too much strain to my brain. Starting at the farmers' market with Reggie on the offense, through several quilters with mixed results, and ending with a runaway accountant who might also be a murderer. I needed time away from the stress of a homicide investigation. It was hard to believe I'd asked for it.

Linda obliged me by talking about a new work project,

updating a collection for the National Postal Museum in Washington, D.C. ("Everything is getting digitized these days.")

"How about that postal inspection job?" I asked.

"I'm still thinking about it, but when I mentioned it casually to Buzz he indicated that I shouldn't make a move without talking to him first. It will be worth my while, blah, blah, blah. So I think I'm in for something bigger around here, which would be easier in the long run."

"I'm glad they appreciate you."

"And to test flexibility theory, by the way, I'm going to take a long weekend and head out there on Friday morning," she said. "I should be there in time to take you to lunch." She paused and I knew what was coming. "North Ashcot does have places to eat lunch, doesn't it?"

I'd long ago decided that, rather than letting it annoy me, I'd have fun with Linda's mocking of small towns. "I'll talk to the town council before you get here," I said.

"You know I'm really coming to meet your mystery man," she reminded me.

Linda had visited only twice in my year here, both of us preferring that I visit her and our posse, as we called our group of friends, in Boston instead. Quinn had been out of town both times, leading her to joke that I'd made him up. I promised that this time he'd be around, though maybe unrecognizable in a Colonial costume.

"Kidding," I shouted, before she lost her breath in a gasp.

When it was Quinn's turn on Skype tonight, I could tell he was tired. But he came to life describing his Saturday purchases: an Etruscan shell pitcher, a pair of mother-of-pearl opera glasses, and a silver gravy ladle one of his regular customers had been asking for. The latter was easy to unpack and he held it up to show me.

"No monos," he said, testing my skills at antique-aficionado shorthand.

"No monogram," I said. I was proud that I'd remembered his tutelage, but embarrassed to admit that I'd forgotten whether that made the ladle more or less valuable.

"I can't wait to shower in my own bathroom," he said, turning his laptop so I could see what might have been the world's tiniest bathroom. He turned the camera back on himself and grinned. "Oh yeah, and to see you."

I grinned back. "I might be around."

After an hour of happy talk with my two favorite people, I was ready for a nap. All that stood in the way as I tried to nod off were images of me, chasing after Jules Edwards, looking for a weapon. In the half dream, the only weapon I could find was a stamp with raised letters. CANCELLED.

I needed to get out more.

Sunni showed up at my house around seven, as promised. I had hopes that this one-on-one meeting with the chief of police would accomplish what my fitful nap hadn't: a clear path forged through the week's accumulation of fact and gossip, thus curing my headache.

Knowing by now that Sunni would never be the first to share her findings, and not wanting to be accused of holding back, I wasted no time. I decided to fill in the gaps from the first of the week, assuring her it was just an oversight that I hadn't told her about the theft of Cliff's files from my car and that, while I appreciated the attention given to my safety, I was sure I didn't need to be a line item in her budget.

She smiled, not budging, except to fold her arms across her chest. "What's up with that first threatening note?"

"It wasn't exactly threatening."

"What's up with it?"

"I tore my desk apart and couldn't find it."

"You think it was stolen? To rattle you, maybe?"

I shrugged, not wanting to say out loud that it certainly did rattle me. "I'm ninety-nine percent sure I put it in my middle drawer. But no one else has a key except Ben and he never goes into the desk drawers."

"It's not that hard to bypass locks and keys if someone is determined."

"That's depressing."

"Do you remember anything about the paper or the handwriting? Was everything the same as with the second note?"

"Except that there was no envelope the second time. Otherwise, they were both on paper you can buy anywhere."

"Okay, let's put that aside for now. Tell me about the rest of your day."

"You mean Ross didn't tell you everything?"

"I'm listening."

I moved on to the events of today while I made coffee, leaving her on the rocker in the living room. I began with my spontaneous talk with Reggie at the market, then reported on my interactions with Fran, Liv, Molly, and Terry.

"Fran brought up an argument Daisy had with Jules in the bank, but I didn't think to ask if she knew what it was about or when it occurred. Dumb, right?"

"Go on," Sunni said, not disabusing me of my self-assessment.

"Liv is the only one who gave me specifics about her alibi," I said, relaying it in more pleasant tones than Liv herself had used with me. "Molly—"

"Molly came by the station after you talked to her."

"What will happen to her? Is what she did . . . ?" I didn't even know what to ask.

"Criminal? We'll figure it out. I want to thank you for encouraging her to come forward. I'm not sure she would have without your urging. Anything more from the others?"

It was hard not to allow myself a moment of pride. My day hadn't been a complete waste. It was also clear that I wasn't going to be made privy to the outcome of Molly's confession.

I outlined the stories and rumors that hinted of trouble in the Harmons' marriage, especially in Terry's outpourings. "I believe the tension was all about Daisy's activism and how it might hurt the fabric shop business. No one said Cliff had any personal issues with his wife or vice versa. I can't bring myself to take him seriously as a killer," I admitted.

"The first thing an investigator has to do is put aside personal feelings," Sunni said.

"And the second?"

"She has to pay attention to her gut. And sometimes those two things have to be reversed."

My confusion lasted only a moment as Sunni broke into a broad smile. "It sounds contradictory, I know, but that is the job."

"Okay," I said, with new appreciation for my simple job of handling the mailing needs of a town with a population of three thousand.

Sunni accepted her cup of coffee and I took a seat opposite her in my living room. Her posture said she was waiting for me to finish before giving me any information.

I covered everything I could think of, including the quasi-secret citizens' meeting last evening, but saved the Jules escape story for last. From her expression, I gathered that Sunni had not yet heard about Cliff's immediate money problems and the reason for them. Cliff was much better at alerting the police to my crises than to his own.

"Hmm," she said. "Does Cliff receive regular paperwork from Jules?"

I shook my head. "From what I understand, Daisy handled the finances. Cliff has only what Jules gave him at the brief meeting the three of us had yesterday. Nothing substantial, which is why I suggested an outside audit. Now I can't help thinking that's what scared Jules away. And what if he's the one who attacked Daisy? I might have put Cliff in danger. I might have—"

"First, let's not do might-haves. Let's stay with what we know."

"But isn't it looking like Jules was embezzling?" I asked. "We know he and Daisy argued. His taking off like this just makes it more likely that he's guilty."

"We can't jump to that conclusion. He's an adult, and not technically missing yet. I'll have to talk to Cliff and find out exactly what Jules has reported as far as the financials go, and when."

"Can you look around Jules's house and office?"

"It's not that simple, Cassie. But given the circumstances, I think I can make a case for it."

"You can't just go to his place? Hasn't he been a murder suspect all along?"

"Not officially. I have no evidence that suggests Jules was involved in Daisy's death." She looked at me sideways. "Unless there's something you're not telling me?"

"Just my gut that I'm supposed to be listening to."

She shook her head and smiled. "Touché. I know Jules. I know he can be short with people, and condescending to say the least. But that's half the people in the town. It doesn't make them criminals, let alone killers."

"Half the people? Really?"

"That might be an exaggeration."

"Tough day?"

"The last person I pulled over this afternoon, a lawyer, told me his intern makes more in his summer job than I do all year."

"Ouch," I said.

"And I can't count the number of times I get 'I pay your salary, you know,' or the variation, 'You work for me.'"

"I get that sometimes, too," I said.

We moved off the "my job is worse than yours" routine and got back to Jules Edwards, fugitive accountant.

"What I don't understand is why he'd embezzle from a small-town fabric shop. How much could he be making from that?" I asked. "Maybe he's been cheating other clients in town also?"

"We'll know soon enough when we check his roster. But don't think it's just a million-dollar score that's attractive to someone who deals with other people's money. And it's not always the finance people. I remember a case where the crook was the director of a library in a small town not far from here. One of the employees got suspicious about some billings and it turned out that for years the director had been skimming. Nothing big, but he had recarpeted his house and was on a buying spree for a new living room set, mega speakers for his stereo, fancy kitchen appliances, that kind of thing."

"Instead of books for the library?" I made a note to rethink my charitable donations for the rest of the year.

"Uh-huh. Or instead of the ten new chairs in his budget, he'd buy six and put the rest of the money toward a new flat-screen for himself. Instead of a new printer for the office, he'd buy one for his home. That kind of thing."

"It hardly seems worth the risk."

"Some people like the risk, and for someone who's into cheating, he'll take what he can get. It's like gambling. Even a small score can be satisfying."

I still had a lot to learn about what motivated people.

Eventually, Sunni owned up to wanting dinner. "Where's all the stuff from your trek to the farmers' market this morning?" she asked.

I showed her the new cutting board I'd bought from a woodworker and pointed to a new plant on my kitchen counter. "It came with papers certifying that it's pest-free," I said.

"It's a good thing I have a couple of bags of real groceries in my car."

"I was kidding. I also bought fresh cauliflower and goat cheese, grass-fed beef, and homemade bread."

"Glad to hear it. And as luck will have it, there's dessert in my car," she said. "I'll bring it in. Then I'll make some calls to get started on Jules's profile while you whip up something we can call a main course."

"Deal."

I gave my hands and eyes to dinner and trained my ears on Sunni's side of her phone conversations once she'd returned. I heard her efficient delegation of look-up tasks to whoever was on duty. I was pleased to hear words like "warrant" and "search" in the mix. My eavesdropping was interrupted by a call to my own cell phone. I dug it out of my pocket. Cliff's name came up. I looked at Sunni, a reflex, and turned my back to her as I slid the phone on and heard Cliff's voice.

"I was going to drop in, but then I saw the chief's car outside your house," he said.

"You can join us," I said, hoping the opposite.

"I don't think so, but I wanted to tell you I got a look around Jules's office a little while ago."

"You what?"

"Yeah, I figured it would be forever until the chief got all the paperwork approved. Especially since she's now having dinner with you."

I chose "no comment" on the half joke. "How did you manage it?"

"Pete and I go way back and I've done a few favors for him lately. Like, his hardware store got broken into last year and I stepped in for security while he was trying to put the place back together. It wasn't hard to talk him into letting me have a quick look upstairs today. It's his building after all. He's the landlord."

Not the strongest defense. "That was not a good idea," I said, imagining charges of tampering with evidence, corrupting the chain of custody of anything that might otherwise have been useful. I kept my voice low, but I had a feeling Sunni was listening and I'd have some explaining to do.

"I didn't touch anything. Pete can tell you. He stayed

there the whole time. I was just trying to see if there was anything obvious, you know. In plain sight."

"In case Jules left a blank check sitting on the table, made out to you?"

Cliff chuckled. "Or a big ledger book with a clear bottom line. As if he'd leave anything like that behind. But I'm kind of desperate here."

I wanted to know if he'd gotten anything useful from his questionable snooping. Aware of Sunni close by, I chose my words carefully. "How did the trip work out?" I asked.

"I think Jules is in the wind, Cassie. I think I can kiss my money good-bye. Maybe he printed out a jet plane on that fancy three-D contraption he has, and flew away." He blew out a breath that sounded like despair. Otherwise, I might have laughed at the image of a 747 taking shape in the little cube in Jules's office.

"Did you check his filing cabinets? Are all his files gone?"

I didn't see how they could be, since Pete had mentioned that Jules had left the building with only one suitcase.

"I didn't check any of the drawers. The only things still around were a couple of pillows on the sofa and the mugs on the coffee bar. But everything looked bare on the surfaces, like on his desk and conference table, which was always piled high with papers. It looked like he might have swept everything into his bag. What we need is for the chief to go in there official-like and figure it out. Open drawers and stuff."

"I'll see what I can do," I said, taking that as a request.

I signed off with Cliff and found Sunni at my side. I cleared my throat, ready to report.

"So, Cliff got into Jules's apartment?"

"His office." I gave her a questioning look. "How did you even know it was Cliff on the phone?" I'd been careful not to use his name. "Is there some X-ray vision that comes with the badge?"

"Oh yeah. Either that or I saw him drive by when I picked up the cake from my car."

"Of course." I pretend-wiped my brow. "You're only human, after all."

"I've already cleared an authorized search with another member of our justice system, who works on weekends."

"For less salary than an intern in a law office."

"Right."

Dinner was remarkably free of shop talk. Or anything substantive. Sunni wondered why we hadn't been going to the Knox Valley Farmers' Market all summer.

"I've never been a foodie," I admitted, and told her about one Boston friend who'd go to great lengths to find just the right tomato for a Caprese sandwich and who refused to eat a pepper that wasn't homegrown.

I imagined someone observing the scene at my kitchen table, hearing our conversation and reading little bubbles over our heads, with what we were thinking. He'd be able to see cogs and wheels in action in both our minds. My machine would be wishing I could go to Jules's home immediately and tear it apart for clues. Sunni probably saw ahead to when she could write "case closed" on the murder of one of the people she'd sworn to protect and serve.

* * *

Was it mere coincidence that my doorbell rang ten minutes after Sunni left? Or had Cliff been sitting nearby in his car waiting till the coast was clear? My vote was for the latter.

"Hey, Cassie," he said. He stood on my threshold, Bruins cap in hand, as if he happened to be in the neighborhood and it was not after ten o'clock at night. "Can I come in for a little while? Just a few minutes?"

As if I could refuse him, or anyone else who looked so needy.

I poured the last of the coffee into a mug for my latest guest. "I suppose you want an update," I said. "There isn't much. In fact, you're ahead of the police if you've already been in Jules's office."

"His home, too," Cliff said. "Same as his office. I'd swear he's not coming back. I'll bet they won't even get fingerprints."

"You realize how much you've compromised the investigation. Any defense lawyer will say you went in to plant evidence."

"Not if they don't know. And you won't be on the spot— don't worry. I'll just deny it, and deny that I told you. If it comes to that. Besides, it was all useless, since there was nothing in either place that told me where Jules was headed. I'm counting on the police to check airlines and bus stations and all. Do you think they will? I'm sure it's too late to set up a roadblock."

"I'm confident our police will be on it. What are you going to do in the meantime?"

"I hit up a friend who owed me a favor and pulled together enough for the trip. The last thing I want is to keep

Daisy's parents waiting." He closed his eyes and let out a long sigh. "I'm really not looking forward to seeing them."

"Don't you get along with them?"

"Oh yeah, they're great people. Her dad is ex-military and he has some great stories. But, you know, their only daughter is dead and—"

And you're not, I thought. I knew how that felt. "Cliff, no one expects a spouse, even one who's in security, to be present and on the watch every minute. Someone took advantage of Daisy's vulnerability during a storm. He's the one who's guilty. There's no way you could have prevented that."

He shook his head, as if he didn't believe a word I said. Was anyone exempt from feelings of guilt when a loved one died? I knew from a nurse friend in Boston that medically trained people felt this way when someone close to them died, no matter the cause. She admitted that there was always that nagging doubt that they didn't do what they should have to save them. Now before me was a member of law enforcement who felt the same inadequacy.

"Yeah, okay," Cliff said, though I knew it wasn't okay, and wouldn't be for a long time. "Anyway, I got a seat on a red-eye." He checked his watch. "I'll be heading for the airport in about a half hour. I'm counting on you to keep the investigation alive while I'm gone, Cassie."

"I'll do my best." What else could I say that wouldn't bring him further down?

A good-night chat with Quinn calmed me down enough to fall asleep the same day I got up, a feat these days. But the dream state didn't last long.

My phone startled me awake.

"I thought you'd want to know right away," Sunni said.

"What happened?"

"Something turned up in our search. If you're not half-asleep, I'll stop by on my way home now and tell you more."

"I'm wide-awake."

And a quick cup of coffee later, I was. Wide-awake, in my living room, waiting for my doorbell to ring.

I switched on my porch light and waited for my late-night guest, realizing that Sunni hadn't said much about what they'd found. Just "something." I'd assumed that by "search," she'd meant Jules's home and office. Where had the "something" been found? And what was it? She hadn't given me a clue.

Maybe she figured a phone line wasn't secure enough for passing on police information. I was pleased that she'd want to share the information with me immediately. That would do for now.

I settled in with old *Boston Globe* newspapers with unfinished jumbles and other word games. I'd long since abandoned the idea of keeping up with the Back Bay social scene. The sound of a car in my driveway interrupted me.

I popped up and held the door as Sunni climbed the stairs to my porch. She was still wearing her uniform, which I'd find unbearable. As much as I loved and was proud of my red, white, and blue outfit, I couldn't wait to get into my jeans and tees or sweatshirt when I left the post office.

Sunni headed straight for her favorite rocker and accepted a cup of coffee. She let out a satisfied grunt.

"So? You found something incriminating at Jules's?" I asked, on the physical and mental edges of my seat.

She nodded. "At the moment we're keeping it quiet. You know how fast news travels in this town."

"Where was it? His office? His house?" No response. "His car?" I refused to allow the notion that she intended to withhold information from me, too, not just from the ordinary citizens of North Ashcot. The ones who weren't more or less deputized. The ones whose food she'd eaten all week.

"It's better that we play this close to the vest. Keep it off the news," said the chief of police, sitting on my rocker, drinking my coffee.

"You're going to keep it from me?" I tried to keep my tone at an even pitch. Not hysterical.

By way of answering, Sunni took another sip of coffee. She cleared her throat, but no words followed.

"You came out of your way to tell me . . . nothing?" I noted the higher pitch my voice had reached.

"I just wanted you to know that, essentially, the case is solved. Our job now is to find Jules. You can relax."

"You're kidding me," I said. But I knew she wasn't. "I'm off the case?"

"As much as you were ever 'on the case.'" She drew quotations marks in the air, which hurt.

I felt almost as bad as when I was dumped by Adam Robinson back in Boston. "I thought we were partners," I wanted to tell Sunni, which was what I'd wanted to say to Adam more than a year ago.

I thought I heard an "I'm sorry" as Sunni took her abrupt leave, but it was probably simply what I hoped to hear.

19

I thought back to the day I entered (not broke in to, I reminded myself) Daisy's shop. I'd just seen someone exit, and followed that person to the corner. Was it only two days ago that I'd skulked around the backyard and heard the intruder? He or she had been carrying something that looked like a USPS Priority Mail Flat Rate envelope.

Now I thought it must have been Jules, whisking off whatever it was Sunni and her crew had found on his property tonight. Most likely a ledger book or financial data of some kind, something that would speak to the motive I'd conjured up: embezzlement, of course, but with nothing to go on other than his hesitancy to show Cliff the books.

It took no time for me to create a story in which Daisy had printed up a ledger sheet showing discrepancies that she wanted to talk to Jules about. Then, after they argued about the numbers, and Daisy was dead, Jules remembered the sheet and needed to retrieve it. He crept into Daisy's on the very day that I was there, and stole the sheet, shoving it into a nearby USPS envelope.

All clear. Why couldn't Sunni have simply told me that?

I wondered if it mattered that I'd seen Jules carrying off the evidence of his white-collar crime. I couldn't identify him with certainty, but the timing might be important to the case in another way. I'd never told Sunni about my venture onto the crime scene and then into the shop. Now was the time. Except it was almost midnight.

Before I could talk myself out of it, I dialed Sunni. She should have this information ASAP. And, by the way, maybe she'd rethink her decision to keep me out of the loop.

She answered after two rings. "What, Cassie?" Spoken with a long breath of annoyance.

"I'm sorry to call so late, Sunni. But I might have something important. I think I know when Jules picked up that evidence you mentioned."

I gave her as brief a summary as I could about my unauthorized visit to Daisy's shop, making sure to mention that the crime scene tape had been removed.

"Interesting," she said.

"Does it matter?"

"It might."

"Can you just tell me if it was a postal envelope that you found? One of the cardboard Flat Rate envelopes?"

"You certainly are persistent."

"Thanks?" I chuckled to show that I wasn't nervous about being a pest, and to remind her that we were BFFs.

"Yes, the item was in a postal envelope."

I suppressed an "aha." "Then he took it from Daisy's shop

while I was in the backyard. That would have been around five thirty on Thursday evening." How was that for being useful?

"Okay."

"I assume it was some kind of ledger sheet or financial stuff?"

"Good night, Cassie."

"Lunch tomorrow?" I asked, but all I got was a dial tone.

On Sunday morning, Eileen called with a reminder that the quilting group would be gathering on Monday evening to scope out and prepare the community room for the quilt display next Saturday.

"I don't have a completed quilt to show," I reminded her.

"First-years never do, dear, but we'd be glad to have your help anyway. We also need people to help at the refreshment table. If you wouldn't mind—"

"Not at all. I'll be glad to."

"Thanks, Cassie. It will be sad with Daisy missing, but nice to have a new face at the show."

The rest of the morning was strange. There was no Officer Ross when I peeked out the window. No one for me to track down and interrogate, since the case was solved. No to-do lists or made-up motives for murder. Not even the chance that Cliff would drop in with food and a new theory.

This should have been good news. Hadn't I wanted Daisy's killer caught? So what if I wasn't the one who found the evidence? I was free now as I'd hoped, to spend a relaxing day decompressing, unstressing my mind, and getting ready for Quinn's return. Maybe bake him his favorite lemon meringue pie. Or order one from our bakery. Linda was due for her visit in a few days. She deserved a clean guest room. And maybe the éclairs that she loved. Definitely a bakery order.

I didn't mind not being in on the search for Jules. I expected a full-out alert for him. If Pete's recollection was correct, he hadn't had much of a head start and he'd be in custody soon.

I forced myself into a round of deep-breathing exercises, a remnant of my halfhearted attempt at yoga a few years ago. It didn't even come close to taking my mind off the case. Was this another occupational hazard of police work? No relief, even after the case was solved?

But that was the problem. I wasn't satisfied with the resolution of the case. I needed one more beat, one more element of closure: I needed to know what evidence Sunni and her crew had uncovered during their search. "Where are they when you need them?" my father had often asked, mostly about doctors but equally for cops. It was clear that Sunni wasn't about to invite me to her briefings or call me with an update. And with no one tailing me, I wasn't likely to run into law enforcement. Getting back in the loop seemed hopeless.

Until I remembered that Officer Ross Little was a big fan of a new item on Mahican's menu: On Sunday morning only they served a Continental breakfast with fruit and breads and their usual good coffee. (The North Ashcot PD were a cut above coffee and donuts.)

Ross's shift ended about fifteen minutes ago. What were the chances? I dressed hurriedly and went forth to find out.

* * *

Sure enough, Ross had shown up at Mahican's. I found him exiting the buffet line and heading toward a table with a blue NAPD windbreaker flung over its accompanying chair. I waved and made a motion for him to save me a seat. No words would have reached him over the din of music and chatter. "All you can eat" was a big attraction in our town.

I tossed a pumpkin scone and half a banana onto a plate and rushed to join the cop, sitting by himself.

"What a nice coincidence, Ross. I miss you on my tail."

Ross smiled. "I'll bet. You're welcome to sit, but I'm not staying long. I'm just off my shift and ready to crash."

"But you want to go home on a full stomach."

"Exactly." He pointed to my place. "No coffee for you?" he asked.

"Later maybe. Right now I'm starving." For information, I meant, and I had a feeling he knew that.

We chatted about what a great idea Sunday brunch was, especially since it was self-serve, and open to seconds and thirds. Ross had loaded his plate with three muffins, a cinnamon roll, and a thick slice of banana bread. A single strawberry hung off the side.

He held up a blueberry muffin. "They make them smaller on Sundays," he said.

A good thing, if they wanted to stay in business. Now for my question. "Hey, Ross, I heard you guys cleared the case last evening." *Reminding you that I'm in the inner circle.*

"Looks that way."

"Sunni told me you found something in Jules's office."

She tells me everything. "In a post office envelope, of all things." A shared chuckle. "I guess it was one of those ledger books accountants seem to carry around."

"Did the chief tell you what we found?"

"She stopped in on her way home. She was in a rush, so she didn't go into detail."

The idea was, she would have, if she'd had time. I so hoped Ross got all my subtext.

"I'm sure she'll fill you in."

"You could save her some time and just—"

"Out with it, Cassie. You think I owe you because you didn't rat me out about working two jobs."

If it hadn't been for Ross's wide boyish grin, I'd have been worried that he'd arrest me for bribing an officer. "I don't want you to get in trouble," I said, stopping short of reminding him that he was a lame duck and had nothing to lose.

He leaned in toward me, but not before downing a large chunk of sugar frosting from the cinnamon roll. "It was a small notebook, like the kind my girlfriend carries in her purse, with a flowery cover."

"Not money related?"

"Didn't seem to be."

"Why would he take something like that?"

"Beats me. I thought it was strange, too. Maybe he thought it was important, then realized it wasn't."

I'd been so sure the police had found financial spreadsheets or pages from a ledger that I had trouble adjusting to this new image of the contents of the Flat Rate envelope. "Why would a simple notebook be incriminating? Just because it was Daisy's?"

"There was also the fact that he happened to close out his accounts and take off." Ross drained his cup and I had a feeling he'd be on his way in a minute. "And then, there was the paint, too," he added, pushing his chair back.

"What about paint?" I asked.

"Gotta go, Cassie."

"Wait—do you think that's it?" I asked. "Is the case really closed?" By now he'd stood, a large man despite his surname, and I was conscious of having to look up at him. I tried not to raise my voice. We'd been lucky so far to have constant upbeat music and a loud group of women two small tables over.

"Until we find him and he hires a lawyer. Less than a week and it won't matter to me."

"Okay. Thanks, Ross."

He grabbed his jacket and held up his hand. "Don't thank me. Please, Cassie. Okay?"

I pressed my lips together in a gesture of silence, went to the counter, and ordered a large cappuccino, double shot.

On the way home I should have felt a sense of satisfaction. After all, I'd played a part in the investigation. The chief of police had given me an assignment and I'd followed through, managing to interview most of the quilters, and annoy some of them. And though she wouldn't reveal the resolution, Sunni had given me credit for getting Molly Boyd to own up to her presence in Daisy's backyard moments before it became a crime scene. It didn't matter that I wasn't the one to have uncovered this last bit of evidence.

I wished I had stuck it out with Ross and pressed him

to tell me about the mysterious paint. He wasn't that hard to manipulate. Had there been paint at the crime scene? Not that I could remember in all the back-and-forth with Sunni. And there was also something funny about the notebook with the flowery cover, but I couldn't put my finger on it.

My car rang, the hands-free link startling me as it always did. With no caller ID screen, I had to take potluck and click the ON button.

"Hey, Cassie," Quinn said in a voice that said he had bad news.

"Are you on your way home?"

"I wish. The big estate sale is great, but I ran out of cash and checks and they won't take a credit card."

"Who doesn't take a credit card?"

"This one dealer apparently. Meanwhile, Fred's away and the kid who's in charge of the store doesn't have access to the accounts, so I have to wait until the bank opens in the morning. I am so bummed."

What good was the Internet when people like Cliff and Quinn had to wait to do business on Monday morning, as if it were 1950? I wanted to explain the many reasons why I was more bummed than Quinn was, but didn't want to make him feel worse. He spent a few more minutes running through all the negotiation it took to have the dealer hold the merchandise and spell out the terms of the transaction.

"I'm not even sure it's worth the haul, but Fred seemed to think so. Now he's off somewhere and I can't get to the money to pay for it."

"You're only a couple of hours away. I could drive out. We could at least have dinner together." Even a long drive by myself seemed better than hanging around my empty house.

"Manchester is over three hours with traffic, and dinner will be at a vending machine. And you'd have to leave at dawn for work in the morning. No, I'll tough it out, and I'll make it up to you, I promise. I already have something very cool that I picked up for you."

"As long as it's not a ten-thousand-dollar mirror."

"Much more personal, I promise."

"Skype tonight?"

"You bet," he said.

I'd pulled over to give my attention to the call and ended up at the curb in front of the police station. Not the best spot in town to put my head down and feel sorry for myself. Not that I had a legitimate reason for whining. Quinn was the one stuck in a motel and working on a Sunday.

Still, I couldn't remember a more upsetting, frustrating week. I gripped my steering wheel—holding fast so I wouldn't do something foolish and storm into the building demanding answers from the chief of police. I came to my senses and drove around the block, parking again behind the bank. I'd decided to storm into Pete's hardware store instead and interrogate the last remaining quilter on my list, Andrea Harris. If anyone knew about paint, she did.

"We don't see you for months outside the post office, and now twice in one weekend? What's up, Cassie?" Pete removed his painter's hat, wiped his brow, and replaced the cap. He seemed nervous and I suspected he thought I was back to quiz him about the meeting in Molly's salon. Unlike his sister and her husband, Pete was known to be politically neutral, avoiding any discussion even the slightest bit political in nature. He was about the same age as my mentor, Ben, I guessed, and had figured out how to get along with everyone.

"I thought it was about time I spruced up my patio, maybe do a little painting. The summer won't last forever."

"Glad to help. What color scheme do you have in mind?"

"I'll bet she's thinking of a shade of red."

Another country heard from, as Aunt Tess used to say. Andrea had come up behind her brother. She wore a standard burgundy apron over jeans and a long-sleeved T-shirt reminiscent of men's underwear.

Pete, his hands in the pockets of a matching logo apron, tilted his head toward his sister. "She's good, isn't she?" He addressed her. "How in the world do you know that, Andy?"

Her crooked smile appeared. "There's a rumor going around about red paint found at the crime scene across the street, and I would have bet money that our own little private eye here would be trying to trace the source."

I was more than a bit annoyed. First, I wasn't "little." More accurately, next to Andrea's pudgy five-two or so, and her shorter-than-average brother and husband, I was an Amazon. Second, I wasn't a private eye; I was a semiofficial deputy with the NAPD. Until last night, anyway. Finally, I wanted to say, "Thanks, Andy, for reminding me about the red blob found on Daisy's wrist." I now knew it was paint, not blood and not ink.

"I guess I have what I came for," I said.

Pete seemed confused, but rose to the occasion. "We should all be relieved that this terrible crime is behind us.

It doesn't matter who solved it." He removed his hands from his pockets and brushed them off, either because his apron was dusty or because he wanted to be rid of the unpleasant topic.

"Amen," Andrea said, turning to walk away.

"You know, I've been meaning to ask you, Andrea," I said to her retreating back. "How come I wasn't invited to the meeting about the farmers' market proposal the other night?"

Andrea grunted. "Why on earth would we include a prodigal daughter who might beat it back to Boston any day?" she answered, still walking.

Pete was clearly dismayed, as he had been when I queried him yesterday. "Anything else, Cassie?" he asked me, extra polite, to make up for his sister's rudeness. "Still want some supplies?"

"Another time," I said. I patted my jacket pocket. "I think that's my phone."

Fortunately, it wasn't, but I could slip away on the ruse.

Home on my rocker, half-asleep from a many-layered sandwich I'd bought from Mahican's packaged-foods counter, I was pleased to have another piece of data. Red paint. I tried to fill in the blanks of why that mattered. Had Jules recently painted something in his office? The only painted surfaces I remembered were the brown baseboards and the white walls. But I'd been there only once and hadn't scouted around, either.

I sat up, flashing on another source. Cliff Harmon, and his semilegal rummaging upstairs in Jules's office.

Was I really about to initiate a call to Daisy's husband, the guy I was purportedly glad to be rid of for a while? I weighed the options. A boring afternoon with a vacuum cleaner and dust cloth, or the chance to put pieces of a puzzle together. I punched Cliff's number.

"Cassie?" Cliff seemed almost happier to hear from me than Quinn or Linda would be. Certainly more pleased than Sunni would have been. "Cassie, I'm glad you called. What's up?"

"First"—(I lied)—"how are you?"

"Good as can be expected, you know. I got here after a layover at JFK, believe it or not. I was a wreck, thinking, what if they took Daisy off the plane in New York by mistake? They didn't, of course, and a friend of Daisy's parents drove them to the Miami Airport to pick me up. Daisy was picked up directly by the funeral home, and now we're all just waiting to be able to see her."

Cliff's voice was shaky and excited at the same time. I imagined he hadn't had much sleep. And facing his in-laws couldn't have been fun. Still, he continued talking, giving me details of the weather ("hot and humid, like home") as well as the service in a couple of days. "Any news there, Cassie? About Jules?"

"They have a warrant out," I said, though I wasn't even sure that was the right term. "They're looking for him."

He blew out a breath and I knew he was wondering if there was any hope that his money was safe, or that he'd see justice for his wife's murder. Before I could gather courage to ask my question, Cliff got ahead of me.

"Do you know anything more about that red paint they're talking about?" he asked. "Did they find the receipt?"

"How did you hear about that?"

"You know I'm friends with Pete. He told me the cops were asking if Jules bought red paint recently."

"I'm surprised Pete was willing to own up to any knowledge of the case. Unless . . . did you bully him again?"

"I might have. He's Jules's landlord, after all, so I might have leaned on him for information. There have to be some perks to this low-paying job. And you got to remember, I know everyone's alarm codes."

It was nice to hear a chuckle from the grieving widower. "Did he? I mean, did Jules buy red paint?" I asked.

"Apparently, some receipts got screwed up on the cash register and they can't tell for sure. Pete doesn't have the most up-to-date system. But there was a small open can of the same color red on Jules's little porch on the second floor."

"I'm not sure why that incriminates him. It might have been bought years ago, even by another tenant. Do you remember seeing anything red in Jules's office when you were looking around?"

"Not really."

"Don't you find that curious?" I asked.

"No, I don't. Maybe he painted something at home. Maybe he helped a friend touch up a red fence." He paused, breathing hard. "Cassie, are you trying to clear Jules?" Cliff's voice turned sour.

I wished we weren't having this conversation over the phone. Or at all. "No, no. I'm just trying to understand." And be sure we had the right person.

"Well, I understand completely. And I hope they catch him pretty quick, before he spends all our hard-earned money."

"I'm with you one hundred percent, Cliff, and I hope the same thing. I'm sorry I upset you."

"It's okay. It's not the greatest time for me, you know. I wish I were home in a way. But in another way, I'd like to stay down here and hide out where there are no memories. I'm not sure I can go back to North Ashcot and just pick up where I left off last week."

I wished I could give him advice, but I knew for a fact that nothing would help until more time had passed. A lot more. "Is there anything I can do for you up here while you're away?"

"Yeah, tell that best friend of yours who's the police chief to get on the ball and find Jules Edwards and slap him in jail."

I promised I'd try. I was glad I'd held back and not admitted that I was leaning toward a rigged-up red paint story.

20

The afternoon news was all Jules Edwards, all the time, his face coming up on the screen continually. There was talk of decades of white-collar crime, citing other cities he'd lived in, other client victims who might be willing to be named. I found it impressive that the media could pull together all that (dis?)information so quickly. The main photo shown was of a much younger man. I guessed it was taken during his college days, which were probably about thirty years ago. That estimate also fit with the eighties hairstyle—longish and straight in the back with a bird's nest on top. Maybe when you strike out as a career embezzler, you make sure you're not looking straight at the camera.

I thought about Jules's office and the lack of personal photos there. Most local businesspeople made sure to be seen around town, donating to academic programs or athletics and hanging the evidence of their generosity on their walls in the form of photo ops with city and state officials. But Jules was not trying to be the face of North Ashcot.

No one offered guesses about where the errant accountant might have gone. He'd apparently never married and had no family anyone was aware of. "I wouldn't be surprised," said one anchorwoman, "if he's lived under more than one name."

One interviewee, a man on the street who was somewhat familiar to me, mentioned that "Edwards was a newcomer. Here only about ten years." That was North Ashcot for you. Ten years barely got you on the voter registry.

Finally, Ben himself had a theory, as laid out in one of our catch-up phone calls. "You say Cliff is in Miami?"

"Yes, you know—to put his wife to rest there."

"And he'll be back?"

"I imagine so, though he did mention he thought he might have a hard time adjusting to North Ashcot without Daisy."

"Uh-huh."

"Uh-huh what?"

"Nothing. Just Jules is gone and Cliff might also be gone. Seem like a coincidence to you?"

I blew out a breath. Here was Ben, not letting go of Cliff as his main suspect. "Yes," I said. "Yes, it does seem like a coincidence."

I hung up, only the tiniest bit of doubt insinuating itself into my mind.

Having exhausted the red paint issue, I turned my attention to the meeting I hadn't been invited to, which I was now convinced had to do with the farmers' market proposal. Was it the ten-year problem? Angela had implied as much, with her accusation that I couldn't be trusted to stay around very long. Or was there another reason?

I thought back to the group of people I'd seen outside the salon. At the time, I couldn't figure out what they had in common. I ran through the list in my head again. Reggie Harris, developer and owner of the property suggested for the market; Andrea Harris, his wife and part-time hardware store employee in the store owned by her brother, Pete, who had also been present; Molly Boyd, beauty salon owner; Fran Rogers, bank teller; Mike Forbes, bike shop owner; Fred Bateman, antiques shop owner. An assortment of other businesspeople I couldn't name, but recognized from the dry cleaners, the phone company store, and Paulie's Party Planet. Plus Catherine Bright, our chief real estate agent, whose face was on every bench in town.

This time, I added a list of people who were not present. Not Liv Patterson, card shop owner, or Rosie Vaughn, who ran the bakery on the corner of Second and Main, or the Chaplin brothers, who operated the convenience market, though the brothers had never shown an interest in being a true grocery store anyway.

Eliminating myself as a newcomer, I examined the groupings. I was sure it had to be their businesses and not their personal lives that brought them together for the meeting or disinvited them. Finally, I had it, so obvious I couldn't believe it had taken me this long. It served me right for focusing on the quilters and on my own small-minded desire to fit in.

The answer: None of the attendees had business interests that conflicted with those of the vendors at a farmers' market. Every one of them was a potential supporter of Reggie Harris's proposal. Not only did they have nothing to lose; they had everything to gain from the influx of week-end shoppers.

I sat back on my rocker, a mug of fresh coffee on the table next to me. One that Quinn had found for me recently. It was time to call in a favor from my absent boyfriend. Hadn't he all but stood me up this weekend? Promising to come back with a present. Putting it off, a day at a time. For all I knew, he was dining in style, not at a vending machine, while I was slaving away, working at my job, plus working overtime, pounding the pavement to help the police with a homicide investigation.

I'd become a drama queen, marvel of exaggeration, but the strategy had worked on my psyche and given me the confidence I needed to approach Quinn. I'd thought of the perfect excuse to query him and, even better, I'd tracked him down while he was enjoying a Sunday-afternoon nap.

"No problem," he said when I gave in and apologized for waking him up. "I sleep when I'm bored."

"I'm feeling down today. Like I'm being left out of things," I said. I refreshed his memory about seeing his boss at the gathering of businesspeople on Friday night. "Can you find out from Fred what that meeting was about? Do you think he'd tell you if I was doing something to alienate people?"

"It was nothing like that, Cassie. I'm sure of it. I'm sorry you've been worried about that."

Was this going to be easier than I thought? The best that I could hope for—that Quinn already knew what the meeting was about? Was I a bad person for taking advantage of a nice guy? I braced myself. I couldn't back down now. "I know I'm still thought of as a newcomer, or even worse, as someone who fled town and came crawling back. But I've been trying my best."

"Trust me, Cassie—that meeting had nothing to do with whether people like you or not or whether you're doing a good job. You're doing a great job, in fact. It's your customers who matter and we know they love you."

I didn't go so far as to sniffle, but aimed for sounding a little hurt. "How can you be so sure?"

He cleared his throat and I heard him take a swallow—sipping his favorite lime-flavored sparkling water, I'd have bet. We called it his comfort drink. "Well, it's supposed to be confidential, but it's not like it's about national security or I'm breaching a legal contract." He took a breath. "The meeting was to gather support for the farmers' market proposal. Reggie Harris pulled together the people who would benefit from having one in town. Including Ashcot's Attic, of course, so Fred was there. There's no doubt that communities benefit from increased shopping opportunities, on weekends especially. And you've always claimed your job prohibits you from participating in political gatherings. I'm sure that's the only reason you weren't invited."

I took a sip of my own comfort drink, now lukewarm. "That makes sense," I said. "I'll bet Reggie's offering incentives for support, since it's his property and all."

"Oh, sure, they're negotiating some kind of deal. But Reggie apparently has much bigger plans for the town. He's calling it 'Plan North Ashcot' or something like that, trying to build on a lot of unused property on the outskirts. New playground, arts center, if I remember correctly. The farmers' market is kind of the kickoff project."

"And he'll be asking for support for all that, I guess. I'll bet the motivation to participate is pretty attractive."

"Yeah, he'll probably include mention of the participating businesses on flyers, call them sponsors or something."

"Or offer kickbacks?"

"Nothing illegal, if that's what you mean. At least not that my boss is involved in. The idea is that eventually everyone will profit. Fred's working with him on a component to make a bigger deal of North Ashcot as an antique capital of the world." He laughed. "I'm glad I'm just a regular employee who has to go on an occasional road trip. Someone else can worry about how businesses work together."

"Some businesses and not others."

"What's going on, Cassie?"

"Just wondering why all the secrecy if there's nothing illegal happening." I thought about my trip to Knox Valley and the shunning I received when I made simple inquiries. "People are slinking around, not answering questions. It sure looks suspicious."

"Understandable when you know about the last time Reggie proposed something like this. It happened just before I arrived in town, and apparently he tried to spread the news about his idea and it was a colossal failure. Vendors copping out, Main Street merchants protesting, customers not happy. I guess this time he decided to strategize first and come up with a more formal, businesslike plan."

"One he wanted to keep tightly controlled, apparently."

"Yup. And also to prevent having it be spun a negative

way and look bad for the vendors that are part of the sponsorship."

"Like maybe that they don't care about their fellow merchants on Main Street? The ones who might be hurt by going elbow-to-elbow with people selling the same wares."

"But business is business, I guess. I'm not that tuned in; it's one reason I never want to have my own place." Quinn uttered a little gasp, then said, "Cassie." As if he'd been talking in his sleep up to now and finally figured out what our conversation was about. "I should have known. Your feelings weren't hurt at all. You're digging for dirt on Reggie." He grunted, half-annoyed, half-proud of me, I thought.

"Thanks, Quinn. You can go back to sleep now."

I refilled my mug, searched out a snack from my kitchen, and returned to my living room. I sat quietly, absorbing the new information. Reggie was stacking the deck. He wanted his proposal to pass through the selectmen. But Quinn was right. That's how business is done, whether in a big city or a small town. It didn't mean that Reggie had to kill someone to get his way, and he certainly couldn't be afraid of blackmail or any exposure of his perfectly legal strategy.

In any case, I was glad I didn't have to be part of such wheeling and dealing, and I was glad my boyfriend didn't want any part of it, either. I couldn't blame him for letting his boss take the lead in business decisions.

My call to Quinn had been so satisfying that I allowed myself a nap, too.

Linda's call woke me up. I guessed that was what Sundays were for. Naps and phone calls.

We talked about her upcoming trip, which might begin as early as Thursday, for a really long weekend.

"We haven't heard much about your case, but someone's picture was on the news today as prime suspect."

I briefed Linda on Jules Edwards and the evidence against him, the most incriminating being his flight from town and all his clients.

"No surprise it's a money guy," she said.

"I'm sure there are some honest ones," I said. "And it doesn't mean they're all killers." I found myself defending Jules, pointing out how weak and maybe suspicious the red paint evidence was.

"Wait, I thought you said two minutes ago that you don't think the farmers' market guy is doing anything sketchy. Doesn't that more or less leave the accountant hanging out there? Who else could it be but a runaway embezzler?"

"There's still something not right."

"What?"

"I don't know. Maybe nothing."

"Probably nothing. I think you're just bored in that little town. Tell me you don't miss the string of bookstores and coffee shops around the Fenway. They still ask about you at Common Coffee. And when was the last time you saw a decent art exhibit? Or heard a live concert?"

I figured the Ashcot High Choral Society didn't count in Linda's book. "Let's talk about your weekend coming up."

"Okay. Tell me again what people are wearing to the party?"

I did my best to explain one more time that Saturday's "party" was actually a parade followed by a community gathering with a quilt display and refreshments. People would probably be wearing what they wore to do their post office errands every day. Except for the ones in Revolutionary War garb.

"Got it," she said.

"Leave your little black dresses and clutch purses at home," I added, in case she really didn't get it.

I was faced with dinner alone again, missing the nearly constant interaction I'd had with Sunni, the high-end takeout from Cliff (with accompanying nagging), and even being tailed by one of NAPD's finest.

Try as I might, I couldn't feel one hundred percent satisfied with the resolution of Daisy's murder. I felt I was betraying her by rejecting her accusations against Reggie Harris. He might be guilty of greed and self-serving business deals, but that wasn't the same as trying to turn a simple farmers' market into a front for illegal substances. Daisy was wrong about that, and I had to face it.

I knew I should also abandon any hope of resolving the niggling doubt I had about Jules's guilt, especially since Sunni had cut me off at the end of the investigation. Ross's hints had been enticing, but without a context, I was left hanging. A splotch of red paint? A notebook with a flowery cover? So what? It would have been different if I could have read the files and had a few complete sentences to work with. Some friend the chief of police was.

My phone rang and my screen lit up with the North Ashcot PD number. I looked around as if I might see Sunni swinging from my light fixture, or watching me through a tiny camera stuck in my pen holder.

I clicked the phone on. Would I have a dinner companion after all?

"We picked up Jules," Sunni said.

"Wow," I said, meaning "Wow" they'd picked him up, and "Wow" she was letting me know personally. "He was ready to cross the border near Montreal. New haircut, a different car, but it was Jules. You'll probably see it on the news in a few minutes."

So, not too much of a heads-up. "How did they find him?"

"A used car salesman, believe it or not, made himself useful. He thought there was something fishy when the guy paid cash, then came out of the restroom with different hair."

"Has he confessed?"

"He's en route. We'll talk to him when he gets here. Probably first thing in the morning. But he had all kinds of incriminating documents with him, stuff he probably should have shredded before he left."

"Maybe he intended to burn it all in Canada."

I wished I knew why Sunni was calling. Was she reinstating me? Apologizing for being so short with me during her little stopover? I didn't know if I should push my luck and ask about Daisy's murder. Not directly, I decided.

"Does that mean Cliff might get his money back?"

"Hard to tell how these things work. The smart ones have all kinds of ways of skirting the law, evading taxes, hiding their money, even after they're caught."

"Good thing Jules isn't that smart," I said.

Sunni laughed, the desired effect. "Good thing."

"Thanks for letting me know."

"Yeah, well, you were a big help with that part of the

case." Making it clear, spelling out what I'd done, lest I have delusions of grandeur. "We should have lunch this week."

"Definitely."

Meaning, peanut butter and jelly alone tonight.

I pulled my computer onto my lap and started a scheduled Skype call to Quinn.

His broad smile told me he wasn't too mad that I'd used him to gain inside information on the farmers' market proposal this afternoon. He didn't have to know that I would have done it so much sooner if I'd known how much he was privy to.

We focused on his return tomorrow, the activities surrounding the Henry Knox celebration, Linda's visit. Happy talk.

I noticed luggage packed up, stacked on the bed behind him.

"I'm getting a head start," he said when I commented. "I don't want to be here a minute longer than I have to."

"Works for me."

Later, when I closed up in preparation for bed, locking doors and windows, I realized it was the first time in a week that I wasn't worried about a note stuck under my door or squeezed into a crack somewhere.

The town of North Ashcot could rest. Daisy's killer had been caught. Jules was in custody. The case was over, all threats gone.

I wished I really believed it.

21

The best thing about Monday morning was that there were no more nasty notes from "Anonymous" telling me to do my job or go home, or otherwise threatening my well-being. The only thing in the delivery room with my name on it was a package containing the new sandals I'd ordered. The heels were a little higher and more pointy than I usually wore, but sometimes style took over practicality when I looked at footwear. Besides, there might have been some element of impressing Linda with a big-city look on my feet.

I was getting used to the idea that Jules really was both an embezzler and a murderer, as well as my stalker. Who was I to question the quantity and quality of evidence the police had put together against him? It was time to give my tired brain a rest and enjoy the job I was getting paid to do.

I stuffed the post office boxes and prepared the retail counter for a normal business day. We were off to a good start with the Raleys showing up first, bearing an already agile, soft-furred baby genet. From birth, its striped tail was at least as long as its body, making it difficult to control the squirming animal on my scale.

"It sure makes him easier to catch, though," George said as the rest of my customers enjoyed the antics of the big-eyed feline.

It felt good to greet new customers and old, to accept letters and packages with goodies going to military addresses. When a middle-aged woman told me she'd read on social media about the great service she could expect at the North Ashcot Post Office, I was pleased, and thought maybe Quinn was right, that I was doing a good job in the way that it mattered.

Ben came around with a dose of reality, letting me know that someone wrote a letter to the editor of the *Town Crier* complaining about the "too-friendly postal clerk" who held up the lines to chat with her friends.

"You can't please 'em all," Ben wisely noted.

I closed up on Monday evening, lowering the flag as usual, feeling cheerful now that Quinn was on his way home. We'd texted throughout the day and I learned the step-by-step process of accessing money from a remote bank. I also had something to look forward to—the quilters and our helpers would be meeting to begin work on the display in the community room adjoining my office, the room that had become the lunchroom where Cliff lured me into helping him with Daisy's case. I gave Quinn my schedule. The plan was that he'd call or text when he was close and find me either at home or at the community room.

There wasn't enough time for me to go home now and

return to the community room in time for the meeting. I headed across the street instead, to Mahican's, where I could pick up a snack that would have to pass for dinner.

I wasn't alone in my decision. Several members of the quilting group—Fran, Molly, and Liv, all of whom worked in the same block along Main Street—plus Eileen and Terry, were seated at one of the rectangular tables along the side wall.

Fran waved me over. "Looks like we all had the same idea," she said.

"Who wants to go home and cook and rush right out?" Molly asked, opening a plastic cup of cut-up fruit.

"Who wants to stay at home and cook for a guy watching football?" Eileen asked.

"Who needs a three-course dinner when there are girl-friends around?" Terry asked, enjoying her usual nut-filled brownie.

We chimed in with a chorus of ayes and nays, making me happy to belong to a social group. Only Liv snuck in a glare in my direction, giving me a thin smile, a step up from nearly throwing me out of her shop the other day. At one time or another, I'd annoyed these ladies, grilling them for alibis or otherwise bothering them with questions or insinuations. I was lucky they were willing to include me tonight.

I took a seat and joined the chatter. How many quilts would we display? (No more than two for each member, preferably of different sizes.) Who would be responsible for the signage? (Liv, who had a background in graphic design.) For organizing the raffle? (Fran, who'd done it several times in the past.) For answering questions during the show? (We needed a schedule for taking shifts.) In what order should the quilts be arranged? (By size, said Terry, overruled by Liv, who said color, and then Eileen, who said complexity of design.) I wondered if the parade organizers had as many details to work out as we did. We agreed on one thing, that next year we'd start the planning sooner.

Everyone was delighted when I volunteered to take care of the refreshment table. I questioned whether I should subject Linda to the task, but she might as well know what small-town life was really like. I had in mind seeking out contributions from known bakers and perhaps trying a recipe or two myself. What would Linda think of that?

About twenty minutes before seven, Andrea came in, apologizing for missing the meeting-before-the-meeting. Pete had to make a last-minute delivery, she told us, and she was left to close out the register.

"Any jobs left for me?" she asked. She listened to the list of tasks, all of which could use extra assistance. "Why don't I help Cassie with the goodies table?" she said.

"That would be great," I said, after nearly choking on a grain of sugar from my muffin. It wasn't good to be surprised while eating.

"In fact, I have an idea for including Cassie even though this is her first year. Why don't we have a special table for a work in progress, to show how far a beginner can get?"

"What a perfect way to encourage new members," Eileen said.

No one else seemed shocked at the good mood Andrea was in, and the enthusiasm and camaraderie Andrea greeted me with. I realized no one could have known how rude

Andrea had been to me in the hardware store, and probably all were grateful that she and Liv had seemed to work things out after Tuesday's rough spots. Plus, they all knew her longer and better than I did.

Before I knew it, Andrea had turned the conversation to Jules Edwards. "Such a relief, isn't it?" she said. "Jules has been caught. I hope we can all move on. Cliff can certainly use our support when he's back."

"I'll bet he's glad he doesn't have an unresolved murder hanging over his head," Terry said.

"I didn't think Jules would be that dumb," Molly said. "To leave things around like that. Taking Daisy's notebook? What was he thinking?"

"I heard there were a ton of meetings scheduled with him on the calendar pages and he was trying to hide the fact that Daisy might be onto him," Fran said.

"Where did you hear that?" Liv asked. "All I heard was that it was the notebook Daisy thought she lost, the one she always had by the register."

"With the van Gogh sunflowers," Molly added. "Isn't that the name of the painting?"

"Yes, and who knows why he'd latch onto that notebook? But leaving the paint can? That was super stupid," Terry said.

There it was again. All the evidence that last night I had thought was confidential was out in the open. The town seemed to get smaller with every gathering like this. Where was the leak? Or leaks? Did Sunni's officers have large families? Were they all, like Ross, vulnerable to a little nudge in the direction of gossip?

I thought of a quote from Benjamin Franklin, the country's first postmaster general, "Three may keep a secret if two of them are dead." That was certainly true of a small town.

But something popped out of all the gossip. "Did you say van Gogh's *Sunflowers*?" I asked.

Molly answered, "Yes, that was her book of the year. Remember every year she had a new one, with some famous painting. This year it was *Sunflowers*."

"Something wrong, Cassie?" Fran asked.

I realized I'd zoned out, focusing on the sunflowers. Wasn't that the notebook I'd rescued from behind the filing cabinets? The book I'd flipped through and then left on a nearby table? But Jules had already accomplished his mission that evening—he'd taken the ledger sheets and walked away before I snooped around and placed the notebook in plain sight. Why would he come back? What if someone else took the notebook after Jules left town, in an attempt to frame him? More likely, what if I was losing control of my ability to focus and think clearly? There was no reason for me to question or care why Jules did what he did.

Andrea and Terry made a few more attempts to keep the Jules Edwards conversation going. One attempt involved praising our chief of police and all her staff. "North Ashcot's finest," Terry said, as if rallying a cheerleading squad.

In spite of my attempts to keep out of it, I felt compelled to add my two cents. "Does anyone else think it's a little too premature to condemn Jules?" I asked. "I mean, we haven't heard his side of the story, and the evidence is kind of thin." Plus, I needed time to process this new wrinkle by van Gogh.

When everyone stopped talking and gave me strange looks, I realized it had not been the greatest idea to speak up.

"Time to pack up," said Liv, who had refrained from the rally, and had decided on her own to put an end to the prattle.

We gathered our things—tossing trash, scraping chairs on the tile, wrapping up bits of conversation—and left the café. Andrea caught up with me as we crossed Main Street, doing her best to match her short strides to my long ones. When we reached the opposite sidewalk, she stopped, out of breath, and motioned me to pause with her.

"I want to apologize for being incredibly rude to you yesterday, Cassie. When Pete pointed it out to me, I was horrified. I guess I've been on edge with this proposal of Reggie's. He worked so hard on it and it's so important for his plans for the future of the town. Nothing matters more to him, but I never wanted to insult you or hurt your feelings. Everyone's glad you're back in town."

It was hard to reconcile this contrite, caring woman with the vindictive Andrea Harris of yesterday, but I did of course accept her apology.

In the community room, the others had already set to work. Pete joined us, bringing the necessary tape measures, sketches of the proposed layout, and hardware for hanging our quilts. A partylike atmosphere prevailed. With Jules's capture in the back of my mind, it should have been easy to relax and get in the spirit of Henry Knox Day.

If only. Now and then, without warning, a last bit of the puzzle called out to be fit into the picture. I felt it was closer now than ever, but still fuzzy, not quite clicking into place.

We were about ready to call it a night when a text came in with good news from Quinn.

An hour out. See you soon!

Just what I needed.

One by one, we left the room, were picked up, or got in our own cars. Eileen, becoming the new mother hen in Daisy's place, volunteered to lock up.

I drove home, thinking that Quinn's return might be the final piece I needed to put things right in my mind. It could be like turning the clock back a week, I told myself. Back to my regular job, lunches with Sunni, dinners with my boyfriend, my best Boston friend coming to visit, and, to top it all off, a parade on Saturday. Perfect.

I'd stopped at the convenience market and found enough food choices to make Quinn feel welcome and now had a rare moment of wanting to prepare a home-cooked meal. I pulled the beginnings of chicken soup from my freezer, added fresh ingredients, and turned on the stove.

I kicked off my new sandals and settled back to wait for a car in my driveway, eventually enjoying the smell of chicken, carrots, and sage. I resolved to cook more often.

Fat chance, said an inner voice that sounded vaguely like Linda's.

One more text from Quinn told me he was close to exiting Route 8 and was stalled by an accident.

Scene clearing up, he wrote. Maybe 30 min more.

I'd nodded off (cooking was hard work) when I heard a knock on my back door. I thought it curious that I hadn't heard a car, and that Quinn had arrived at the back instead of the front of my house. Maybe his idea of a romantic surprise.

I shook myself awake, straightened my clothes, and smiled my way to the door. I opened it as wide as it would go, hindered as it was by a lineup of potted plants waiting for attention, and greeted—Andrea Harris.

22

I tried to cover my amazement that it was not my wandering boyfriend who'd returned at last, but Andrea Harris at my back door.

She wore a heavy jacket, a double-breasted navy blue knee-length with large buttons, the modern equivalent of my dad's old pea coat. Not what I would expect on a typical August night, not cool enough for most of us, maybe seventy degrees, even a couple of hours after sundown. She sniffed the air and breathed out appreciatively. "Smells wonderful. Too bad I can't stay for dinner, but I have to make this quick."

I stammered out a few syllables and ended with "Hey, Andrea," spoken as a question.

"I'm sure this is a surprise, but I find I have no choice."

I gasped as my mind locked on to the reality of the moment. This was not overkill to make amends for a brief exchange of unpleasantness. This was a woman who realized that I'd figured out how Daisy's notebook came to be in Jules's office. She'd been wrong until now, but she wouldn't believe that.

I screamed, something akin to "No," as loudly as I could. I tried to close the door on her, but she'd already shoved her chubby knee and equally heavy elbow into the wooden panels and pushed me inside. I stumbled back and she pushed both of us over the threshold, back into the kitchen, wrecking my counter organization in the process.

She reached into the pocket of her heavy jacket. And pulled out a gun.

I screamed again (I think) and stepped back, nearly knocking over a kitchen chair. "Andrea . . . ," I stammered.

"Don't worry, Cassie. I'm not going to shoot you." She looked at the gun, and for a long minute I thought she was going to kill herself. "It's my brother's," she said, as if I'd asked or might care about its ownership. "He has it for protection in the store, and I wouldn't want Pete involved in this. He's too law-abiding. Some might say wishy-washy." She waved her hand in a wishy-washy gesture, making me back away a few more steps.

I almost asked why—why was Andrea holding a gun on me? But we both knew why. Andrea was giving me more credit than I deserved. She'd guessed correctly that I figured out the notebook was planted to frame Jules. What she didn't know was that I hadn't fingered her. Yet. I wondered if I could convince her now that I knew nothing and therefore was not a threat to her. Too late? Probably. I tried anyway. There was, after all, a gun pointed at me. I'd try anything.

"I didn't know it was you," I said. Pitiful.

"You would have, eventually. I saw it in your face. And being best friends with the chief, well, you'd never give up trying to figure it all out. I had the paint and I went looking for something else to frame Jules with. Dumb," she said, knocking the gun on the side of her head.

"Andrea, I—"

"Stop. You've done enough. I'm not sorry it happened. I couldn't let Daisy ruin our lifestyle. The things she was accusing Reggie of would have ruined him and all his plans. And what else could we have done in this town?"

When she waved the gun for emphasis, I held my breath, half thinking I might be able to wrestle it from her, but I couldn't take that chance. I was taller, but she was probably heavier. And armed. And still talking. That last was a good thing, I figured.

"We work hard for what we have, Reggie and me. Daisy didn't seem to get that. She called us royalty, as if everything has been handed to us."

"I know how hard you work, Andrea. Daisy was just focused on her own survival in a small business." What was I doing defending the victim to her killer?

"It's a little late to sort all that out, isn't it? And you, you just wouldn't let it drop. So what if Jules paid a little more for his crime? He stole on purpose; I never meant for Daisy to die."

Andrea's logic left a lot to be desired, but I did understand that it made sense to her. Did it matter that she would have left me alone if I hadn't turned into an investigator? I felt drunk, though I'd had nothing but coffee and a spoonful of soup to drink. Was it too late to take it all back? I had to try.

"The police will understand that Daisy's death was an accident, Andrea. You didn't mean to kill her. You were arguing and it . . . it just happened." Speaking as one who was at the crime scene? Not. Another brilliant tactic.

Andrea put the gun to her head—not pointing as if to shoot herself, but using it to massage her scalp. "I just wanted to talk some sense into her." She seemed near tears; I thought I heard sniffling. "She didn't even have a big stake in the outcome of Reggie's project. Our project, which will put North Ashcot on the map. Daisy just needed some cause, some reason to speak out."

I tried my most soothing voice, fraught though I was with anxiety. "You can just tell Sunni that, Andrea. We're friends, you know, and I can go with you and—"

"No, no, no." Her sobs turned to angry screams and she began another gun-waving episode. "That's not how this is going to work. You're going to have an accident just like Daisy did, except we don't have a storm to help out. But we'll manage. You're going to follow me out of your house and down the back stairs, and we're going to take a ride in your car."

I froze. I didn't want to leave the safety of my home, even though it was now populated by a killer with a gun. "Quinn, my boyfriend, is going to be here any minute."

Andrea threw her head back and laughed. A crazy laugh. I saw the extent of her fury in her eyes. "Nice try."

I looked at the kitchen clock. Only twenty minutes since Quinn's last text. My nap couldn't have lasted more than ten minutes. I had to stall only another ten, and Quinn would ride up and rescue me. I smiled in spite of my terrifying situation.

As if I could count on a travel estimate when Route 8 was involved.

I saw our plans for the rest of the summer and early fall disappear. No walking the Ashuwillticook Trail, hiking our little section of the Appalachian Trail, taking selfies on the way. I saw our post office flag at half-mast. My senses peaked and I smelled the sage in the pot next to me, heard the bubbling chicken broth. I considered dumping the Crock-Pot on the floor as a distraction, but then what? She'd still have the gun. I needed something more than hot soup as a weapon.

Andrea had no such problem. It seemed she had a plan in place. "Grab your keys," she said. "And go ahead of me to the back door. You'd better put on your shoes. You're driving."

"I don't know where my—"

"Your shoes are by the rocker and your keys are right on the table near the front door. Walk over there slowly, no funny business. I'll be here waiting. With the gun."

I turned and started back toward the living room, measuring each step, stalling for time. Where was Quinn? Would he ever forgive himself if he dallied and couldn't get to me in time? I gasped. Did I want him here at all? Andrea could shoot both of us. That wasn't what I wanted. Unless I could warn him to bring the entire NAPD.

I found myself studying every object on the way as I crossed my small living room rug. The blue ottoman, an old afghan knitted by Aunt Tess, the small table with a lamp and a few newspapers. I'd decluttered to prepare for Linda's visit, even removing my sewing chest with its long pins and eight-inch scissors, and taking away the remnants of my last meal alone with a knife resting on a plate. I made a note to myself to always leave potential weapons handy. If I lived for another quilting session or for another meal.

I had no choice but to obey Andrea. I picked up my keys and dragged my feet back toward her. She'd stepped to the side and indicated that I should lead the way out the door. My phone rang, echoing through the house. Quinn, I was sure. Andrea stepped closer to check and apparently saw his name.

"Move it," she said. "The last thing I need is two people to deal with. Move it," she said, louder, and I did.

The walk down the back steps and around to my car in the driveway seemed endless, and yet not long enough for Quinn to arrive. We climbed into my car and I drove as instructed. So close, I thought. Quinn had almost made it. Would he suspect something was wrong when I didn't answer? Probably not.

I headed west, toward the end of town. My car had a pocket on the driver's-side door. I'd stuffed it with necessities like tissues and change for toll roads. What else was in there? Could I rummage around without Andrea knowing? I had to give it a try.

I dropped my left arm and felt around the pocket. I felt a small tube of hand lotion, cough drops, a pen. Would the pen work? Not unless I was within an inch of her neck. I put my hand back on the wheel and shifted my weight. I needed to get my arm back farther. But Andrea was leaning over toward me. Suspicious? I straightened up and drove with both hands until I could get another opportunity.

Andrea ordered me to put my lights out and pull into a wide driveway, clearly a construction zone, with heavy industrial equipment locked inside a chain-link fence. Not just any construction site, but one with a large sign with HARRIS CONSTRUCTION in thick black letters. Another sign warned DANGER: ELECTRIC FENCE. A few small red-and-yellow lightning bolts radiated from the letters in case it wasn't clear. I stopped a few feet from the fence.

"Why are we here?" I asked, not sure I really wanted to know.

"Everyone knows you've been questioning Reggie. It makes sense that you'd head out here after dark to break into his trailer."

"I didn't even know it was here."

"You'd have found out."

I wished Andrea didn't think I was so smart. "But why would I do that?"

She shrugged. "Maybe to find some evidence. I know you're dying to prove he's getting kickbacks from everyone he deals with, even though he's the most honest guy around. Anyway, the story will be that you came out here to snoop around, and you had an accident."

She reached into her pocket and pulled out what looked like a remote control device. She pressed it and the fence crackled.

I had no question about the kind of accident I might have.

"This will have to do as a plan," she said.

A pretty good one, I thought, and shivered.

I reached down into the door pocket again. One last shot. This time I hit on a possibility. A flashlight. I had no idea whether it had batteries or not, or how bright it was if it did. I'd used it recently but couldn't remember how bright it was. Neither had I been under such stress.

I clutched the metal casing and felt for the slide to turn on the light. Wasn't there a saying about taking a flashlight to a gunfight? But it was my last remaining chance for survival. Once we stopped and I got out of my car, I felt, it would be over.

I hit the lever to move my seat to the farthest back position, then quickly slid the flashlight lever to ON with my thumb. I coughed to cover another movement and swung the light directly into Andrea's eyes. Back and forth, first one eye, then the other, as close as I could get, reaching at the same time for the gun, which she'd forgotten momentarily in her struggle to protect her eyes. I managed to hit the gun to the floor—her side of the floor, unfortunately, but at least it was out of her hands.

Hand-to-hand combat had not been in my training for the postal service. I flailed around, using my long legs and pointy-heeled sandals to pin Andrea's midsection to the door. She groaned in pain as I doubled over to scramble for the gun. Not exactly one of those graceful yoga moves I'd seen on exercise videos, but working for now. Andrea (foolishly, I thought, but I wasn't the one with a sharp heel in my gut) opened the door and tumbled out, falling on her back. She scrambled up and stumbled toward the fence, this time using the remote to open the lock. This time the fence swung open.

I wondered if I'd punctured an organ with the heel of my sandal. I looked down and, in the dim overhead lights strung around the site, thought I made out stains on the car seat that could be blood. But it was not time to be worrying about Andrea's well-being.

I stayed in my car, not trusting the reach of the electricity in the fence, and tried my phone. Not surprising, I was well beyond the reach of phone service. Meanwhile, I found Andrea's gun on the floor of the car and picked it up. Andrea had headed into the darkness of the construction site. I guessed she knew it well and therefore knew where there might be another gun.

I thought of chasing Andrea, but then what? A shoot-out? Not in my skill set. And besides, I had no confidence that I could get past the fence uncharred.

I wished I knew Andrea's overall plan. Maybe Reggie or one of his henchmen was right behind me. Or maybe he was in my house, waiting for me. Their plan B. I wished I knew if Reggie was in on plan A.

If I drove away, I'd avoid Andrea, but only for now. She'd be at large and who knew how long it would take to find her? Or whether she'd pop up again in my home?

I decided the safest thing was to drive away, head out, and hope for a cell phone signal soon. How to get to Andrea wasn't really my problem.

I backed down the driveway, happy to be putting distance between me and the evil fence. Almost immediately, I heard a car rumbling down the road toward me. An SUV from the height of the headlights. Quinn? Please, Quinn, and not a construction worker.

I stopped, my foot on the gas pedal, ready to slam into the vehicle if I had to. The SUV stopped within a few feet of my back bumper; the driver jumped out. Quinn? Yes!

"I missed the turn when your lights went out," he said,

banging his fist against his thigh. I barely heard him. I took a breath, maybe my first one since the knock on my back door.

"She went back there," I said, pointing madly, skipping the welcome-home hug I'd planned. "That fence. Don't touch it. I was supposed to be electrocuted."

The last words slipped off my tongue as I collapsed on the rough gravel, my new sandals ruined. All I could see were red-and-yellow lightning bolts that seemed to be aimed at my chest: DANGER: ELECTRIC FENCE.

23

Ben insisted I stay home for a couple of days, though the biggest casualty of my altercation with Andrea was my newest pair of sandals.

Andrea, on the other hand, who was in custody, had a serious wound in her gut. She'd fled into the construction site hoping to lay her hands on another gun, Reggie's this time. But my quick-witted friends had come through. Quinn had arrived at my house to find a burned pot of soup. He suspected my snooping had caught up with me and alerted Sunni. Her entire force of five officers and three patrol cars were engaged to find me.

"It was all about Quinn's quick-witted response to a burned pot of soup," Sunni said when she and her crew arrived with a fresh pot.

"And Cassie's flashlight-as-weapon training," Quinn said.

"I'm going out with a bang," Ross had said. "Pun intended.

I may have underestimated the excitement of small-town policing. I doubt my new job will be as action-packed."

Reggie was apparently as shocked as anyone, never suspecting that his wife was that wedded to their prosperous lifestyle or that easily moved to violence.

One surprise came when Sunni shared the solution to the mystery of my missing note from Anonymous. Jules had admitted to writing the warning notes to me. Once he learned that Cliff was involving me in the investigation, inviting me to discuss the finances of Daisy's Fabrics, he decided to try to cut me off at the pass. "His words," Sunni said.

"You mean I have a reputation as a . . ."

"'Troublemaker' might be the word you're looking for," she said. "And I'm only sharing this with you because you might want to do something about the ease with which he was able to get into the post office. He simply printed out a key." I gulped at the idea of printing a key until I remembered Jules's state-of-the-art three-dimensional printer. "He admits he was just messing with you, all in an effort to dissuade you from pursuing an investigation. He'd been experimenting with fashioning a skeleton key for a while and it was handy to try it on you."

"And I obliged by sticking the note where everyone sticks notes, in their middle desk drawer."

"Exactly."

I had a vision of a time when physical keys would no longer be viable. "We're all going to be carrying around a key card or some kind of retinal scanning device," I said.

"Or we'll all have chips in our hips," she offered.

We laughed at that, realizing it wasn't much of a joke anymore.

* * *

Linda arrived on Thursday, as planned, and was introduced to Quinn and all my favorite people at a gathering at my home in the evening. Cliff Harmon had returned from Miami, expressing his undying gratitude to all of us. I declined any special thanks, mostly to assure Sunni that I was not considering a change of career. Most of the quilters had adjusted to the fact that one of their longtime members was guilty of the most grievous crime.

"How does someone go from making warm, beautiful quilts to being capable of such a violent act?" Linda asked.

"Her quilts weren't that beautiful," Liv said, earning a smattering of applause.

"You were right to believe in this guy," Ben told me, his arm around Cliff. "In spite of my advice."

A pile of presents had arrived, too, as if it were my birthday.

"Since you're not going to tell us when it is, we'll keep celebrating on random days," Sunni said.

"Such a deal," I said.

"They've all been offering me a nice chunk of change to tell them the real date," Linda said.

"What makes you think you know the right one?" I asked.

"Uh-oh, she's back. Snarky as ever," Linda said.

More applause.

Besides lavishing large amounts of TLC on me since he returned, Quinn had a special gift for me: a soft mauve pillow imprinted with an image of the 1963 Eleanor Roosevelt stamp. THE REAL DEAL, it read, next to her picture, and 5¢

U.S. POSTAGE in the corner. It had been cancelled at Hyde Park, New York 12538.

"How much is it worth?" Sunni asked.

Linda answered, "Cancelled, about twenty cents. On a pillow? I don't know. However much Quinn paid for it."

"I spared no expense," Quinn said.

"Talking about that, I haven't heard the end of the money-man story. What's happening with Jules Edward?" Fran, the banker, asked.

"He's in the hands of the commonwealth," Sunni said. "They'll straighten it out. He stole from more than just Cliff, and he'll pay. He's just relieved that he's not facing a murder charge."

"Yeah, what's a little embezzlement charge?" Ben asked, shaking his head.

"I heard they found plastic keys that he made from that three-dimensional printer he was always showing off," Molly said.

"I heard he was working on a kind of skeleton key that would open just about any door," Liv said.

"I hope not," Fran said.

"Is that right, Sunni?" Molly asked. "Skeleton keys from a printer?"

I held my tongue.

"Maybe, maybe not," Sunni said. I wondered if she held out hope of ever being in a gathering as an ordinary citizen.

"I can't figure out why he didn't fool around with my books," Liv said, "but our auditors say everything was clean."

"Same for me," Molly said.

"I guess I'm just lucky," Cliff said.

"I'm guessing he was only beginning to test the waters at home," Sunni said.

"What's that expression?" Cliff asked. "Don't steal where you sleep."

"Something like that," Ben said. "How about cutting the cake, Linda?"

She was happy to.

After the relief of a murder solved, the weekend parade and quilt show seemed anticlimactic.

My order of eight-cent Henry Knox stamps had come through and I decided to give a few to special friends. You never knew when you'd need exactly eight cents to complete the postage on a package. How cool to use the smiling face, topped by a wig, of a former bookseller turned Revolutionary War hero.

According to a spoilsport reporter for the *Town Crier*, further research into Henry Knox's trek across the state cast doubt on the legend that he passed through what was now North Ashcot. No matter—no one wanted to give up a parade.

"I can see why not," Linda said. "It's been more than a month since the Fourth of July Parade. And isn't that what small towns are for?"

She was singing a different tune, however, when her cake was judged the best at the refreshment table. She "Woohoo'd" with the rest of us as she took possession of the blue ribbon. She promised all her new friends that she'd be back soon.

* * *

North Ashcot folks were happy that peace was restored. Linda had a new appreciation of small-town life. And Quinn and I had a growing appreciation for each other. Quite enough to ask of a week in the summer that had started out promising one kind of storm and hitting us with another kind.

I was ready to start my second year as postmaster.

POST OFFICE STORIES

Cassie Miller has been a fan of the U.S. Postal Service since she was a kid, sitting on her porch in North Ashcot waiting for the mail, crossing her fingers that there would be a letter with her name on it. She admits to sending away for things, just to receive letters or packages addressed to her. Free information kits for home improvement or health, brochures for colleges and universities all over the world—it didn't matter. Looking back, she figures she needed something to affirm her rightful place in the busy world she lived in. Cassie saved everything the mail carriers delivered in a special box that she'd covered with colorful adhesive paper. Now and then she'd pull the box from under her bed and go through the treasures: a flyer advertising the flea market in her school parking lot on Saturdays; information about life insurance that was secure and affordable; a catalogue of new toys from a big store across the ocean in London (her father explained the meaning of the funny *L* that was like the dollar sign in the United States).

She still collects trivia and stories that involve the postal service. Here's a sampling, some funny, some strange, all very interesting.

INTERESTING COMMEMORATIVES THROUGH THE YEARS

Today, if they're in mint condition, some of these stamps are worth about fifty dollars, some not much more than their face value. If they're used, you can count on collecting about twenty cents.

1920: one-cent stamp commemorating the pilgrim tercentenary. THE MAYFLOWER.

1954: three-cent stamp commemorating the two hundredth anniversary of Columbia University. MAN'S RIGHT TO KNOWLEDGE AND THE FREE USE THEREOF.

1957: three-cent stamp honoring the fiftieth anniversary of Oklahoma statehood. ARROWS TO ATOMS.

1961: four-cent stamp honoring Frederic Remington. ARTIST OF THE WEST.

2000: thirty-three-cent stamp honoring *Seinfeld*. SITCOM SENSATION.

CHILDREN, FIRST CLASS

What was the easiest way to send your child for a visit to her grandparents across the country at the beginning of the twentieth century? Attach postage and mail!

In the early 1900s, it was legal to mail children through the U.S. Post Office. Hard as it is to picture, stamps were affixed to the child's clothing, and the child rode the rails accompanied by a letter carrier.

Cassie's favorite is the (true) story of a little girl who was sent by railway mail from her mother's home in Pensacola, Florida, to her father's home in Christiansburg, Virginia. Her weight was recorded as just under the fifty-pound limit, costing fifteen cents in parcel post stamps. Another well-documented shipment involved a two-year-old boy who was sent from Oklahoma to Kansas, at a cost of eighteen cents. A special delivery package if there ever was one!

The practice continued for a while even after a law was passed prohibiting humans in the mail.

POSTAL MUSEUM

Cassie loves to visit the National Postal Museum in Washington, D.C., associated with the Smithsonian Institution. The museum's galleries offer a comprehensive view of postal history from Colonial times to the present. On exhibit are items as small as a postal uniform button and as large as a retired delivery bus.

One of the highlights is an exhibit of an early mail crane,

a system of collection begun in 1869. A town's bag of outgoing mail was attached to the arm of a crane erected along a train track. As the train approached, a clerk on board used a hook to snatch the bag from the crane. The clerk then tossed the incoming mail onto the track for distribution to the town citizens. Except for a few timing glitches, the system worked pretty well for a while.

FUN FACTS

- The highest-elevation post office is in Alma, Colorado, 10,578 feet above sea level.

- The lowest-elevation post office is in Death Valley, California, 282 feet below sea level.

- The post office in Peach Springs, Arizona, has walk-in freezers for food destined for delivery to the bottom of the Grand Canyon by mule train.

- The five most common street names in the country are Main, Second, Oak, Maple, and Park, in that order.

Finally, Cassie's good friend in Boston, Linda Daniels, is a font of post office humor. Here are two of her favorites, though she admits she's paraphrasing classics.

- *Consider the postage stamp: Its usefulness consists in the ability to stick to one thing till it gets there.*

- *I'm tired of being* FED EX*cessive numbers of post office jokes.*